DARK SEDUCTION

AN AGE GAP, OFFICE ROMANCE

K.C. CROWNE

DESCRIPTION

What's more humiliating than the walk of shame?
Walking into your new job...
Locking eyes with the dominating stranger.
And realizing *he's* your boss.

Lev Ivanov.
Dark. Commanding.
The most irresistible silver fox I've ever seen.

After rescuing me from a sketchy situation,
He didn't just suggest dinner—***he demanded it.***
Curiosity won over caution, and that night became the most passionate of my life.
By morning, he was gone.

Fast forward to today:
I choke on my coffee as I spot Lev in the CEO's office.

Turns out, he's not just my boss...
He's a mob boss.

Then, two life-changing revelations hit:
***"You're having a baby,"* says the doctor.**
***"We're getting married,"* says Lev.**

And one thing about Lev...

He doesn't ask.
He commands.

Readers note: This is full-length standalone, Russian mafia/bratva, age-gap, office romance romance in the bestselling Chicago Bratva series. K.C. Crowne is an Amazon Top 6 Bestseller and International Bestselling Author.

PROLOGUE

"What if we get caught?" I gasp, my breath shaky, my pulse racing.

His lips curve into a dark, confident smile, his eyes locked onto mine with a fire that makes my stomach flip. "Let them watch," he growls softly, his voice dripping with hunger. "All I care about is you... right here, right now."

His words send a shiver down my spine, and before I can respond, his mouth crashes against mine, fierce and unyielding. His hands slip under my shirt, rough fingers tracing a line up my back, igniting a fire in my skin.

"You're insane," I whisper, breathless, my fingers tangling in his hair, pulling him closer. "We shouldn't—"

"I don't care," he cuts me off, his voice a ragged whisper, his lips brushing mine as he speaks. "I need you. Now."

His hands are relentless, pushing my body back against the elevator wall, his hips pressing into me, letting me feel just how much he needs this—needs me.

I let out a low whimper as he nips at my bottom lip, tugging it between his teeth before his mouth trails down my neck, his breath hot against my skin.

My hands fumble with his belt, desperate to free him, to feel him inside me.

He groans, making a deep, primal sound that sets my blood on fire.

This is insane, but I don't care.

All I want is him, right here, right now.

He quickly opens the button and zipper on my jeans, exposing my lacy black panties.

His hand slides across my flat belly, then down into my panties.

The second his fingers make contact, I moan, a desperate sound that echoes in the small space of the elevator.

This is what I've been craving.

"You're so fucking wet for me," he murmurs.

I moan and nod, my hips instinctively bucking against his hand. He teases me at first, his fingers skimming over my clit, then dipping lower to explore my slick folds.

The teasing drives me wild, and I whimper with need.

Then, without warning, he inserts two fingers deep inside me, his thumb circling my clit with perfect pressure. I cry out, gripping his shoulders as waves of pleasure crash through me.

He works me expertly, his fingers moving in a rhythm that has me teetering on the edge of release.

"Come for me," he demands, his voice a low growl.

CHAPTER 1

DALIA

A Few Days Earlier

"Caught my husband screwing his secretary. In our bed."

The words spill out like word vomit.

The tow truck driver, a grizzled old man, glances over, his expression a mix of shock and disbelief. For a moment, I worry the poor guy might keel over right there.

"Damn," he mutters, his voice heavy with empathy. "That's... quite a story. You wanna talk about it?"

I chuckle. "Trust me, you're better off if I don't."

"I've got time, Miss. Try me."

I sigh, surrendering to the odd comfort of confessing to a stranger. "Where do I start? Well, for starters, I'm broke because my husband cleared our bank accounts. So that's fun. Turns out our marriage wasn't even legal. Half a decade, living a lie. And then, catching him in the act with his secretary in our own bed? The cherry on top."

The driver remains silent, a respectful audience to my calamity.

"And if that wasn't enough," I continue, my voice as sharp as broken glass, "I lost my job today. Fired by my boss, who happens to be my ex's best friend. Betrayal seems to be a common theme in my life right now."

He lets out a low chuckle, not mocking, but understanding.

"What's so funny?" I ask, my irritation evident.

"Sounds like when it rains, it pours."

I snort, a humorless sound. "Yeah, you could say that."

We pull into the mechanic's lot, and I hand him the last of my cash. "Thanks for the ride... and for listening."

"No trouble at all, Miss," he says, his voice as steady as ever as he hops out to unhook my pitiful excuse of a car. Just as he's about to leave, he pauses and turns back toward me, a thoughtful expression crossing his face.

"Life's funny, you know," he begins, his voice soft but firm. "Sometimes it helps to believe everything happens for a reason. Never know what's around the corner."

I manage a faint smile, the warmth of his words cutting through my exhaustion. "I appreciate that. *Really*."

With a small nod and a final smile, we say our goodbyes.

As he drives off, his words stay with me, lingering like an unexpected comfort on this otherwise shit show of a day.

I step into the garage, only to be greeted by a mechanic who looks like he's allergic to soap.

His greasy hair, stained clothes, and overall demeanor scream *this day isn't getting any better*.

"Hello. I'm having car trouble," I say, trying not to sound as defeated as I feel.

"No kidding." His voice, thick with a Russian accent, doesn't exactly ooze sympathy.

"Do you offer payment plans?" I ask, trying to keep my voice steady.

He laughs, but it's not a pleasant sound. More like someone revving an engine too hard. Then he mutters something in Russian that I'm pretty sure wasn't "Welcome to our fine establishment."

Great, I think.

Another fucking winner.

This day just keeps getting better.

The man calls over his shoulder. "Take a seat. I'll take a look."

I hand him my keys as he walks by, watching him disappear into the garage. With a heavy sigh, I plop into a chair in the dingy waiting area, feeling totally defeated. The seat feels as broken as my bank account.

If this guy rips me off, I have no idea what I'll do. My stomach churns with anxiety.

I thank my stars for the interview my friend lined up for me tomorrow.

It's truly my last lifeline.

I sit there, fidgeting and biting my nails, trying to ignore the rising tide of dread. An hour drags by, then finally, the mechanic returns.

He wipes his greasy hands on an even greasier rag. He doesn't waste time on pleasantries. "Your car's a mess," he snaps. "Come out and look."

My legs shake and anxiety takes hold as I get up and follow him out to the shop floor. My car—a non-descript little Nissan—sits there, the hood open. The sounds of power tools and the smell of oil are thick in the air. Some of the other mechanics glance in my direction. I can't help but wonder if I appear more like a money sack to them than a woman.

The mechanic starts throwing a barrage of jargon at me—something about a busted transmission, worn-out brake pads, and a failing alternator.

I can barely keep up with the onslaught of technical terms.

"You haven't been taking care of it," he scolds, his tone dripping with disdain. "Typical woman driver. You probably don't even know how to check the oil."

I narrow my eyes at him. "Excuse me? Just tell me the cost without the condescension, alright?"

He sneers, tossing the rag aside. "Fine. It's gonna run you about fifteen hundred. Maybe more, depending on how bad the transmission is."

I feel the blood drain from my face. "Fifteen hundred? That's insane. I'll take it somewhere else."

His laugh slices through the tense air, harsh and mocking, tinted with the unmistakable edge of a Russian accent. "Good luck with that. All the mechanic shops around here are controlled by the same family. You'll get the same price —or worse—anywhere else."

My temper ignites like a flare. "Are you kidding me? This is highway robbery!"

He crosses his arms, leaning back against the counter with a smug grin that seems all too common among the tough, cynical men of his heritage. "Call it what you want, sweetheart. That's the price. Take it or leave it."

I stammer, scrambling for a solution, "I... I'll find somewhere else. I'm not paying that much."

His sneer widens, his eyes cold and mocking. "You're not going to find anywhere else. You're stuck, just like all the other clueless idiots who wander in here."

My blood simmers with fury.

"I'm not clueless, and I'm certainly not an idiot. I'll figure something out."

He rolls his eyes dismissively, a gesture so characteristically disdainful it's almost a caricature. "Yeah, good luck with that. Maybe next time you'll learn to take care of your car. Or better yet, find a man who can do it for you."

My fists clench at my sides, the urge to retaliate growing stronger. "I don't need a man to take care of my car, or anything else for that matter. You can take your sexist attitude and shove it."

He straightens up, his face contorting with anger. "Watch your mouth, lady. You're lucky I even agreed to look at that piece of junk."

I glare at him, my resolve steeling. "And you're lucky I don't report you for this shakedown. Now, give me my keys. I'm done here."

He smirks again, shaking his head as he carelessly tosses the keys my way.

"Bitch," he mutters under his breath in a low growl.

I'm about to unleash a torrent of anger when a booming voice cuts through the cacophony of the shop, the words sharp and commanding in Russian.

The mechanic stiffens, his previous arrogance evaporating as he turns toward the source of the voice.

A man strides out from the shadows, an imposing figure whose very presence seems to command respect and fear.

He's dressed impeccably in a tailored dress shirt, the sleeves rolled up to reveal tattoos that whisper tales of his roots—vivid, intricate designs possibly symbolic of Russian folklore or military service.

His pleated slacks and polished shoes speak of a life that straddles worlds both rough and refined. An expensive watch clings to his wrist, a beacon of his status.

"What is going on here?" His voice booms, thick with a Russian accent, firm and cold as the Siberian winter, echoing through the garage with undeniable authority.

As he steps into the light, his features come into sharp focus —rugged yet strikingly handsome, with a jawline chiseled from stone and eyes that burn with a fierce intelligence.

His presence is not only magnetic but also slightly intimidating, embodying the fierce pride and resilience of his heritage.

Holy shit, is he hot.

The mechanic's arrogance vanishes instantly, replaced by a nervous tension. He turns to address the newcomer, stuttering slightly, "Sir, I meant no disrespect—"

"Silence," Ivanov commands with a flick of his hand. His authority silences the entire garage; every worker stops to witness the scene unfold.

Turning his penetrating gaze towards me, his face softens ever so slightly, though the intensity never leaves his eyes. "Miss, I apologize for this encounter. It seems we have some reevaluation to do here."

He then speaks to the mechanic with a stern finality that brooks no argument, "This is your only warning. Fail, and you will answer to me."

CHAPTER 2

DALIA

I've never been so intimidated and turned on at the same time.

He's tall, easily six-foot-six, with a physique that screams power and control. His black hair is impeccably styled, and those piercing gray eyes—my God, they flash with a quiet intensity that makes my heart skip a beat.

His forearms are ropy and toned. I spot a deep scar on his neck and another on his right arm, hinting at a past that's anything but ordinary. Everything about him exudes strength and dominance, like he's a force of nature packaged in perfect human form.

Tall, dark, and handsome don't even begin to cover it. His entire aura is magnetic, pulling me in. As much as I try to stay focused on my crappy situation, I can't help but feel a wave of heat spreading through me, pooling low in my belly. My panties are getting soaked just looking at him. What the hell is wrong with me?

I shake my head slightly, trying to clear the fog of lust clouding my mind, but it's no use. The way he moves, the authority in his voice—everything about him has me completely entranced.

The well-dressed man tears into the mechanic in Russian. The mechanic, now meek, tries to stick up for himself, stammering out some weak excuses, but the big man quickly shuts him down, making the mechanic look more like a scolded puppy than the arrogant jerk he was a few minutes ago.

The other mechanics around the shop stop what they're doing to watch the show. For a brief, wild moment, I wonder if Mr. Tall, Dark, and Dangerous is going to grab a wrench and club the mechanic to death right in front of me. He certainly looks like the kind of man who's seen his share of violence.

But the man barks out one more thing to the mechanic in Russian, and the guy practically scampers off like a little boy sent to timeout. With a casual sweep of his large hand, the well-dressed man smoothes his hair back into place and then, in English, commands the other mechanics to get back to work. They snap to it without hesitation.

Finally, his eyes lock onto mine. For a split second, the intensity in his gaze sends shivers through me, making me think I might come on the spot.

"Miss, would you mind coming to my office so we can further discuss the matter of your car?" he asks in a stern yet polite tone. His English is flawless, his accent slight.

My breath catches in my throat, but I manage a nod. "Sure," I say, trying to keep my voice steady.

As he leads the way, I can't help but admire the confidence and control in his stride. We enter a small, cluttered office, and the man's eyes immediately zero in on a nude pinup on the wall. "Pigs," he mutters under his breath as he tears it down and tosses it in the trash.

I get the distinct impression that this guy isn't just the boss of the auto shop but the boss of many other thing as well. He gestures for me to sit and I instantly comply.

He leans against the desk, arms crossed, and looks down at me. "I was watching the floor on my phone," he begins, his voice calm but firm. "I apologize for the way my employee spoke to you."

I raise an eyebrow. "I was handling your mechanic just fine, but thanks."

He smirks, clearly amused by my response. "I was watching that, too. You've got quite the spirit. But all the same, I don't tolerate that kind of behavior from my employees. And it shouldn't be your job to handle them, regardless."

"Okay," I reply, crossing my legs and leaning back in the chair, trying to relax despite the situation. "So, what's the plan for my car?"

He straightens up, his expression turning serious. "We'll fix your car, and it'll be on the house. Consider it a courtesy to make up for the way you were poorly treated just now."

I blink, a bit taken aback. "Just like that?"

"Just like that," he confirms, his eyes boring into mine. "You deserve better than what you got out there."

I can't ignore the danger I sense from this man. He's not just a businessman; he exudes an undercurrent of something far more sinister, like the city's criminal underworld.

I clear my throat, feeling the need to assert some control over the situation. "Thanks, but I'm willing to cover the costs as long as they're fair."

He raises an eyebrow, his piercing grey eyes on me. "Are you sure?"

It's like he can see right through me and read my every doubt and fear.

I hesitate, then admit, "Well, in installments."

He thinks it over, then nods. "Fine, an installment plan it is. But what you were quoted is bullshit. You'll pay half the quoted amount—a hundred-dollar payment a month until it's covered. Does that work?"

I'm momentarily stunned by his generosity but quickly gather myself. "Yeah, that works," I say, my voice steady despite the whirlwind of emotions swirling inside me.

He leans back, a hint of a smile playing on his lips. "Good. We'll get your car taken care of."

He checks his watch, then looks back at me. "I'll make sure your new friend"—he says the words with a wry tone—"stays late to ensure your car is ready by the end of the day. And if the job isn't done right, his career as a mechanic in this town is over. I'll see to that personally."

"Thank you," I reply, still unsure of what to make of this man who exudes authority and danger in equal measure. I watch the way he moves and sits behind the desk, like he was born to be in control, effortlessly commanding respect and fear.

A small smile curls his lips, making my heart skip a beat. "I'd like to add one more thing to our arrangement," he says, his eyes never leaving mine.

"What's that?" I ask, my curiosity piqued.

"I'd like to take you out to dinner," he says smoothly.

My heart races, my pussy clenches, and a wild image pops into my mind—this man bending me over the desk, filling me with his almost-certainly huge cock, making me come until I can't think straight. I clear my throat, forcing myself back into the moment.

"Dinner?" I echo, trying to keep my voice steady despite the heat coursing through my body.

"Yes, dinner," he repeats, his eyes glinting with amusement as if he knows exactly what's going through my mind.

"I'm not really hungry," I object, trying to keep my composure. But just as the words leave my mouth, my stomach betrays me with a loud growl.

He gives me a slight smile, his eyes twinkling with amusement.

"Your body says otherwise." My heart races.

"My name is Lev. And you?"

I can barely speak. "Dalia."

"A pleasure, Dalia. A pleasure, indeed."

CHAPTER 3

DALIA

"I want to know everything about you," he says, his voice smooth and inviting.

I blink, feeling like I'm in a dream. We're seated in a luxurious restaurant in downtown Chicago, the city glittering outside the windows. The atmosphere is almost surreal.

A tinge of nervousness creeps into my voice. "You can't possibly want to know everything about me."

"Au contraire," he replies, a twinkle in his eye. "Spare no details."

I laugh, trying to shake off the nerves. "Do you want me to start with the tragic story of how my car ended up in the shop? The mechanic wasn't entirely wrong, you know. I hadn't been taking the best care of it." I lean in closer to him as I confess.

He laughs, a rich, deep sound that makes my heart skip a beat. "You can start there or anywhere else you'd like. As long as I get to learn more about you."

I take a deep breath, looking into those piercing gray eyes, feeling a strange comfort in his attentive gaze. He sits back, giving me a thoughtful look. "How about you start with what's troubling you?"

My eyes flash with surprise. "How do you know something's troubling me?" I ask shyly, glancing down at my simple jeans and blouse, a stark contrast to the luxury of the restaurant. I can't help but feel out of place while he appears completely at ease, fitting right in as if he owns the establishment.

"In my line of work, understanding people and their motivations can be the difference between life and death," he says calmly.

I narrow my eyes, suspicion growing. He's not using a figure of speech. "What exactly do you do for a living?"

He smiles, but it doesn't quite reach his eyes. "I'm a manager in my family's business."

I can sense he's leaving a lot out. "Uh-huh, and what kind of business is that?"

He leans in slightly, his gaze intense. "We manage... a variety of enterprises."

I raise an eyebrow, not buying it for a second. "A variety of enterprises, huh? Sounds like something straight out of a mafia movie."

He chuckles, clearly amused by my sass. "You've got a quick wit, Dalia. I like that."

I smirk, feeling a bit bolder. "And you've got a knack for avoiding questions. I'm *not* sure I like that."

He nods, acknowledging my point. "Fair enough. Let's just say it's complicated. But right now, I'm more interested in hearing about you."

I take a deep breath, deciding to let it slide for now. "All right, well, you were right. A lot is troubling me. Besides my car being a mess, my ex-husband cleaned out our bank accounts and was cheating on me with his secretary."

His eyes widen slightly, but he stays silent, letting me continue.

"And to top it all off, I lost my job because my boss is best friends with my ex."

He leans back, his expression thoughtful. "That's quite a lot to deal with."

I nod, feeling the weight of it all again. "Yeah, you could say that."

He reaches across the table, taking my hand in his. "I'm sorry you've been through so much. But tonight, let's focus on you. Tell me more."

The dinner flies by, and our conversation flows effortlessly. I find myself opening up to him more than I ever thought I would. Between the food, the wine, and his company, I feel happy for the first time in a long while. As I finish my dessert—a rich, velvety chocolate mousse—I look around, expecting the check.

He notices and asks, "What's wrong?"

"I'm just waiting for the check," I reply, a bit sheepishly. "I want to contribute to it."

He laughs, a deep, warm sound that makes me smile. "There's no check; it's all on my tab."

I frown slightly. "Well, in that case, let me pay you back by taking you out to dinner. Though on my budget, it might have to be Chik-fil-A."

He leans forward, his eyes locking onto mine with an intensity that causes my blood pressure to spike. "The only thing I desire is more of your company."

I sense a sexual undertone in his words, making my pulse quicken. He glances out of the window toward a nearby skyscraper, then looks back at me.

"I own a penthouse in that hotel," he says smoothly. "If you'd like a change of scenery."

My pussy clenches at the thought, and I can barely suppress the excitement in my voice. "Sure," I say, my heart racing.

He smiles before standing up and offering his hand. "Let's go."

As soon as the elevator doors close behind us, we're all over each other. Our lips collide in a hard, deep kiss as his big, strong hands roam over my body with a possessive urgency. I can feel his hardness through his slacks—there's no doubt his cock is huge.

The elevator starts to ascend, and Lev pulls back just enough to growl, "I want you right here, right now."

A jolt of nerves hits me. "What if we get caught?" I gasp, my voice breathy with excitement.

He smirks, hitting the stop button. "This is the penthouse elevator—nice and private."

Before I can respond, he pounces on me like a wild animal, pressing me against the elevator wall. His hands slide under my shirt. His touch sets my skin on fire, and I moan into his mouth as he kisses me fiercely.

The thrill of the moment, the danger, and the sheer intensity of his desire make me feel alive in a way I haven't felt in ages. My hands fumble with his belt, desperate to free him, to feel him inside me. Lev groans, making a deep, primal sound that sets my blood on fire.

This is insane, but I don't care. All I want is him, right here, right now.

He quickly opens the button and zipper on my jeans, exposing my lacy black panties with a delicate floral pattern that's just a little bit naughty. His hand slides across my flat belly, then down into my panties. The second his fingers make contact, I moan, a desperate sound that echoes in the small space of the elevator. This is what I've been craving since that first moment in the garage.

"I love that you're so fucking wet for me," he murmurs.

I moan and nod, my hips instinctively bucking against his hand. He teases me at first, his fingers skimming over my clit, then dipping lower to explore my slick folds. The teasing drives me wild, and I whimper with need.

Then, without warning, he plunges two fingers deep inside me, his thumb circling my clit with perfect pressure. I cry out, gripping his shoulders as waves of pleasure crash through me. He works me expertly, his fingers moving in a rhythm that has me teetering on the edge of release.

"Come for me," he demands, his voice a low growl.

With a final thrust of his fingers, I explode, my orgasm ripping through me with incredible intensity. I cling to him, gasping for breath as pleasure floods every nerve in my body. He continues to work me through it, his touch both commanding and surprisingly tender.

He's dominating, and to my surprise, I like it. As I come down from the high, I look up at him, my eyes glazed with satisfaction and awe. He pulls his fingers from my panties, licking them clean with a satisfied smirk.

"That was incredible," I whisper, still trembling.

He chuckles softly, brushing a strand of hair from my face. "We're just getting started, Dalia."

I shiver with anticipation, knowing that this night is far from over.

We stumble out of the elevator and into the penthouse suite. The living room is stunning—plush carpets, sleek modern furniture, and floor-to-ceiling windows offering a breathtaking view of the Chicago skyline. But I barely register any of it; my focus is entirely on the man in front of me.

He looks at me with the eyes of an animal who's just spotted his prey, like a beast in desperate need of a rut. His gaze is intense, almost feral, and it makes my heart race.

"That was so fucking sexy, watching you come like that," he says, his voice dripping with lust. The words make my knees weak, my body trembling with anticipation.

He steps closer, his presence overwhelming. "From now on, you'll refer to me as sir. Understood?"

Sir? Why the hell not?

I nod, feeling a thrill run through me. "Yes, sir."

"Say it again," he commands, his tone leaving no room for argument.

"Yes, sir," I repeat, loving the way the words sound coming out of my mouth.

"Good. Now, strip," he orders, his eyes never leaving mine.

"Yes, sir," I reply, my tone lusty and low. I begin to undress, my hands shaking slightly as I peel off my clothes, one piece at a time. His eyes darken with desire as I reveal more of my body, and the anticipation builds with every second.

Standing naked before him, I feel a mix of vulnerability and power. I can tell he's holding back, but the intensity in his gaze tells me he won't be able to for long.

"Go to the bedroom and lie on your back," he commands.

I turn to obey, but he grabs me by the jaw, pulling me into a hard, deep kiss first. His tongue probes my mouth, tasting delicious and intoxicating. When he finally lets go, I'm breathless. As I walk away, he gives my bottom a firm swat.

I gasp, a smile creeping onto my lips. It's surprisingly hot.

I lie down on the bed, completely bare, feeling the cool sheets against my skin. He removes his shirt, revealing a physique that's nothing short of breathtaking—powerful and muscular—every inch of him exuding strength and control.

"Show yourself to me," he orders, his eyes dark with desire.

I know exactly what he means. Reaching down, I part my lips, exposing myself to him. His eyes devour the sight, and a low growl escapes his throat.

"You're sexy as hell," he murmurs, his voice thick with lust. "Are you ready for me?"

"Yes, sir," I whisper, my body trembling with anticipation.

He climbs onto the bed, positioning himself between my legs. The heat of his body is almost unbearable, and the look in his eyes makes my heart race. This is more of what I've been craving, what I've needed since the moment I laid eyes on him.

"Take off my pants," he orders, his voice rough with desire.

As I reach down to unbutton his pants, he covers my neck and breasts with kisses, his mouth hot and urgent. He sucks on my nipples, sending jolts of pleasure through my body. I manage to get him out of his pants, and when his cock is finally exposed, it takes my breath away. It's long and thick, the sight of it making me even wetter.

"Do you want protection?" he asks, his eyes locking onto mine.

"No," I whisper. "I'm on the pill. I want to feel you."

"Show me where you want me."

I grasp his warm, thick cock, guiding it to my entrance. The anticipation is almost too much to bear. As it presses against my pussy, I shiver with excitement. Slowly, he glides into me, and it feels like his cock was made for me.

A low moan escapes my lips as he pushes deeper, the sensation overwhelming. He moves with a steady, deliberate rhythm, each thrust sending waves of pleasure through my body. It's like he's claiming me, and I love every second of it. The stretch is deliciously intense, and I respond eagerly to every inch of him, tightening around him and drawing him in even further.

He feels incredible inside me, his cock filling me completely, hitting all the right spots. The heat between us builds, the connection growing stronger with every thrust. I wrap my legs around him, pulling him closer, needing him deeper.

"Fuck, you feel amazing," he groans, his voice strained with the effort of holding back. "Do you like the way my cock feels inside of you?"

"Yes, sir," I breathe, my hands gripping his shoulders. "Don't stop. Please."

He begins to thrust into me with raw power, each movement sending shockwaves of pleasure through my body. My breasts bounce with the force of his collisions, and I can see his muscles flexing and tensing, a beautiful display of strength and dominance.

"I'm going to come," I gasp, my voice shaky with impending release.

"Do it," he growls, his eyes never leaving mine.

With his command, I let go, a second climax crashing over me with incredible force. My body convulses around his cock, the pleasure so intense it leaves me breathless.

When my orgasm finally subsides, he doesn't miss a beat. He grabs me by the hips, flipping me over as if I weigh nothing at all. His thick, muscular arm wraps around my waist, pulling my ass into the air. Without hesitation, he plunges his cock back into me, the new angle sending a fresh wave of ecstasy through my body.

"Fuck," I moan, the sensation overwhelming. His grip is firm and possessive, and I can feel his raw strength as he drives into me.

His thrusts are relentless, each one pushing me closer to yet another orgasm. I brace myself against the bed, my body responding eagerly to his every move.

He fucks me with a primal intensity, the force of his movements causing my body to rock forward. I brace myself against the bed, surrendering to the passionate energy he pours into every stroke. His cock drives into me, filling me completely, hitting all the right spots with a precision that leaves me gasping for breath.

My moans mix with his grunts, the sound of our bodies slapping together echoing in the room. I can feel the heat building inside me again, my climax approaching rapidly under his relentless assault. He grips my hips tighter, his fingers digging into my flesh as he pushes us both to the edge.

"You feel so fucking good," he growls, his voice thick with desire. "I want you to come with me."

"Yes, sir."

With a final, powerful thrust, my orgasm hits, crashing through me with a force that leaves me breathless and trembling. My pussy clenches around his cock, milking him as I scream out in pleasure. The intensity of the moment is overwhelming, and I feel like I'm floating, completely consumed by the sensation.

He joins me, erupting inside me with a guttural groan. I feel the warmth of his cum, each pulse sending aftershocks of pleasure through my body as he spills himself deep inside me.

The feeling is indescribable, his release amplifying my own pleasure. We ride the wave together, his body tensed and powerful above me, mine trembling and spent beneath him. As the intensity slowly fades, we collapse together, our breathing heavy, hearts racing, and bodies entwined.

He slowly pulls out of me, and I can feel him dripping from my pussy as he gently maneuvers us into a spooning position. His strong arms wrap around me with surprising tenderness, his lips trailing soft kisses along my shoulder and neck before finally capturing my own in a sweet, lingering kiss.

"Thank you," I whisper, feeling total contentment. "I needed that."

He chuckles softly, his breath warm against my skin. "The pleasure was all mine," he murmurs. Then, with a grin I can almost hear, he adds, "Well, maybe not all of it."

A big smile spreads across my face, and I snuggle closer to him. As I drift off to sleep, wrapped securely in his arms, I realize that this night has just changed everything.

I know I've experienced something incredible, something raw and real that I never knew I needed until now.

I begin to open my eyes, early morning light pouring in through the windows. I'm in that hazy, in-between state where I can't tell if I'm awake or dreaming. I'm still in the hotel, and through bleary eyes, I watch Lev as he slips out of bed.

I get a wonderful view of his perfect ass, toned and muscular, the kind of ass that looks like it's been sculpted by the gods themselves. My gaze drifts up, and I notice something I hadn't seen last night. His back is covered in scars. Faint, crisscrossing lines that tell a story of a past I can't even begin to imagine.

Who is this guy?

He glances over his shoulder, catching me watching him.

"It's early—go back to sleep."

Just like all the other commands he's given me, I obey. My eyes flutter closed, and I drift back into the comforting embrace of sleep, my mind swirling with thoughts of the mysterious man I've just spent the night with.

I wake up a couple of hours later, this time to the bright light of late morning.

Lev's no longer in bed beside me. I assume he's somewhere else in the penthouse, so I throw on a robe I find hanging on the back of the door, taking a moment to savor the amazing room and the breathtaking view of the city.

I glance at the clock and remember my interview is at eleven—I can't linger for too long. I start looking around for Lev, but there's no trace of him. The penthouse feels strangely empty.

As I wander into the kitchen, I spot an envelope on the counter. My heart skips a beat as I open it. Inside is a note and, to my shock, a thick stash of cash. I'm stunned, my mind racing with questions.

I unfold the note, my curiosity piqued. It's short and to the point, written in a bold, confident script:

Dalia,

Last night was amazing. I hope you feel the same way. The money is for you to get a fresh start. You've been through enough. Before you object, you don't owe me anything.

I spoke with your "friend" at the repair shop. Your car is ready to be picked up, and there will be no charge.

Sorry to renege on our payment plan arrangement.

— Lev

I read it twice, a mix of emotions swirling inside me.

Well, Lev, you certainly know how to make an exit.

Gratitude and relief bubble up, but there's a tinge of reluctance, too. I don't want to take the money, but I know I'm in no position to turn it down.

I look at the thick stack of cash, knowing this is my ticket to a fresh start, even if it stings my pride a bit. I fold the note and slip it back into the envelope, determination settling in. Time to face the day and make the most of this unexpected twist.

I get dressed and slip the money into my purse, still grappling with the idea of taking it. Who the hell is this guy? I only got his first name. I consider asking the front desk, but then I realize they're not going to give his info to some random woman who stayed over.

I step over to the window, looking out at the sprawling city below. Despite the whirlwind of the past twenty-four hours, I feel a newfound confidence rising within me. Ready to put my past behind me, I take a deep breath and smile.

Time for act two of my life.

CHAPTER 4

DALIA

L ev's powerful body is on top of me, muscles flexing as he drives his thick cock into my eager pussy over and over. Each thrust is deep and powerful, sending waves of pleasure through me. His hands grip my hips firmly, holding me in place as he claims me completely.

"Call me sir," he growls, his voice dripping with lust and dominance.

"Yes, *sir*," I moan.

The way he commands me, the sheer power in his movements, is intoxicating. His cock fills me perfectly, and my body is overcome with pleasure. I'm getting closer to the edge; I can feel the tension coiling tighter and tighter inside me, ready to snap. He leans down, his breath hot against my ear.

"Come for me," he says, his voice a low, sexy growl.

Just as I'm about to lose myself in the fantasy, a loud horn honks, jolting me back to reality. I blink, shaking my head to clear the haze of arousal.

The real world comes rushing back.

I snap back into the moment, finding myself stopped at a red light in downtown Chicago. It has turned green, and I give a little wave to the annoyed driver who honked at me, watching him speed past with a scowl on his face.

As I continue driving, I can't help but notice how well the car seems to run—it's better than ever. A grin spreads across my face as I remember the mechanic who'd been so rude to me when I first entered the shop. When I picked up my car the other day, however, he'd been meek and apologetic, practically tripping over himself to make sure everything was perfect.

Lev, whoever he is, sure has a way of putting the fear of God into people. And damn, am I grateful for it. The thought of him brings a warm flush to my cheeks, but I shake it off. Time to focus on the road ahead, both literally and figuratively. With my car purring like a kitten and the city stretching out before me, I feel a surge of confidence.

I drive through the bustling streets, passing the towering skyscraper of Ivanov Holdings—the company where I'd interviewed. The interview had gone well, I think, but Bailey failed to mention that the position was for the personal assistant to the COO. That's a far cry from the administrative role I'd expected.

It'd be a hell of an upgrade for my career, but the thought of working directly for one of the bosses of that enormous company is more than a little daunting. The interviewer's comments about how demanding Mr. Ivanov could be had been enough to give me pause. Still, the challenge intrigues me.

I glance up at the impressive building, its glass facade reflecting the late morning sun, and wonder what it would be like to work in such a place. It's been a few days now since I interviewed, and I haven't heard anything. I can't help but wonder if they decided I was not suitable for the role and went with someone else. Screw them if they can't see my potential. Still, I'm determined to make my own way.

At least I've got Lev's money for some breathing room. I came here to Chicago to make it, and that's what I'm going to do. The last thing I want is to go back home to Rhode Island.

I park in front of the charming brick walk-up I've rented for the month, thanks to Lev's cash. I step out and stretch as I take in the quiet neighborhood. After a minute, I grab my bag and head inside, ready to kick back and figure out my next move.

I step into my temporary apartment, a charming and cozy one-bedroom that feels like a perfect little retreat. The living room has a comfy couch and a small but cute kitchen area. It's not much, but it's all mine for now.

Just as I'm about to toss my purse on the couch, my phone rings. I quickly grab it, hoping it's Ivanov Holdings, but no such luck. It's Mom and Dad.

"Hey, Mom. Hey, Dad," I answer, trying to sound upbeat.

"Hi, sweetie," my mom's warm voice comes through. "How are you doing? How's the new place?"

"Hey, kiddo," my dad adds, his tone a bit sterner. "Everything okay over there?"

"Yeah, everything's fine," I reply, walking over to the window and looking out. "The new place is nice. Cozy. Just getting settled in."

"How are things after... everything with Chad?" my mom asks gently.

I take a deep breath, steeling myself. "It's been a whirlwind, but I'm managing. You know, taking things one day at a time."

"Have you heard back from that company yet?" my dad asks, an edge of expectation in his voice.

"Not yet," I reply.

"Well, get your resume out there. Don't just sit around waiting for someone to reach out," he instructs, a hint of his Egyptian accent surfacing.

"Dad, I'm on it," I say, suppressing a sigh. "I've got a few more places in mind."

"Good. You need to keep pushing," he continues. "Don't ever stop."

"Have you met anyone new or are you not ready for dating yet?" my mom asks, her voice softer, more encouraging.

I grin, unable to resist. "Actually, I did meet a nice guy the other day."

"Oh, that's wonderful!" my mom exclaims, sounding genuinely happy. "Tell us more!"

"Nothing much to tell yet; it was just an unexpected date with a nice guy I met at the auto shop."

Nice is the last word I'd use to describe Lev. But what the hell was I supposed to say, that he ordered me to call him "sir" and I happily obliged?

"Is he worthy of you?" my father asks.

"Dad, it was just dinner," I say, rolling my eyes. "Nothing serious."

My mom is thrilled. "I'm glad you're getting your toe back in the water, sweetie. It's good for you."

"Thanks, Mom," I say, appreciating her support. "I'm just taking things slow and seeing where they go."

My dad grumbles something under his breath, but I know he's just worried about me. They both want what's best for me, even if they have different ideas about what that looks like.

My father clears his throat. "There's still another option, you know if you can stop being stubborn and consider it."

I sigh, already knowing where this is headed. "Dad, it's not going to happen."

"It's a good plan," he insists. "You move back in with us, and we'll pay your way while you look for a job. In the meantime, I can set you up with a suitable man."

I can picture his hopeful expression through the phone. "A suitable man? Do you have someone in mind?" I cringe. I know I'm opening a can of worms.

"Ahmed. He's a doctor, a very respected dermatologist," he says, sounding a bit too pleased with himself.

"Dad, arranged marriages aren't really a thing here in America," I reply, rolling my eyes again, glad he can't see me. "I appreciate the thought, but I need to do this on my own."

"It's not an arranged marriage," Dad says, quick to dispute me. "You meet him, you see how it goes. You ask me, it's a win-win if we approve of him and Ahmed's family approves of you. That's ninety percent of it."

"Dalia, it's just an introduction. You don't have to marry him tomorrow," my mom chimes in, trying to smooth things over.

"I know, Mom. But I need to figure things out for myself."

"You're so stubborn," my dad mutters. "Ahmed's not going to stay single forever; men like him never do."

"If I'm stubborn, I get it from you," I tease, trying to lighten the mood. "Look, I'll be fine. Just give me some time."

"All right, all right," he concedes. I can hear the concern in his voice. "Just know we're here for you."

"I know. Thanks, guys. I'll talk to you later, okay?"

"Be safe," my dad adds, still sounding a bit gruff.

"I will."

"Take care, sweetie," my mom says warmly.

I feel more grounded after the call. I sigh, knowing my father is right—not about the Ahmed thing, but about how I need to keep pushing and keep applying to places. Deciding to relax a bit before spending the rest of the day looking for a job, a fantasy with Lev flashes in my head again.

With a naughty smile, I decide to unwind.

I draw a bath, the sound of the water filling the tub instantly soothing my frazzled nerves. As the steam rises, I slip out of my clothes and step into the hot water, letting out a contented sigh as the warmth envelops me. Leaning back, I close my eyes and let my mind wander.

Lev's image comes into focus, and I feel a rush of excitement. My body reacts to the thought of him, and I can't help but grin. Reaching for my wand, I turn it on, the vibrations immediately sending a shiver of anticipation through me.

Settling back into the tub, I close my eyes and let the fantasy take over. In my mind, Lev's powerful body hovers over mine, his hands exploring every inch of me. The thought makes my heart race, and I press the wand against my clit, the sensation making me gasp.

"Beg for it," I imagine him growling, his voice commanding and rough.

"Please, sir," I whisper to the empty bathroom, my voice trembling with need. The vibrations from the wand mix with the heat of the water, creating a whirlwind of pleasure.

In the fantasy, Lev's hand comes down on my ass a few times; the combination of the sting and pleasure is perfect.

His deep voice fills my mind with dirty talk, each word making me hotter, more desperate.

"You're such a good girl, taking your punishment so well," he says, his hand coming down on my bottom again. "Does that feel good? Do you like it when I spank you?"

"Yes, sir," I moan, the words spilling out as I imagine his commanding presence.

"Beg for my cock," he demands, his voice rough and insistent. "Tell me how much you want it."

"Please, sir, I need your cock," I whisper, my breath hitching. "I want you to fuck me so badly."

"Good girl," he purrs. "I love hearing you beg. You're going to come so hard for me."

His words, combined with the sensation of the wand, drive me to the brink. Just as I'm about to lose control, my phone rings.

My first instinct is to turn it off and finish my fun, but then I see the words "Ivanov Holdings" flash on the screen. I freeze, torn between the intense pleasure coursing through my body and the potentially life-changing opportunity calling me.

I sigh and set the wand aside before answering the call, putting it on speaker.

"Hello?"

"Hi, is this Dalia?" a professional voice asks.

"Yes, this is her," I reply, trying to steady my breath.

"This is Melissa Barnes from Ivanov Holdings HR. I'm following up on your interview."

My heart skips a beat. "Yes, of course."

"I'm pleased to inform you that we've finished vetting the applicants, and we've selected you for the position. Can you start on Monday?"

I blink in disbelief. "Wait, really? Just like that?"

"Just like that," Melissa confirms with a smile in her voice. "Mr. Ivanov was very impressed with your qualifications. Are you able to start on Monday?"

Hell, yes.

CHAPTER 5

LEV

Dalia's on her knees before me, looking up with those gorgeous, chocolate-brown eyes that make me want to melt. A smile spreads across her face, and I can see she's ready to please me.

"What would you like, sir?" she asks, her voice soft and inviting.

"Put your mouth on me."

She complies, leaning in and slowly licking the tip of my cock, sending a jolt of pleasure through me. Her tongue is warm and wet, teasing me just enough before she takes my length into her mouth, enveloping me in a hot, tight embrace. The sight of her, so eager and submissive, only fuels my desire, and I can't help but let out a satisfied groan.

Her eyes never leave mine as she pleasures me, her mouth working skillfully over my cock. She licks and sucks with an exquisite rhythm, her tongue swirling around the tip before taking me deeper. Now and then, she pays special attention to my balls, gently sucking and licking them, sending waves of pleasure radiating through my body.

"That's it," I groan, my voice husky with desire. "I want to watch you drink every last drop of me."

She nods, her eyes full of determination and lust as she takes me back into her mouth, her movements becoming more urgent. I can feel the tension building, my release imminent. But just as I'm about to reach the peak, a door opens and closes, snapping me back to reality. I blink, the fantasy dissolving as I take in my surroundings.

My eyes shift to the sprawling view of downtown Chicago before me. I take a moment to focus, banishing thoughts of Dalia from my mind. I've been thinking about her a lot, too much, in fact. But it's hard not to fantasize about those full lips, those plump breasts, the sensual, olive complexion.

I turn, coming face to face with Sean Winter, the vice president of marketing. "Sean," I greet him with a firm handshake.

"Mr. Ivanov," he replies, his tone respectful.

More people filter into the conference room, filling it with a low hum of chatter. I straighten my tie, feeling the weight of my responsibilities settling onto my shoulders. Once everybody is seated, I clear my throat, commanding the room's attention.

"Is everyone ready to begin?" I ask.

Heads nod, and the room falls silent, all eyes on me. Time to focus on business, push aside distractions, and get things done. The company needs my full attention, and that's exactly what it's going to get. I begin the meeting.

"Let's start with a review of our second-quarter performance. Our investments in green tech and healthcare have shown a steady increase, contributing significantly to our overall growth. However, we need to address the underperformance in our retail sector. Sean, I need you to present a strategy for revitalizing those assets."

As Sean launches into his presentation, I can't help but become distracted yet again by images of Dalia flashing through my mind, her full lips, her tight pussy, and how she writhed beneath me. All of it makes it hard to focus.

I force myself back to the present as Sean finishes. "For the third quarter, we're looking at expanding our portfolio in renewable energy. The market trends indicate a strong potential for growth, and I believe we should capitalize on that."

Heads nod in agreement, but my mind keeps wandering. I envision Dalia on her knees, looking up at me with those chocolate-brown eyes.

Damn it.

I grip the edge of the table, trying to banish the thoughts. "Additionally," I say, trying hard to keep my voice steady, "we need to streamline our operations in the logistics sector. I've noticed some inefficiencies that are costing us valuable time and resources. Let's focus on tightening those processes."

I power through the meeting, giving each segment the attention it deserves, but the lingering thoughts of Dalia make it difficult. By the time we wrap up, I'm mentally exhausted, but at least I managed to maintain my composure. "Any questions?" I ask, opening the floor for discussion.

There are a few questions, and I handle them smartly, keeping the conversation focused and productive. As the meeting comes to an end, the attendees file out, leaving me with a brief moment of quiet. That is, until Melissa Barnes, the HR director, approaches me.

"Lev, are you OK?" she asks, concern evident in her voice.

"I'm fine," I reply brusquely, not in the mood for small talk.

She smiles, clearly used to my stern disposition. "You know, it's OK to take a day off now and then. Most people aren't built to handle eighty-plus hour work weeks."

I'm not like most people, I think. *I can't afford to be.*

"Your new PA started this morning," Melissa continues, not missing a beat. "She's in orientation now. Having an assistant should ease your workload a bit."

I nod, taking in the information. "Good. I need someone who can keep up."

"Don't worry," Melissa says with a reassuring smile. "I hand-picked her myself. And you already approved her qualifications. I think she'll be a winner."

I give a curt nod, appreciating her effort but not showing it. "Thank you, Melissa. I'll make sure to meet her soon."

"Actually, you can meet her now," Melissa says with a smile.

"Fine. Send her to my office."

Melissa nods. "Will do," she says before departing.

I make my way out of the conference room and through the bustling executive floor to my office. Stepping into the massive, modern room, I take a moment to appreciate the view. The Chicago skyline stretches out before me, the lake's vast expanse extending to the horizon. It's a view I've seen countless times, but today, it does little to distract me from my thoughts.

I can't believe I've been fantasizing about Dalia the way I have. No woman has ever gotten into my head like this. Shaking off the thought, I try to refocus on the tasks at hand. Before I can delve too deeply into my work, a knock sounds at the door.

"Come in," I call out.

My jaw nearly drops to the floor when Dalia walks into my office.

At first, I think I'm imagining things, but when Melissa walks in with her, I know it's real.

"Lev, this is Dalia Abbas," Melissa says, introducing us. "Dalia, meet Lev Ivanov."

Dalia looks as surprised as I feel, but she recovers quickly, extending a hand.

"Nice to meet you, Mr. Ivanov."

"Likewise," I manage to say, shaking her hand. Her grip is firm and confident.

Melissa continues giving a rundown of Dalia's qualifications. "As we discussed, Dalia has a degree in art history from Brown and a master's in business from the University of Chicago. She's highly recommended and comes with excellent references."

The qualifications sound familiar, but Melissa and I hadn't gone over names when discussing the applicants. Regardless, I'm impressed, but I'm also struggling to keep my mind professional.

Dalia looks stunning—her hair is pulled up in a sleek, professional style, and she's wearing an off-white blouse and a black pencil skirt. The outfit is a delicious contrast to the image of her in her bra and panties from the other night, stripping at my command, her gorgeous, heaving breasts pouring from her bra as she undid the clasp.

"Impressive credentials," I say. "Welcome to the team."

"Thank you," Dalia replies, her eyes meeting mine with a mix of curiosity and something more playful.

Melissa smiles. "I'll leave you two to get acquainted. If you need anything, Dalia, my office is just down the hall."

"Thank you, Melissa," Dalia replies.

Melissa leaves my office, closing the door behind her. I take a moment to compose myself, then gesture to the chair in front of my desk. "Have a seat, Dalia."

She sits, her posture perfect, her eyes never leaving mine. I sit across from her, wondering how in the hell I'm going to ever get any work done.

CHAPTER 6

DALIA

"This is quite a surprise, isn't it?"

The memory of Lev seated at the desk in the mechanic's shop flashes through my mind. I had no idea who he was then, though I believed he was definitely a man of importance. But the sight of him now, seated behind the desk in this massive office of the COO, leaves no doubt, making me feel things I didn't know I could.

His hands are clasped together before him, and all I can think about is him bending me over the desk, hiking up my skirt, and swatting my rear with those hands.

Great, I think. *I'm already soaked.*

There's a charged silence between us, the air thick with unspoken desire. I manage a smile, trying to keep my cool. "Yeah, you could say that."

His eyes darken slightly, a hint of a smile playing on his lips. "I didn't expect to see you here, Dalia."

"Same for me," I admit, shifting in my seat slightly. "Small world."

He leans back in his chair, regarding me with an intensity that makes my heart race. "So, tell me what you know about our company and what you hope to achieve here."

I take a deep breath, willing myself to focus. "Ivanov Holdings is a diversified holding company with interests in technology, healthcare, and retail. It's the biggest holding company in the city, in fact. You've been expanding aggressively into renewable energy, which I find particularly exciting. As for what I hope to achieve, I'm looking to bring my skills and experience to the table, help streamline operations, and support your initiatives in any way I can."

He nods, his gaze unwavering. "Impressive. And how do you handle stress, Dalia?"

I can't help but let my mind wander back to our night together, the way he commanded my body and made me beg for more. I swallow hard, keeping my expression neutral. "I thrive under pressure," I reply, my voice steady. "I've learned to manage stress by staying organized and focused. And I'm always up for a challenge."

A slow smile spreads across his face. "Good to hear. I have high expectations. I think you'll find working here to be quite stimulating."

The double entendre isn't lost on me, and I feel a flush rise to my cheeks. "I'm looking forward to it, sir."

Sir. Shit. I just had to say that word.

He arches an eyebrow but doesn't expand on it.

"Excellent," he says. "Let's get started, then."

He stands up, moving with a slow, deliberate grace. He makes his way around the desk and sits in the chair next to me, his eyes never leaving mine.

"Your duties will include managing my schedule, handling correspondence, preparing reports, and coordinating meetings," he begins, his tone all business. "I expect nothing less than perfection. Mistakes are not tolerated."

I swallow hard, the weight of his words sinking in. It's clear that, while he'd shown kindness to me the other night, here in the office, he's all business. Still, I can't help but let my eyes drift down to the slight bulge in his pants when he looks away, well aware of the thickness that he's packing.

"Understood."

He nods, satisfied. "Good. I'll give you a brief tour of the executive floor before my meeting with my brothers."

I stand, smoothing down my skirt, and follow him out of the office. As we walk, he points out the various departments, introducing me to key personnel along the way. His demeanor is stern, and it's clear he commands respect from everyone around him.

We pause in front of a large conference room, the door closed. "This is where we hold our executive meetings," he explains. "I expect you to be prepared at all times, as meetings are sometimes last-minute. Understand?"

"Yes, sir."

God, I need to stop saying that.

"Good."

He continues showing me around the executive floor, his voice a steady stream of information. I try to focus, but my eyes keep stealing glances at his rear, the way it looks in those perfectly tailored slacks. The man is a walking distraction.

His voice drifts in and out as my mind wanders, fantasizing about him on top of me, taking me from behind like he did before. I imagine all the places we could have an office tryst —quick fucks in the supply closet, me on my back with my legs spread on the conference table as he pounds me after hours, him reaching up my skirt and fingering me in his office as I struggle to explain the day's itinerary.

"And this is the main break room," he says, snapping me back to reality. "It's stocked with snacks and coffee. You'll find most of the team here during lunch. Though, you're more than welcome to take lunch out of the office, provided that you're not a minute late getting back."

I nod, trying to keep my thoughts professional. "Got it."

As we continue to walk, he points out various offices, introducing me to a few more key people. Each time he turns away, I can't help but admire his form, my mind running wild with images of our night together.

Finally, we stop outside another office. "This will be your workspace," he says, opening the door to reveal a sleek modern office with a view almost as impressive as his own. "You'll have everything you need here to assist me efficiently."

"Thank you," I say, stepping inside and taking it all in.

He watches me for a moment, his eyes dark with an intensity that makes my pulse quicken. "I expect you to be thorough and diligent. We have high standards here, Dalia."

"Yes, si—" This time, I manage to stop myself, thankfully.

He nods, satisfied. "Good. Now, I have a meeting with my brothers. You'll come with me to take notes."

I grab my notebook and follow him to one of the smaller conference rooms. Inside, two men in sharp suits are waiting for us. One looks to be in his late thirties, a bit older than Lev. The other is younger, maybe late twenties, tall and lanky, with the same black hair and gray eyes.

"Dalia Abbas, meet my brothers," Lev says, gesturing to them. "This is Luk, our CEO," he nods to the older man, "and Yuri, our CFO."

Luk gives me a curt nod, his demeanor stern like Lev's. "Nice to meet you, Ms. Abbas."

"Pleasure," I reply, feeling the weight of his intense gaze. "And please, call me Dalia."

Yuri, on the other hand, has a wild glint in his eyes, a mischievous smile playing on his lips. "Welcome aboard, Dalia. I hope you're ready for a challenge."

"I am," I say confidently.

"Good to hear."

Lev takes a seat at the head of the table, and I settle in beside him, notebook and pen at the ready.

"Let's get started," Lev says, his tone commanding as always. "We have a lot to cover."

As the meeting begins, I do my best to focus on taking notes, but it's hard to ignore the dynamic between the brothers. Lev and Luk are both all business, and their discussions are efficient and to the point. Yuri, though brilliant with numbers, injects a bit of levity into the conversation with his quick wit and sharp observations.

"We need to finalize the budget for the new project," Lev says, turning to Yuri. "Do you have the projections?"

Yuri nods, sliding a folder across the table. "I've crunched the numbers, and I think we're looking at a solid return on investment within the first quarter."

Luk reviews the documents, his expression serious. "This looks promising. We'll need to ensure the execution is flawless."

I scribble down their key points, doing my best to keep up with the rapid exchange of information. Despite the intensity of the meeting, I can't help but feel a sense of excitement. Being part of this high-powered team is exhilarating, and I'm determined to prove myself.

The meeting goes on, and once more, my thoughts drift to Lev and all the things I want him to do to me. I know it's impossible now, with us working together, but I can't help myself.

"Dalia, do you have the notes on the meeting schedule for next week?" Lev asks, his eyes piercing into mine. "They should've been emailed to you early this morning before your arrival."

Without thinking, I respond, "Yes, sir."

Lev allows himself a small smirk, and I can sense that he knows exactly what's on my mind. The realization sends a jolt of arousal through me, and my pussy clenches at the thought of him thinking about me in that way.

I clear my throat, trying to recover. "I mean, yes, I have them right here. The schedule includes the marketing strategy session for our new tech division, among others."

Lev's smirk fades into a more serious expression as he nods. "Good. Make sure everything is in order. I want you to coordinate closely with the marketing team to ensure all preparations are flawless."

"Of course," I reply, scribbling it all down, my heart still racing.

The rest of the meeting continues smoothly, but I can't shake the lingering tension between Lev and me. His knowing grin, his domineering presence—it all keeps my mind spinning with possibilities.

Every time he looks at me, I imagine his hands on my body, his low voice telling me exactly what to do.

This job, I realize, is going to be a hell of a lot harder than I bargained for. Working so closely with Lev, balancing professional duties with the simmering tension between us, is going to be a test of my self-control.

As the meeting wraps up, I gather my notes, taking a deep breath to steady myself. I'm determined to succeed here, but I can already tell it's going to be an interesting ride.

I can't wait to see where it takes me.

CHAPTER 7

LEV

"Dalia, are you ready for the meeting with the board at ten?"

It's the following morning, and I'm going over the day with Dalia in my office.

I've been facing the window while detailing the schedule. I finally turn to her, taking her in. She's dressed in a distractingly professional way—though almost certainly unintentionally so. A woman like her can't help but be sexy.

God, the things I want to do to her.

"Yes, sir," she replies, her voice steady.

There it is again, that word, *sir*. My mind flashes back to our night together, and I have to force myself to stay on track.

"We'll also need to prepare the quarterly reports for my review," I continue, my eyes involuntarily drifting to the curve of her waist and the way her blouse tugs slightly as she leans forward to make a note.

She nods, jotting down the details. "Got it. Is there anything else you need me to get ready?"

"No, that should be it for now," I say, finally tearing my gaze away from her and back to the agenda in my hand. "Just make sure everything is in order for the board meeting."

"Of course, Mr. Ivanov," she says, looking up at me with those chocolate-brown eyes that have been haunting my thoughts.

"Do you remember what time the call with the European partners is scheduled for?" I ask as a little test.

She pauses, her brow furrowing slightly. "I believe it's at two p.m.," she says, but there's a hint of uncertainty in her voice.

I take a stern tone with her.

"Dalia, as my PA, you're going to have to have an encyclopedic understanding of my schedule. You can't afford to hesitate."

She looks a bit chastened, and I realize my tone might have been too harsh.

"I have a private meeting in a few minutes," I say, softening my voice. "I'll let you know when my guests and I need coffee."

She nods, standing up and gathering her notes. "Understood, Mr. Ivanov."

"Good," I say, watching her for a moment longer than necessary. "You can go now."

Dalia turns and leaves the office, and I can't help but admire the way she moves, the sway of her hips. Once the door closes behind her, I take a deep breath, trying to regain focus. Having her as my PA is going to test my self-control in ways I never anticipated.

Ten minutes later, there's a knock at my office door. "Come in," I call out. The door swings open, and Vladimir Smirnov strides in, followed closely by Ivan "Vanya" Korolev. Vladimir is a key ally and partner in our operations, and Vanya is my right hand and close confidant.

"Gentlemen," I say, my voice firm. "Take a seat. Let's get started."

The three of us exchange pleasantries, but I keep it brief. Time is valuable.

"All right, let's get down to business. The company is growing nicely. We're quickly becoming one of the largest holding companies in the Midwest."

We discuss possible expansions to the East and West Coasts, plans that are ambitious but necessary. "We need to build a stronger base here before making those moves," I say, my tone firm.

Vanya smirks, making a crack. "Lev, you've always imagined taking over the world."

I allow myself a smirk of my own. "True, but I'll start with the U.S. first."

Vladimir interjects, his expression serious. "There's a growing problem we need to address. A man named Alexei Plushenko has been swooping in and buying properties we've been looking to acquire."

My eyes narrow. "Plushenko. What do we know about him?"

"He's a cunning operator," Vladimir explains. "Seems to have deep pockets and good intel on our moves. He had the audacity to have his personal assistant inform us that he's willing to sell the properties to us for a 'fair and reasonable price.'"

I glance at Vanya. "Look into it."

Vladimir continues, his tone heavy with annoyance. "And, of course, the prices are anything but reasonable. He's playing games, trying to undermine us at every turn."

I feel my jaw clench. The nerve of this Alexei, thinking he can toy with us like this. "We'll see about that," I say, my voice low and dangerous. "Vanya, I want you to dig up everything you can on him. I want to know his every move before he makes it."

Vanya nods, already formulating a plan. "Consider it done."

Vladimir adds, "We can't let him think he has the upper hand. We need to make a move, and soon."

I agree. "We'll strategize our next steps carefully. But make no mistake, we will put Alexei in his place." A charged silence fills the room, each of us aware of the stakes.

I muse aloud, a trace of confusion in my tone. "It's odd—no one in Chicago's Russian American community would dare challenge Ivanov turf like this. By this point, they all know better."

Vanya leans forward. "There are always new young guns trying to make a name for themselves by targeting those at the top."

Vladimir, however, isn't convinced. He shakes his head dismissively. "Even the ambitious ones here know better than to take a direct swing at us." He pauses, his gaze sharpening. "We need to exercise caution with Alexei. He's clearly not a typical brash youth; he's astute, hungry for power, and obviously well-connected if he can afford the real estate."

I nod, absorbing their perspectives. "Agreed, Vladimir. Underestimating him would be a mistake. His audacity implies he has support and resources we haven't fully accounted for yet. Not to mention the kind of nerve that could prove dangerous."

Vanya interjects, "I'll look into his networks. Understanding his backers will reveal their confidence in challenging us."

"Excellent," I respond. "And Vladimir, monitor his movements closely, especially around the properties he's targeting. We need to anticipate his strategies."

Vladimir nods firmly. "I'll ensure our real estate team is on high alert. If he tries to outsmart us, we'll catch him swiftly."

Leaning back, I consider our strategy. "We must handle this delicately. Alexei is looking to provoke us, but we will dictate the terms of our response. His ambition will be his downfall. He will fall in line or be crushed under my boot."

The atmosphere is charged with tension. I look between Vanya and Vladimir. "Stay sharp. This isn't just about defending our assets—it's about reinforcing the stature of the Ivanovs."

Their nods of agreement affirm their readiness. Alexei Plushenko might think himself a formidable challenger, but he's about to learn the harsh reality of going against the Ivanov family.

I sit back, letting the conversation wash over me. "A bit of coffee before we go on, gentlemen?"

"That would be heavenly," replies Vanya.

I place my finger on the intercom to Dalia's office. "Coffee, please. Cream and sugar."

"Yes, Mr. Ivanov."

"How's the new personal assistant?" Vanya asks, turning his cane over in his hands.

God, what a question. "Working out well so far. No major mistakes—yet."

Vladimir smiles. "Perhaps she'll free up your schedule enough to take a day off every now and then, maybe some time to hit the links with me like I've been pestering you to do."

I chuckle. "You know golf's never been my thing; it's too slow."

"Just think of it as a lovely walk through the park," Vladimir replies, "one where you get extremely frustrated now and then."

Vanya laughs. "You sure know how to make a case, Vlad."

Dalia enters the room with the coffee; her movements are fluid and alluring. As she bends over slightly to hand out the cups, her posture accentuates her curves, and I find myself struggling to maintain my composure. Underneath my desk, I feel a familiar stir of arousal, making it increasingly difficult to focus.

Vladimir, noticing my distraction but misinterpreting the cause, gives me a ribbing smile. "Lev, you look like you've seen a ghost. Too much on your mind?"

I clear my throat, adjusting slightly. "Just thinking about the next steps," I reply, trying to keep my tone even.

Dalia, seemingly oblivious to the effect she's having, smiles politely and asks, "Anything else you need right now?"

Vanya, ever observant, gives me a quick glance but remains silent, sipping his coffee. "Just the coffee, thank you, Dalia," I manage to say, my voice slightly strained.

She nods and exits the room, and I take a deep breath, trying to refocus on the men in front of me.

Vladimir leans back. "You know, Lev, it's good to see you taking charge like your father did. He'd be proud."

I nod, appreciative of the sentiment. "Thanks. We've come a long way from the old days, haven't we?"

"Indeed, we have," he agrees, his tone reflective. "I remember when we used to run around causing more trouble than it was worth. Now look at us—strategizing about expansions and dealing with corporate espionage."

Vanya chuckles dryly. "Speak for yourselves. I was always the responsible one."

"You? Responsible?" Vladimir laughs, the sound booming around the room. "Let's not rewrite history too much."

The light banter helps ease some of the tension, and I find myself grateful for the moment of levity.

"Now, about those expansion plans," I say, steering the conversation back to business. "We need to be two steps ahead of Alexei and anyone else who thinks they can take a piece of what we've built."

"Agreed," Vladimir says, his expression turning serious again. "We'll do whatever it takes. You can count on that."

The meeting concludes with strategic decisions mapped out and the team reinvigorated. I stand up, signaling the end of our session. "I'll have Dalia schedule a follow-up in a few days," I tell Vladimir and Vanya, shaking their hands firmly.

"Sounds good, Lev. We'll be ready," Vladimir responds.

CHAPTER 8

DALIA

One week later...

My phone buzzes loudly on the desk, jolting me out of my workflow.

I've been grinding away at this late hour—my new norm since starting to work for Lev. I'm deep into organizing his schedule and typing up emails that need to go out during tomorrow's business hours.

I glance at my phone. The Thai food delivery I'd completely forgotten about is here.

I stretch, feeling the stiffness in my shoulders from hours of being hunched over my laptop. I grab my phone and head to the lobby to pick up my dinner, thankful for the break and the chance to refuel.

As I head out, I notice that the only lights still on are those in Lev's office.

I grab the food and wait for the elevator to take me back up, reflecting on my job. Lev is demanding, but he's also a surprisingly fair boss. The more than generous salary makes the late nights and high expectations worth it.

When I return to my office, I decide to check in with Lev about tomorrow's schedule and offer him some food. I knock gently on his door, and in that deep, gruff, and insanely sexy voice, he calls out, "Come in."

Pushing the door open, I find him seated in the meeting area of his office, his feet propped up on the table, sleeves rolled up, revealing his ropy forearms. His collar is undone, lending him a more relaxed charm, and his face is knitted in concentration as he pores over a form in his hands. Just the sight of him like this, effortlessly sexy, sends a rush of heat through me.

"What do you need, Dalia?" he asks, not looking up from his paperwork.

I clear my throat, trying to steady my voice. "Dinner," I manage to say.

He looks up, confusion crossing his features momentarily. I can tell he forgot all about eating—something he tends to do when he's buried in work. "Dinner?" he echoes.

"Yes, you know, that thing people do in the evening when they're hungry," I say with a light laugh, trying to ease the sudden tension I feel. "I figured you might have forgotten, just like I almost did. You're not the only one who skips meals when busy."

He sets the papers down and rubs his eyes, a faint smile breaking through. "That was thoughtful of you. Thanks for looking out."

I set the food down on the table and hand him a container. Watching him ease back into his chair and start to unwind causes desire to bubble to the surface.

He cranes his neck to peek into the bag, noting there's more food than one person could possibly eat in one sitting. "I'm hungry, but not *that* hungry," he jokes.

I laugh, picking up my own container. "That one's mine."

"Join me then," he offers, gesturing to the space across from him.

The invitation sends a thrill through me, and despite the nervous flutter in my stomach, I accept. He hops up from his chair and grabs a bottle of mineral water for each of us from a small fridge under one of the shelves.

We both dive into our food, devouring it in silence. The intensity of my hunger surprises me.

Sitting across from Lev in the quiet of his office, sharing a simple meal, feels unexpectedly intimate. The lines between boss and assistant blur just a bit, making this ordinary moment feel like something more.

After polishing off half his meal, he takes a long swig of water, and I find myself fixated on the bobbing of his Adam's apple as he drinks.

I press my thighs tightly together under the table, trying to quell the growing heat within me. I silently curse, knowing I'll have to change my panties if I get any more aroused.

Lev wipes his hands on a napkin as he shifts his focus toward me, his expression turning slightly more serious.

"So, tell me, how are things going with you? That prick of an ex-husband causing any more trouble?" he asks, his tone protective.

I correct him quickly, a slight flush coloring my cheeks, "Well, we weren't technically married."

Lev's eyebrows knit together, showing his curiosity is piqued. "What do you mean by 'not technically married?'" he probes gently.

I let out a heavy sigh, the memory still sour. "It was a big mess," I begin, feeling the frustration anew. "He faked the marriage certificate and had someone who wasn't even ordained conduct the ceremony. It was cheap and quick. I didn't know about any of this until I tried to take legal action against him for what he did with the bank accounts."

Pausing, I collect myself before revealing more. "By the time I figured out what had happened, he was long gone, and so was my money."

I watch Lev's reaction, a storm of anger brewing in his eyes, a fierce, protective rage that looks as if he wouldn't hesitate to tear Chad apart with his bare hands.

But instead of acting on his fury, he reins it in, his voice calm but stern as he says, "Bad deeds always catch up to you; trust me, I know."

Revisiting the topic of Chad stirs a mix of emotions within me, casting a slight shadow over our dinner. Lev seems to pick up on my discomfort, his gaze softening as he leans back slightly in his chair.

"You're doing really well, Dalia," he offers. "Despite my demanding expectations, you've handled yourself excellently."

His words lift my spirits. "That might be the first nice thing you've said to me since I started here."

Lev raises an eyebrow, a hint of surprise in his expression. "Really?"

I nod, a playful smile tugging at my lips. "Yep. You've more or less been barking orders at me and little else for the last couple of weeks."

He grins, his demeanor easing into a more casual, almost teasing posture. "I just like to get things done with no fuss," he explains. "My military background has made me accustomed to a certain level of discipline."

My curiosity piqued, especially by the scars that marked his skin, I venture cautiously, "Can you tell me about your military background?"

As soon as the words leave my mouth, I gasp, realizing that I might have stepped into sensitive territory.

"Sorry. I just want to get to know you better, not trying to dredge up memories you might not want to talk about," I add quickly, hoping to ease any discomfort.

There's a flash of something—pain, perhaps remembrance—in his eyes, but it quickly vanishes as his expression softens. "It's fine," he assures me, his voice steady. "It was a long time ago. I was in the Russian army, in military intelligence. I served in Crimea."

He pauses, the memory seeming to weigh on him. "I was medically discharged after an injury."

Curiosity again getting the better of me, I gently probe, "Your arm?" remembering the scars I had seen.

His expression darkens slightly, and he shakes his head. "No," he replies, his voice lower.

I nod, understanding that some stories are more difficult to tell due to the complexity and pain they entail. I decide not to press further, giving him the space to share what he's comfortable with.

Wanting to steer the conversation away from sensitive territory, I shift gears slightly.

"So, military intelligence... that must mean you're good at reading people?" I ask, hoping to lighten the mood a bit.

Lev nods, a knowing smile slowly forming on his face. "Yes," he affirms confidently.

Then, leaning forward, his gaze intensifying, he adds, "For example, I can tell that you've been turned on since the moment you walked into my office tonight."

I gasp, caught off guard by his blunt observation, my eyes going wide.

"Is that right?"

He nods confidently, "Of course."

"How can you tell?" I ask despite the embarrassment.

He chuckles deeply before sitting back in his chair, completely at ease. He starts to list the signs: "The flush in your cheeks, dilated pupils, the way you frequently tilt your head, exposing your neck to me..." He pauses, his eyes locking with mine, "and other more subtle cues you're probably not even aware of."

I'm both impressed and a bit alarmed at his perceptiveness. But then he goes a step further, his voice lowering, "I'd also bet that your pussy is soaking wet right now."

I let out a strangled noise, my face heating up at his boldness.

"Am I right?"

Swallowing hard, I nod, barely whispering, "Yes."

He smiles slightly, satisfied with the confirmation.

"Good. Now, I want to see just how wet you are."

My eyes widen, my heart racing. "What do you mean?"

"Stand up," he commands, his tone brooking no argument.

I stand on shaky legs as adrenaline mixes with raw lust.

"Go over to the desk and bend over."

Obediently, I walk to the desk. I bend over the surface, feeling the cool wood against my skin, exposing myself in a way that feels both daring and natural under his watchful eyes.

"Hike up your skirt," he orders next.

I reach back, my fingers trembling with a cocktail of nerves and excitement as I lift my skirt, revealing more of myself to him.

"Now, slowly take off your panties."

Taking a deep breath to steady my racing heart, I hook my fingers into my panties and slide them down over my hips, letting them fall to my ankles. Stepping out of them, I am completely exposed, my compliance complete, my body tingling with desire.

He rises from his chair, his movements deliberate. "Keep your eyes forward."

I obey, staring out at the cityscape of downtown Chicago, the lights glittering like distant stars. The tension in the room climbs as I hear his footsteps approaching.

Then, I feel his hand on my ass, a firm squeeze that sends a jolt of desire straight through me. I half-expected, half-hoped he might take me right here, bent over his desk, with the city as our backdrop.

But instead, his hand travels lower, resting momentarily on my exposed pussy.

"You're body temperature has spiked—another clear sign of your arousal."

His fingers then slip between my thighs, exploring the wetness there before pushing into me. The sensation is electric, and as he moves them inside me, the pressure builds, making me gasp at the intensity.

"You're soaking wet, just as I thought," he states, a hint of satisfaction and raw desire in his voice as he continues to move his fingers, exploring and stretching me. He leans in close, his breath hot on my ear, "You like it when your boss fingers you here in the office, don't you?"

I can't help but squirm against him, pushing my ass into his hand, guiding him deeper as the orgasm starts to build. "Yes," I manage, totally caught up in the moment.

He tightens his grip a bit, a firm reminder of who's in charge.

"Yes, *sir*," he corrects me, his tone strict.

"Yes, sir."

"You want to come?" he asks with a hint of authority.

"Yes, sir," I reply, desperation in my tone.

"Then beg for it," he orders, speeding up his fingers and driving me crazy.

I don't hesitate, my voice breaking with the intensity of my need. "Please, sir, please let me come."

He keeps going, his fingers moving with a fervor that's about to break me completely.

"Show me how much you want it," he urges, his words as charged as his actions.

Driven over the edge by his commands and the relentless pleasure, I finally tip over the edge, my body shaking with a powerful orgasm that tears through me. I cry out, gripping the desk as waves of intense satisfaction roll over me, leaving me shivering and completely undone under his expert touch.

With a surge of animalistic strength, he wraps his arm around my waist and spins me around, planting me firmly on the edge of the desk. He swiftly drops to his knees, his intense gaze never leaving mine until his lips meet my skin.

He starts kissing along the inside of my thighs, his movements slow and deliberate, sending shivers up my spine as he builds anticipation with every breath.

As he reaches my pussy, his approach changes; he's no longer teasing. He parts my lips with his fingers, his eyes locked on mine for a moment before he dives in. His tongue works with precision and hunger, licking and flicking with a purpose that has me gripping the edge of the desk.

"God, yes, just like that, just like that."

He sucks on my clit gently at first, then with increasing pressure, driving me wild. His mouth is relentless, devouring me with total lust, each movement of his tongue designed to draw deeper moans from my throat.

The room fills with the sounds of my escalating pleasure and his deep, satisfied groans as he indulges in me.

He brings me to another orgasm, his lips and tongue working in perfect harmony, sending me over the edge yet again into a blinding release that eclipses the first. This climax is earth-shattering, much more intense, rippling through me in powerful waves.

I cry out, my body trembling uncontrollably, completely at the mercy of his skilled mouth. As I come down from the high, he slowly eases up, placing soft kisses on my thighs, giving me a moment to catch my breath in the afterglow of mind-blowing pleasure.

He stands up, his lips glistening with my juices. Casually, he licks them, his eyes locking onto mine as he murmurs, "You're delicious."

Noticing the bulge in his slacks, I place my hand on his cock, feeling it pulse beneath the fabric. I can't help but tease, "Looks like I'm not the only one who's turned on here."

He chuckles. "Seems so."

"I can return the favor, y' know," I offer, licking my lips at the thought.

He pauses, a thoughtful look crossing his features.

"Perhaps another time. All I wanted tonight was a little dessert. And what a sumptuous one it was."

He hands me my panties, which I slip into with a small smile. Then, he hands me the container of my leftover food. "You might want to take the rest to-go if you don't mind. I've got a long night ahead," he says, hinting at the mountain of work still waiting for him.

"Go home and get some rest," he advises, opening the door for me, his demeanor shifting back to the composed, authoritative boss.

I nod, my body still tingling from our encounter as I prepare to step out of his office.

"One more thing," he calls after me.

I pause, turning to face him. He closes the distance between us and plants a slow, deep kiss on my lips. The world seems to blur and fade into the background; all I can focus on is the warmth of his lips on mine, the firmness of his hands on my waist. I feel like I'm melting into him.

Then, just as I'm getting lost in the kiss, he pulls back slightly, gives me a firm swat on the ass, and says, "Good night."

I leave his office, my legs still a little shaky. I go back to my own office to grab my things, still buzzing from our interaction. As I pack up, it hits me—this is his game. He turned me on, made me crave him, then left me wanting.

It dawns on me that even though our encounter seemed like he was giving me everything, it was all orchestrated for his amusement.

Stepping into the elevator, a grin spreads across my face. I realize that Lev and I have just escalated our sexy little contest.

It's a thrilling realization, one that makes me eager to see how far it will go and what kind of move he'll make next.

CHAPTER 9

LEV

I'm getting in too deep, and I know it.

I'm seated at a fancy French bistro called Le Loup, tucked away in a quiet corner of downtown Chicago. The place is quaint, featuring old-world charm. It's decorated with antique light fixtures and intimate tables for two, the walls lined with vintage posters featuring scenes of France from the early 1900s through the present day.

I arrived early, needing some time to think away from the office and its constant demands.

As I sip my espresso and watch the hustle of the midday crowd from my secluded booth in the back, my thoughts drift to Dalia. The more time I spend with her, the deeper I find myself being drawn into something I know is dangerous yet irresistibly compelling.

What if she's the one? The one who might finally give me the family and love I've secretly yearned for all these years? Dalia, with her resilience and warmth, who's never been loved properly herself, deserves so much more than what she's had.

She deserves someone who will give her everything she wants and needs, and I find myself wanting to be that person for her. It's a risk, a huge one, given my life's complexities, but the thought of not exploring what could be with her feels like an even greater risk.

As I stir my coffee, I resolve to find a way to make this work, to give us both a chance at something real and lasting.

Through the glass front of the bistro, I watch as my guests arrive, stepping out of sleek, black cars that glide to a stop. Vladimir, Luk, Yuri, and Elena—my younger sister, a bona fide tech whiz and the head of the IT department—make their way inside.

Dalia steps out next, and my breath catches. She looks incredible and effortlessly sexy in a way that draws every eye to her.

I unconsciously lick my lips at the sight of her—memories of the other night in my office flooding back—how goddamn good she tasted, how fiercely I craved more. If all's going according to plan, she's been consumed with thoughts of nothing but me and how I made her feel.

As they enter the bistro, I hop up from my seat and weave my way through the bustling lunch crowd, approaching with a confident stride and greeting them with a warm, "Good to see all of you. Vladimir," I nod with respect. "Luk, Yuri," I add, clapping each on the shoulder in a brotherly fashion.

Turning to Elena, I give a slight smirk, "Always a pleasure to see our tech wizard in the flesh and not through a Zoom call."

Elena grins. "You're all better looking from behind my computer," she retorts.

The hostess, recognizing the others, swiftly leads us back to the secluded booth where I had been seated, perfect for both privacy and conversation. As we settle into our seats, I catch Dalia's eye, giving her a knowing look that makes her cheeks flush a deep, delightful red against her rich olive skin.

"So, Elena, still terrorizing the IT department with your ruthless efficiency?" I tease, knowing full well she runs a tight ship.

She chuckles, her eyes twinkling with mischief. "Only the lazy ones. Someone has to keep them on their toes. How about you, Yuri? Still trying to convince everyone to adopt your latest crypto investment strategies?"

Yuri rolls his eyes, a grin spreading across his face. "It's not my fault none of you understands the beauty of blockchain. One day, you'll thank me."

Luk chimes in, his voice dry, "Or blame you when it all crashes. Again."

"Hey, at least I'm not the one who tried to teach Lev how to use Twitter last Christmas. That was a disaster waiting to happen," Yuri shoots back, pointing at me with a laugh.

I raise my hands in surrender. "Guilty as charged."

The table erupts in laughter.

Elena decides to shift gears. "Enough with the frivolities, let's talk shop."

As the discussion prepares to become more serious, Vladimir, with a thoughtful glance, turns his attention to Dalia, who has been quietly observing the conversation.

"Can we trust her with this level of private business?" he asks me in a low voice, the rest of the group busy chatting amongst themselves.

I'm about to vouch for her myself, but Dalia beats me to it.

She speaks up, her voice confident and clear. "I was hired for my discretion and professionalism. And if it makes you feel any better, I had to sign an NDA on top of it."

She doesn't stop there; her gaze sweeps across the table as she continues. "Furthermore, as Lev's personal assistant, I'm fully integrated into the organization. I'm in the loop now, and while I understand and respect the need for caution, I don't appreciate having my competence and loyalty questioned."

I lean back, silently observing her, impressed by her fortitude and the ease with which she asserted herself at a table full of seasoned executives.

Vladimir, after a moment's pause, chuckles lightly, nodding in acknowledgment.

"Point made and taken," he concedes. It's clear that Dalia's forthrightness has made an impression.

Elena laughs lightly, teasing, "Glad to see there's another ballsy woman in the company. Welcome."

Dalia flashes a quick smile and shoots back, "Well, last I checked, I don't have any balls. But I did inherit a strong will from my parents."

Luk leans in a bit. "Speaking of which, what's your story, Dalia? Where are you from?"

Dalia relaxes into her chair. "I'm from Maple Grove, a little town in Rhode Island, not far from Providence. My mom's a schoolteacher, loved by everyone. And my dad is a second-generation Egyptian-American and runs the general store there—your typical middle-class businessman."

Watching her, I'm struck by her poise and the way she articulates her background with such pride. Her confidence is incredibly appealing.

The contrast between her public persona and our private encounters is strikingly sexy. Dalia handles herself with a no-bullshit attitude that commands respect from everyone around her.

Yet, in the privacy of the bedroom, she transforms into a yielding plaything, eager and pliant under my control. This duality fascinates me, and as much as I admire her assertive side, the thought of her sweet submission is enough to get the blood pumping to my cock.

I want more.

And I'll have it.

CHAPTER 10

L unch concludes and we stand outside the restaurant, saying our goodbyes.

I turn to Dalia. "I'll take you back myself."

We walk toward my car, a sleek Mercedes-Benz S-Class, its glossy obsidian-black finish catching the afternoon sun.

"Nice car," she says as we approach.

"Thanks."

As I open the passenger door for her, she teases, "A bit old-fashioned, aren't you?"

I flash a quick smile. "I assure you, I'm anything but old-fashioned. If anyone should know that, it's you."

She glances back at me as she slips into the car, a tinge of blush on her cheeks.

Once we're both settled inside, I turn to her with a proposal. "How about we both take the rest of the day off?"

She looks surprised, eyebrows raised in curiosity. "Why?"

Leaning back, I meet her gaze directly, the intensity clear in my eyes.

"Because all I could think about during the meeting was how much I wanted to make you come again," I confess.

She gasps at my frankness, but the mischievous sparkle in her eyes betrays her intrigue.

"You're the boss."

I start the car and pull into the stream of city traffic, the engine purring smoothly.

"Where do you live?" I ask, glancing over at her as we navigate the bustling streets.

"In Wicker Park, on Pierce Avenue near the park entrance."

"Have you ever given road head?" I ask with as much nonchalance as if I'm asking her favorite color.

She laughs for a minute before realizing I'm serious. "Uh, no, I haven't," she admits, but I can see her interest is piqued.

"Well, then, you should try it. As in right now," I say. I watch her squirm in her seat out of the corner of my eye.

As I return my focus to the road, she reaches over, unzipping my slacks with a delicate yet eager touch.

Her hand finds my hardness, stroking it slowly, exploring as she acquaints herself.

After a few minutes of her stroking me, she unhooks her seatbelt and leans over, taking charge of my eager manhood.

She starts slow, with gentle licks and teasing kisses, before diving in.

Her mouth feels like pure heaven as she takes me deeper, her technique a mix of tender laps and determined suction.

Her handwork is just as expert, one hand firmly at my base while the other ventures to add more thrill. I let out a low groan, the car filling with the wet sounds of her enthusiasm.

She's got me on the edge, and every muscle in my body tenses with the need for release.

But I've got other plans. Just as we pull into her apartment block, I lay a firm hand on her head, easing her off.

"Enough for now," I manage to say, my voice thick with restrained need. The restraint only sharpens my anticipation.

She licks her lips, a satisfied look in her eyes. "You're delicious," she comments with a playful smirk.

"I'm glad you enjoyed it," I respond, the corner of my mouth lifting slightly as we exit the car.

As we walk toward her building, I take in the sight of the charming brick walk-up.

Her place is a small, cozy studio that reflects her style: functional yet inviting.

While I appreciate the charm, part of me feels she deserves something more.

But there's no time to dwell on that thought as we're quickly wrapped up in each other. The moment her door shuts behind us, we're kissing fiercely, hands roaming as we peel away each other's clothes.

I squeeze her breasts and her ass, each touch making her moan as she presses herself closer to me. The world outside her apartment fades away, leaving just the heat and urgency between us.

She pulls back slightly, her expression turning serious for a moment. "Is this really a good idea? I am your employee, after all."

I chuckle softly. "We crossed that line the moment I ate your pussy on my desk," I remind her.

A mischievous grin spreads across her face, her thoughts obviously drifting back to that night. Encouraged by her response, I cup her cheek gently, making sure she understands my next words, "We won't do anything you're not comfortable with."

She steps closer, her body language signaling her decision. "We'd be idiots to think we could just ignore what's between us."

Responding to her admission, I lean in and kiss her deeply, my hand finding its way between her thighs, caressing her over the fabric of her panties. Her body responds immediately, pressing into my touch, the connection sparking with undeniable intensity.

I quickly yank down her panties and toss them aside, eager to feel more of her. My fingers slide easily into her wetness, her body already primed from our heated kisses. I work her slowly at first, feeling her warmth clench around me, then pick up the pace, driving her wild.

My other hand roams her body, grasping her hips and pulling her closer.

Her moans fill the room, driving me crazier with each breathy sound.

"I'm going to fuck you right here against this wall," I growl into her ear.

"Yes, sir," she breathes out.

That's all the confirmation I need. I pull my fingers from her, her slickness making them glisten in the low light.

I lift Dalia effortlessly, her legs instinctively wrapping tightly around my waist as I pin her against the wall. I position myself at her entrance before I slide my cock into her, relishing the slick warmth of her pussy enveloping me.

I start to move, each thrust deep and forceful, the primal rhythm matched by the slap of skin on skin. Our moans fill the space, hers high and wanting, mine low and guttural.

"You're going to come on my command," I growl into her ear.

"Yes, sir," she gasps out, her voice sultry, her body taut with anticipation.

I increase my pace, driving into her with unrestrained force. Watching her face contort with pleasure, her eyes glazed with lust, I wait for the perfect moment.

"Come now, Dalia," I command, my voice sharp. "Come all over my cock."

Her response is immediate and intense. Her pussy clenches tightly around my cock as she comes undone, her body shaking against mine as she screams out in pleasure. I hold her against the wall, feeling her convulse around me.

I gently set her back on her feet, her legs trembling from the intensity of her climax.

"I want to see you on top of me," I command, watching her struggle to steady herself.

"Yes, sir," she replies, her voice breathless.

We move over to the couch, where I take a seat, my cock erect, glistening with her juices.

"Ride me."

She positions herself above me, taking hold of my cock and slowly lowering down until I'm fully sheathed within her. I grasp her hips, guiding her movements initially. Watching myself disappear inside her, coupled with the way her eyes flutter closed in pleasure, is intoxicating.

She begins to ride me, finding her rhythm, and I let my hands roam over her body, feeling every shudder and tremble. The way she moves, how she takes control yet submits to the pleasure, quickly drives me to the edge.

Dalia's movements soon become more fervent and deliberate. The sight of her above me is mesmerizing—her breasts bouncing rhythmically with each thrust, her toned muscles flexing, her hips grinding down on me in a dance of both control and surrender.

"You feel so good wrapped around my cock," I groan, my hands moving up her body to her breasts, pulling her closer to taste her.

"I love feeling you so deep inside me," she breathes out, her voice laced with lust as she leans down, allowing me better access to her dark, hardened nipples. I take one into my mouth, sucking and flicking it with my tongue, eliciting moans of pleasure from her.

Her movements intensify, driven by the dual sensations of my mouth on her breast and my cock filling her repeatedly. "I'm close," I warn her, feeling the familiar build-up within.

"I want it, sir. Come inside me," she responds, her voice desperate with need.

Her words push me over the edge. I grip her hips tightly, guiding her down as I thrust up, synchronizing our movements to chase our climax together. As I erupt inside her, the sensation of releasing deep within her is overwhelming —hot, intense, and profoundly satisfying. Her own orgasm ripples around my cock, her inner muscles clenching, milking me for every last drop.

The shared intensity of our release binds us for a moment longer, our bodies quivering in pleasure simultaneously, her head thrown back in ecstasy.

When our orgasms have faded, she falls to my side and curls up against me, her body fitting perfectly into the curve of my arms as we share tender kisses.

I study her face, looking for any hint of regret, but find none.

"Are you enjoying our games?" I ask, genuinely curious about her feelings.

She nods, a slight blush coloring her cheeks.

"Yes, surprisingly so," she admits, her voice soft but sure. This admission sends a wave of satisfaction through me, knowing she's as caught up in this as I am.

We settle back on the couch, my arm securely around her, drawing her close. The comfort of her body against mine is soothing, and without intending to, I feel myself drifting toward sleep.

It's been a long time since I've felt this peaceful and content with someone. As sleep claims me, I'm aware of a profound connection that I hadn't realized I'd been missing.

CHAPTER 11

DALIA

I wake up, snuggled against Lev's impossibly sexy body. We've shifted during our nap and are now lying next to one another. He's still asleep. Moving a bit to get comfortable, I catch our reflection in the mirror across the room.

That's when I see them—huge, jagged scars crisscrossing his back. I hadn't noticed them until now.

Carefully, almost without thinking, I start tracing the rough lines with my fingers. What kind of hell did he go through to get these? It's clear he's lucky to be alive.

Lev stirs awake, and when he catches me tracing his scars, his eyes flash with annoyance.

"Stop touching them," he says sternly.

I jerk my hand back.

"I'm sorry," I stammer.

He doesn't respond; he just slides off the couch and starts gathering his clothes. There's a sudden coldness to him as he avoids further discussion, focusing instead on dressing.

"I need to get back to the office," he says, voice gruff. "Need to spend the rest of the day catching up on work."

I watch him dress, unable to take my eyes off the powerful play of muscles across his back, that perfect ass of his, firm and just begging to be grabbed. Each movement is efficient, almost mechanical, as he slips back into his professional armor.

He seems distant now, and I can't help but wonder if I crossed a line by touching his scars. Or maybe he's upset with himself for letting things go too far.

"I'm happy about what happened between us," I say, trying to reassure him or perhaps myself.

He doesn't respond. He taps away at his phone before slipping into his shoes, his movements precise and detached. Sensing the growing distance, I venture cautiously, "Do you want me to come to the office with you?"

"No," he answers quickly, almost *too* quickly, as if the idea is something he needs to shut down immediately. "Take the rest of the day off."

As if to cement the distance between us further, he adds, "I'll be out of the office tomorrow so that you can work from home."

Once he's all suited up, Lev stands tall in front of me, the epitome of a boss, with his hands assertively planted on his hips. Even though I'm miffed by his sudden shift to ice-cold professionalism, I can't deny that the guy looks drop-dead gorgeous, wielding that much authority. Part of me, annoyingly enough, knows I'd melt in a heartbeat if he decided to take me again right here and now.

He clears his throat, pulling my thoughts back from the edge. "Do you remember what tomorrow night is?"

I nod, recalling the scheduled event. "It's the annual gala at the Art Institute of Chicago."

He confirms with a nod before scanning me up and down. "Got something appropriate to wear for that?"

I hesitate, then admit, "Just work clothes."

He shakes his head slightly. "That won't do. Go pick out a nice dress, put it on my tab." His statement leaves no room for argument.

"I'll see you there," he adds sharply, turning to leave without any of the warmth we shared just hours ago.

He's out the door before I can even process what's just happened, leaving me alone and confused.

Sitting there, stunned, I try to wrap my head around Lev's abrupt switch of character. Is this just another part of his game?

As I get dressed, I mull over everything, trying to find some sense in his actions. The shift felt too sharp, too sudden. I make myself a cup of tea, letting the warm liquid ground me as I consider tomorrow night. Ivanov Holdings poured a lot of money into refurbishing an entire wing of the art museum.

It's more than just a party—it's a showcase of Lev's influence and power. Maybe that's why he's so tense, why he pulled back into that commanding shell of his. But where does that leave me in the grand scheme of things?

I sip my tea, but the warmth does little to soothe the rising irritation within me. We've shared something intense and personal, and I've opened up to Lev in ways I never thought I would with anyone.

Shutting me out the minute things get a bit uncomfortable for him is infuriating. Maybe it has nothing to do with me; maybe he's just grappling with his own choices and lashing out.

Enough is enough. I've decided that if Lev wants distance, he's going to get it. From now on, I'll be nothing but professional. No more blurred lines, no more late-night escapades in his office.

If he wants a PA, that's exactly what he'll get and nothing more. I need to protect my own heart in this, even if part of me dreads the thought of losing the connection we have.

CHAPTER 12

The next evening…

I pull up to the Art Institute in an Uber, my nerves tangling up inside me. I feel out of my element in this gown—it's stunning and definitely the most extravagant thing I've ever worn. The only reason I even dared to indulge in something so luxurious was Lev's insistent message last night.

His text still burns in my memory.

Don't even glance at the price tags. Choose something that dazzles. Also, ensure your hair and makeup are done by professionals. And one more thing... visit La Seduction Lingerie.

As much as his demands frustrate me, especially with what happened yesterday afternoon, they also thrill me in a way I can't deny. There's a part of me that revels in trying to meet his high expectations, a rush I get in satisfying his specifications. I find myself struggling to hold onto my self-declaration last night: to be nothing more than his employee. I both hate and love my reaction.

I hate that he knows just how to pull my strings, but at the same time, I love the attention he gives me and the way he makes me feel so sensual and beautiful.

I take a deep breath, ready to step out into the night that Lev has so meticulously orchestrated.

As I approach the entrance of the Art Institute, a sea of glitz greets me. Swarms of elegantly dressed people, women in luxurious and flowing gowns, men sporting sharp, tailored tuxedos, mill about. My nerves spike—I'm so out of my element here, a girl from a small town where the most exciting event is the annual Fourth of July parade.

Amidst the crowd, I spot Lev and his family, the picture of class and power. He catches sight of me and quickly strides over.

He greets me with a warmth that makes my heart race. "You look absolutely stunning; your gown selection was perfect."

I had promised myself I'd keep things strictly professional, but my resolve begins to crumble the instant I see him, all dashing and devastating in his tuxedo.

He wears it with such an air of nonchalant elegance. And that voice... that voice that always sends shivers down my spine; it's unfair how quickly he can make me forget my own rules.

Lev guides me through the crowd, his hand lightly resting on my lower back. "How are you holding up?" he asks.

"I'm fine," I reply, trying to sound more confident than I feel. Part of me clings to the hope that he'll apologize for his abrupt departure yesterday, for the cold distance that seemed to spring up out of nowhere. But he doesn't mention it. Instead, he's all smiles, as if eager to sweep past any lingering tension between us.

"There's someone I really want you to meet," he says as we weave through the growing crowd of attendees.

We approach his family, who are clustered together, chatting animatedly. Luk, Yuri, Vanya, Vladimir, and Elena all greet me warmly, making me feel surprisingly welcome. A stunning woman with striking Irish features—fair skin contrasted by dark red hair—stands beside Luk.

Luk steps forward, a proud smile lighting up his features, and gestures to the woman beside him. "Dalia, I'd like you to meet Maura, my wife," he says affectionately.

"Hello, Dalia. It's so lovely to meet you," Maura says, her voice warm and inviting.

Her presence is elegant yet approachable, and she extends a hand, which I shake, feeling the genuine kindness in her gesture.

Maura leans in with a conspiratorial smile, her eyes sparkling as we step aside from the group. "So, Dalia, how are you settling into our little Ivanov universe? It's quite a world apart, isn't it?"

I nod. "It's definitely a whole new dynamic for me, but everyone's been incredibly welcoming so far."

She gives a knowing nod, her voice lowering a bit. "Lev is a good man, really. He might seem all tough on the outside, but he's got a softer side, too, just like my Luk." Her gaze briefly flits to her husband, filled with tenderness and affection.

I can't help but laugh, the sound bubbling up from deep within.

"Lev? Sensitive? Now that's something I'll have to see to believe." The idea of Lev being anything other than the stern, commanding figure I know strikes me as both amusing and oddly intriguing.

Maura's laughter is a light trill that draws me in further. Curiosity piqued, I lean closer, "So, how did you find yourself part of this world? With the Ivanovs, I mean."

Her green eyes flash with mischief as she begins, "Oh, it's a funny story, actually, filled with arranged marriages and a bit of old-world intrigue."

I laugh, already captivated and wanting to know more. "You can't start with that and not finish. I need to hear the whole story."

Maura's smile widens. "It's quite a tale. I'd love to share it over a glass of wine sometime."

"It's a deal."

"As a matter of fact, let's grab that glass as soon as we get inside," she adds.

I hesitate as a sudden wave of nausea washes over me. "I think I'll wait a bit, actually," I reply, placing a hand on my stomach. "I'm feeling a bit squeamish. Must've been something I ate."

Maura nods understandingly. "It could just be nerves. The Ivanovs can be quite the intimidating bunch."

I exhale a long sigh. "You've got that right."

"Don't worry too much," Maura continues, her voice lowering slightly. "They might appear tough to outsiders, but once you're part of their inner circle, they're incredibly protective."

I half-smile. "That's a nice thought, but I'm just Lev's PA. I hardly think that puts me in any inner circle."

Maura gives me a look and a smile that suggests she knows better. "Oh, I wouldn't be so sure about that. I've seen the way he looks at you."

Her words catch me off guard, stirring a flutter of surprise and curiosity in my stomach.

Maura nods toward where everyone else is mingling. "Let's head back," she says.

Chatting with her was a breath of fresh air. "It's been really nice talking to you, Dalia," Maura tells me, her smile genuine.

"I feel the same," I reply, returning the smile and warmed by our conversation.

Heading back to the group, I feel a bit more relaxed thanks to Maura's kindness. Yet, as I sneak a glance at Lev, I can't shake off the uncertainty about where I stand, especially after his distant behavior yesterday.

It doesn't take long before Lev sidles up next to me. "Glad to see you and Maura hit it off," he says, a hint of approval in his voice.

"Yeah, she's really nice," I respond, glad that he noticed.

He gives a small nod, and then his eyes wander down to my dress. "You really do look absolutely gorgeous tonight."

"Thanks," I manage, his penetrating gaze feeling like a physical touch.

Leaning in, his voice drops to a whisper. "Did you make it to La Seduction Lingerie like I suggested?" he asks, a predatory gleam in his eyes.

A blush creeps up my cheeks. "Yes, I did," I admit quietly.

"And what treasure did you find?" His curiosity hangs between us, thick and palpable.

I hesitate for a second, then share, "A midnight blue set."

His eyes light up with dark mischief. "I can't wait to see you in it," he murmurs, his lusty tone sending shivers down my spine. "And out of it."

"I'm not sure that's a good idea," I reply, trying to keep it professional, but his commanding presence and proximity make it hard to think straight.

He grins, that hungry, knowing smile. "I always get what I want, Dalia."

Lev leans in closer, his lips barely brushing my ear, sending a thrill of anticipation through me. His voice is low and sultry, dripping with promise.

"If we were alone right now, I'd peel that stunning dress off you inch by torturous inch," he murmurs, his breath warm against my skin. "I'd explore every curve of your body with my tongue, tasting your sweet pussy until you're writhing and begging for more."

His words ignite a fire within me, arousal washing over me in an overwhelming tide. The image of him doing just that —his hands and mouth all over me—makes my knees weak. My brand-new panties dampen as he continues, the huskiness in his voice expressing his barely contained desire.

"And when you're desperate for it, I'd slide deep inside you, taking you hard and fast, until you scream my name."

His words send a fire racing through my veins, and I feel my face flush with heat. My body responds viscerally, my pulse quickening, a slick warmth spreading between my thighs.

But before I can reply to Lev's steamy whisper, he's all business again, checking to see if everyone's ready to head inside. I'm still standing there, dazed and more turned on than I should be, when I hear the distinct growl of motorcycles. Turning toward the noise, my heart drops.

Three bikers race down the street, pulling up sharp, right in front of the bustling crowd. They're decked out in all black, faces hidden behind dark shielded helmets. A cold wave of realization washes over me as I spot the guns they're casually brandishing. I grab Lev's arm, my fingers tight against his sleeve.

"Lev, look," I whisper urgently, trying to keep my voice steady despite the sudden spike of adrenaline.

His reaction is instantaneous, his body shielding me as the bikers wield their pistols.

The air cracks with gunfire as bullets begin to fly. Panic grips the crowd as screams and shouts fill the air, echoing through the night.

In the thick of the bedlam, the Ivanovs spring into action. Luk, despite the confusion and danger, manages to grab Maura. He yanks her behind a decorative statue, an improvised shield from the imminent danger.

Amid the sound of shattering glass and the sharp zing of bullets ricocheting, I catch a glimpse of blood spreading across Luk's sleeve, stark against the white of his shirt.

He doesn't flinch or groan, his focus is entirely on Maura, his movements protective and precise. The stark fear for her safety overshadows his own, his arm hanging limply by his side as he checks her over for injuries.

The crowd scrambles amidst the panic, driven by sheer survival instinct. Elena, Vladimir, and Yuri jump into action, barking orders to get everyone to safety. It's all happening so fast, like a scene from an action movie, except it's terrifyingly real.

Lev yanks me behind a car, using it as a makeshift barrier. He's in protective mode, checking me over quickly, making sure I'm not hit. "You okay?" he asks, his gaze sharp and assessing.

"Yeah," I answer, barely hearing my own voice over the chaos.

"Stay down and keep hidden, no matter what. Don't lift your head," he commands, his voice firm, brooking no argument. "Do you understand?"

I nod, trying to process an impossible situation.

"Tell me with words that you understand."

"I understand," I assure him, my voice gaining a bit of strength.

He places his hand on my shoulder, grounding me.

As he prepares to stand, I latch onto his shoulder, my voice spiked with fear. "What are you going to do?"

"I'm going to protect my family," he declares without a hint of hesitation. Suddenly, he pulls out a large silver pistol from under his jacket, and my breath catches.

Why on earth does the COO of a holdings company carry a gun like it's second nature?

Before I can voice my shock, he's already moving. He darts out from behind our makeshift cover, firing off rounds with a practiced hand. One of the bikers makes a beeline for Luk and Maura, but Lev's shot catches him in the shoulder, halting him in his tracks.

I'm stunned, watching Lev maneuver with a cold, calculated precision that chills me to the bone. He's not just some corporate executive; he's trained and lethal. It was one thing to hear about his military background but a whole other thing entirely to see him in action.

I can hardly make heads or tails of what's happening, but it soon becomes clear that the attackers are retreating.

Lev continues to fire, the sharp reports of his gun slicing through the evening. Suddenly, a burst of gunfire erupts near him, and he groans, ducking swiftly behind cover.

Panic seizes me, overriding caution. I can't just sit back; I need to make sure he's okay. Ignoring the danger, I dart out from behind the car, crouching low to the ground. The remaining bikers are making a quick getaway, the wounded one struggling to get onto his bike.

Heart pounding, I rush toward Lev, desperate to reach him, praying he's not hurt.

His eyes flash, sharp and commanding. "Get the hell down!" he snaps, scanning the area for more threats. "Get behind cover, now!"

"Not a chance!" I shoot back, unwilling to leave him exposed. My heart slams against my ribs, the air thick with danger.

Suddenly, the wounded biker lifts his gun, aiming directly at me. My breath catches as time slows down. But before he can fire, Lev swings his pistol up and squeezes the trigger. The shot rings out, striking the biker, causing his aim to veer off wildly, the bullet zinging past me and hitting nothing but air.

With a curse, the biker revs his engine and takes off in pain and desperation, losing control. His motorcycle bounces off a parked car with a crash that echoes down the street.

The bike, still careening wildly, rockets toward me, its rider half-slumped over, grappling to maintain control. It's like everything shifts into *Matrix* mode—the roar of the engine, the cries from the crowd, Lev's voice shouting my name.

Fear roots me to the spot; I'm a deer caught in the headlights of an oncoming disaster.

The bike is closing in, too fast for me to react. Desperate fear grips me, and all I can do is throw my hands over my eyes, bracing for the impact. My heart pounds against my ribcage; each beat a drum of impending doom.

Then, suddenly, everything goes silent.

CHAPTER 13

"Not a chance in hell! I'm going with her!"

Lev's booming voice pulls me back into the moment.

The world feels like it's spinning out of control, everything fuzzy and surreal.

I catch glimpses of flashing red and blue lights and the urgent wails of ambulance sirens slicing through the night air. Scenes flicker in and out, disjointed and hard to grasp.

I see Lev, his face a mask of concern, arguing heatedly with the EMTs, insisting on riding in the ambulance with me.

The interior of the vehicle is stark and clinical. Lev is there, his hand gripping mine tightly, his presence a comforting anchor in the whirl of chaos.

EMTs hover over me, their voices a distant buzz as they work. I try to speak, to ask what's happening, but a gentle "shush" from one of the EMTs stops me.

"Save your strength," they advise in grim tones.

Panic claws at my insides. Am I going to die? The thought terrifies me, making my heart race even faster. Lev's face swims into view again, his eyes intense and full of concern.

"You're going to be fine," he says, but the worry I see in his gaze makes me doubt his words.

I struggle to stay conscious, fearing that if I close my eyes, it might be for the last time.

Once we arrive at the hospital, I'm wheeled through the ER on a stretcher, everything blurring around me as we zip past bright hospital lights. Lev's right there, squeezing my hand, trying to calm me down with words I can barely hear over all the noise.

The shock is too much for my system, and I succumb to the darkness.

When I come to, I'm in a hospital bed, groggy and confused. I try to piece together what went down. That crazy moment with the motorcycle speeding toward me snaps back into focus. I brace myself and check my body, half-expecting to see a broken mess, but it's just a few cuts and bruises.

I scan the room, and my heart jumps when I see Lev slouched in a chair, looking like he hasn't slept in days. The moment he notices I'm awake, he's on his feet, his eyes scanning me like he's checking for any missed injuries.

"Don't move; just stay still," he says as he rushes over.

He grabs my hand and gently squeezes, and I grip his right back tightly. I'm hit by a wave of relief and weirdly thrilled that he's here.

"What happened?" I ask, my head pounding like it's hosting its own little rock concert.

Lev looks at me, a serious expression crossing his face. He looks so worn out. "Well, there was an incident at the gala," he cautiously begins to explain.

The memory of bikers and gunshots starts to click into place. "The bikers, the shooting..."

He nods, his expression grave. "Exactly. One of the riders lost control of his bike and nearly ran you over. You fell and smacked your head on the pavement, trying to get away."

Rubbing the back of my head, feeling the tender lump there, I quip, "Well, that would explain why my head feels like it's been used as a drum."

My thoughts dart as more details come back to me. "Luk and Maura. Are they okay?"

Lev nods reassuringly. "Luk's tough. Took a bullet in the arm, but it was clean through and through. He'll be fine." His voice steadies me. "Maura and everyone else are safe, too. It's a damn miracle nobody was seriously hurt—it could've easily turned into a bloodbath."

Relief washes over me, but it's mixed with the realization of just how close we all came to something far worse.

I struggle to sit up, my voice edging with frustration. "Lev, I need to know what's going on. What was that? Why do you carry a gun? Who is trying to hurt your family?" My questions tumble out, each one sharper than the last, demanding answers.

He opens his mouth, but just then, the door swings open, and a doctor comes in.

"Sir, I'll need you to step outside," he says to Lev.

He reluctantly agrees and leaves the room.

As the doctor examines me, my mind races through the possible explanations of what Lev hasn't told me yet, of how deep I'm getting into whatever world the Ivanovs belong to.

Maura's words echo in my head, hinting at some intense and secretive lifestyle. It's a lot, and here I am, smack in the middle of it, still trying to piece together the full picture while lying in a hospital bed.

"You're very fortunate," the doctor says. "Just a few minor scrapes and a mild concussion. Nothing that won't heal with a bit of rest."

He continues, adjusting his glasses, "We'd like to keep you here overnight for observation, but your husband was quite adamant about taking you home. He's arranged for private medical care to monitor you through the night."

I open my mouth to correct him about Lev not being my husband, but then I think better of it. The thought of spending a night in the hospital sounds less than appealing. "Thank you," I say instead.

The doctor pauses, his expression softening as he glances at his notes again. "Were you aware that you're pregnant?"

His words hit me like a tidal wave. My eyes widen, and the room starts spinning. For a moment, I feel like I might faint again.

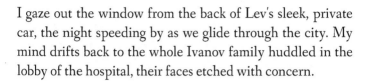

I gaze out the window from the back of Lev's sleek, private car, the night speeding by as we glide through the city. My mind drifts back to the whole Ivanov family huddled in the lobby of the hospital, their faces etched with concern.

The doctor was right about Lev being adamant about keeping me safe. He insisted that I stay over at his place—in my own room, of course. I'd agreed without much thought.

Wrapped in my thoughts and the quiet of the car's back seat, Lev breaks the silence. "Do we talk about the big news now or wait until we get back?" he asks, his voice low and careful.

I sigh, feeling the weight of the revelation still settling in my chest. "I need some time to process it," I admit, turning to look out the window and watching the city lights blur past.

He nods in understanding, letting the silence envelop us again, giving me space to think.

We pull up to a towering skyscraper smack in the middle of downtown. Lev's casual declaration of, "This is my place," nearly knocks me off my feet. Like his place is just some average Joe's pad and not this glittering column scraping the sky.

As we exit the car, he mentions he's got some top-notch medical specialists on site if we need them.

The lobby is as grand as you'd expect, spacious and swanky, and the tight security gives me a bit of reassurance. I wonder briefly if Lev is expecting more trouble or if this is just an everyday precaution for the high-flying Ivanov lifestyle.

As we step into the penthouse, two doctors approach, their professional demeanor evident. Lev introduces them with a nod. "Dalia, this is Dr. Simon Hale," he gestures toward a tall, silver-haired man with a reassuring presence, "and Dr. Laura Chen," pointing to a petite woman with an attentive yet warm gaze.

Dr. Hale speaks up, his voice calm, "We've prepared one of the spare rooms with everything you might need, including a call button should you require us during the night."

Dr. Chen adds with a smile, "We'll be staying in the guest rooms downstairs, just in case." She scans the expansive layout of the penthouse.

Lev's tone carries a deeper note of seriousness as he adds, "I trust them with my life. And I mean that quite literally at times."

As they turn to leave, Dr. Chen stops and turns back toward me, offering a gentle smile. "Oh, and congratulations on your pregnancy," she says.

They retreat down the sleek, modern staircase to the lower floor, leaving Lev and me alone in the quiet luxury of his massive penthouse.

When they're gone, I look at Lev, confusion etched on my face. "How do they know about the pregnancy?"

He reaches for a glass and fills it with water from the tap. "I wanted them to have your full medical picture. They needed to know. But I promise you that I haven't spoken a word to anyone else about it."

He hands me the water, and I gulp it down, the cool liquid a small comfort.

Lev pours himself a glass of whiskey, and I can't help but think how much I'd love one myself right now.

He sits down beside me. "How are you feeling?" he asks, his eyes searching mine.

"Totally overwhelmed," I admit. "I want to know everything about you and your family and what I'm walking into here."

Lev gives a small smile. "There's time for that. But right now, we need to discuss what happens next."

He takes a sip of his whiskey, then looks me straight in the eye. "We're getting married."

I blink, taken aback. "Married? Listen, I'm not one of those old-fashioned—" I start to say before he cuts me off.

Lev's expression hardens. "You don't have a choice. If I'm the father of your child, I'm going to be there for you and them. And I'm going to do it the right way."

His words hang in the air.

I respond, my voice sharp. "You've got some nerve to put my life in danger, then make demands like that."

My head starts to throb as my anger flares. He places his hand on mine, and somehow, his touch calms me right away.

"You're more than entitled to tear into me," he says, his voice steady. "But now's not the time. You need to rest and recover."

I realize he's right, though it frustrates me. "Fine," I mutter. "But don't think this conversation is over."

His lips twitch in a small, almost amused smile. "I wouldn't dare."

I sigh, leaning back in the chair. "And don't think for a second that I'm going to make this easy for you."

He chuckles. "I would expect nothing less."

CHAPTER 14

DALIA

I'm caught in a whirlwind of memories from that night—the adrenaline, the fear, the bikers, the guns, the screaming—they play over and over on repeat in my mind. I remember the sound of gunshots, the weight of Lev's body shielding me, the feel of cold pavement against my skin.

It's all so vivid, so terrifyingly alive in my mind.

Snap back to now. I'm sitting at my desk in the office, trying to catch up on a week's worth of missed work.

Vanya sits next to me in Lev's place, going over some upcoming meetings, his voice steady and reassuring, but I'm barely holding it together. I scribble down notes, my handwriting shaky.

He pauses, glancing up with a knowing look. "You're still shaken up about that night, aren't you?" he asks gently.

"Yeah. You could say that." I nod, swallowing hard. "How do you deal with it? The trauma?"

Vanya smiles sadly and taps his leg, the one supported by a cane. "We all carry our burdens," he says softly. "But we learn, we adapt. You will, too."

I force a smile, grateful for his attempt to ease my mind. "Thanks, Vanya. I guess it's just going to take some time."

He nods understandingly. "Take all the time you need. We're all here for you."

I nod, his words making me feel a little better. Maybe he's right. Maybe I can get through this, just like he did. But for now, I need to focus on simply getting through today.

I try to turn my attention to the tasks at hand, but my mind keeps drifting. Vanya, catching on to my distraction, tilts his head and lowers his voice, "What's really on your mind, Dalia?"

I hesitate, the secret of my pregnancy with Lev pressing against my lips, but I decide against sharing it. Too much, too soon. "I haven't seen much of Lev lately," I admit instead, trying to sound casual.

Vanya nods understandingly. "He's been tied up with clients, wining and dining, you know how it is. He should be back soon, though."

He gives me a sly grin, teasing, "Why, do you miss him?"

I laugh, more out of relief than amusement, and shrug nonchalantly. "Maybe just a bit. He certainly makes the office more interesting."

Vanya chuckles, tapping his cane lightly on the floor. "That he does. Lev tends to leave a void when he's not around. But he'll be back before you know it, stirring up trouble and making your days less predictable."

I smile, grateful for the lighthearted tone of our talk. It's nice, the normalcy of it, even if just for a moment. "I guess I'm getting used to that certain something he brings."

"Sounds like you're fonder of him than you let on," Vanya observes, raising an eyebrow.

I wave him off, but the warmth in my chest tells me he's right.

He gets up, pushing his chair back with a thoughtful nod. "Let's wrap this up for now. Whatever's left can wait for an email, right?" he suggests with a gentle smile. He pauses at the edge of my desk, his expression softening. "And Dalia, if you ever need someone to talk to about that night or anything else, I'm here."

"Thanks, Vanya," I manage, genuinely grateful for his support.

As he walks away, my mind wanders back to Lev. Things have shifted between us, and it's unsettling. There's no proposal, no ring, nothing concrete.

The night of the attack, he was my rock, but now, he's distant, almost absent. What's going on with him? Why the sudden coldness?

It's been a whole week since Lev dropped that bombshell about marriage, and he's been as elusive as a ghost. Each day drags on, leaving me to wonder if his comforting words that night were just a knee-jerk reaction to what happened or if he's having second thoughts.

I rest my hand on my belly, still in disbelief that I'm actually pregnant. The whole idea of becoming a mom is overwhelming, and I have no idea how I'm going to break the news to my parents. I mentally kick myself for being so careless with birth control.

I need some answers soon. This waiting game is driving me up the wall, and with a baby on the way, I don't have the luxury of time to waste on uncertainties.

I definitely need a break from my spinning thoughts, so I head out of my office toward the break room, aiming for some much-needed tea. Just as I walk in, I spot Vladimir closing his laptop, his eyes lighting up a bit when he sees me.

"Care to join me for a coffee?" he asks, already rising from his seat.

"Actually, tea for me," I reply, sliding into a chair opposite him.

He raises an eyebrow, then asks, "What kind?"

I shrug, feeling a bit out of my depth. "Something calming."

He gives me a look that makes me feel like he's reading more into my words than I intended. He reaches for the box of chamomile tea and pulls out a bag.

"Chamomile," he explains as he heats the water, "is good for relaxation. Might help with any stress you're dealing with."

The way he says it, so casually yet pointedly, makes me wonder just how much he's picked up from our little interaction. I nod, grateful for the suggestion, and watch as he carefully prepares the tea, his movements precise and practiced.

"You sure know what you're doing," I say.

As Vladimir carefully pours the steaming water over the tea bag, he speaks. "My mother used to brew tea whenever she felt stressed," he begins, a hint of nostalgia in his voice. "Back in Moscow, she was the pillar of our household, never allowing any worry show—especially in front of my brothers and me."

He chuckles lightly, continuing. "As a single mother, she had a lot on her plate. But the one tell she had was her tea. Whenever I saw her with a cup, I knew things were weighing on her."

With a playful grin, he adds, "That was my cue to ease up on the mischief. Well, for a little while at least."

He hands me the mug of tea, the steam curling up gently.

"Maybe it's a bit of inherited wisdom, handing you this cup," he says, smiling, his eyes meeting mine with a warmth that's both comforting and slightly piercing.

I wrap my hands around the warm mug, grateful for the story and the tea. "Thanks, Vladimir," I say, smiling back.

He gives me a knowing nod. "You're welcome," he replies, then falls silent for a moment as he stirs his coffee. With a half-smile, he continues, "You know, my mother also taught me never to pry into a woman's affairs, but I must confess, I never quite mastered that lesson."

He leans forward slightly, his expression turning serious. "How are you doing after what happened at the gala? It was quite a night."

I take a moment, sipping the tea to gather my thoughts before answering. "Honestly, I'm more worried about Lev than anything. It's been a lot to process."

Vladimir chuckles softly, his gaze thoughtful. "Don't worry about him. Lev is tough. Trust me, what we saw the other night was child's play compared to some things he's faced. But," he says, pausing, his voice softening, "he's been quite concerned about you, Dalia. He talks of little else."

A warmth spreads through me at his words, comforting yet tinged with the complexity of my feelings about Lev. "That's reassuring to hear," I admit, allowing myself a small smile. "Thanks, Vladimir. It means a lot knowing that."

"Well, Dalia, since we're chatting like old pals now, just call me Vlad," he says with an easy grin.

"Ok, Vlad, in that case, what can you tell me about all these things he's faced? I know he was in the military, but the way the whole family reacted that night..." I trail off.

Vlad nods. "That really is something you should hear from Lev himself," he says.

I groan, frustrated. "Yes, in a perfect world, but he's been pretty scarce lately. If I'm going to stick around, do I need to be worried about the threat of another shootout? Please, Vlad, help me out here."

He thinks for a moment before speaking. "Lev's family is part of a very old tradition in Russia."

"Are you being cryptic on purpose?" I ask him.

He offers a smile. "The Ivanovs are Bratva."

The word sounds vaguely familiar. "Bratva?"

"Yes. Much like the Italian mafia, Russians also have powerful families, and the Ivanovs are among the most powerful of them all."

The puzzle pieces start clicking into place. "Ah, I see."

What the fuck have I gotten myself into?

Sensing my unease, Vlad goes on. "We are not criminals. We own businesses, legitimate ones, and try to give back to our community. The Bratva is a brotherhood, and we protect our own."

I nod, urging him to continue.

"Here in Chicago, the Ivanov family is top dog. That should mean things are calm and stable. But apparently, someone's got an itch to stir the pot if that insanity the other night is any indication."

He leans in closer, lowering his voice as if sharing a state secret. "And trust me, in this game, it's all about keeping your friends close and your enemies on speed dial. Sounds like someone's looking to reshuffle the deck."

His casual mention of espionage reminds me of all those twisty mob plots in the movies, except this is real life, and somehow, I've found myself in a supporting actress role.

"Between trying to decode Lev and dodging bullets, I think I've accidentally signed up for a spy thriller, not a job."

Vladimir nods solemnly. "What we witnessed the other night, Dalia, was a horrendous violation of Bratva code. Civilians, especially those uninvolved directly, are off-limits. Whoever orchestrated that stunt has essentially signed their own death warrant in our world."

He takes a sip of his coffee, his expression hardening. "Lev made me promise to spare you the gritty details, but you should know—he's been scouring every corner of Chicago since the attack. He's hell-bent on unmasking whoever dared disrupt our peace."

I lean in, soaking up every word. It's like a window has opened into Lev's world, one that I've only glimpsed through veiled curtains until now. "So, that's where he's been all week? Hunting ghosts in the underworld?"

"Exactly," Vladimir confirms. "It's not just about retaliation; it's about sending a message that the Ivanovs will not be challenged without consequences. He's determined, perhaps more than I've seen him in years. It's a side of him that takes no prisoners."

He sets his cup down, his gaze meeting mine with intensity. "I know this world is new to you, and frankly, it's not one I'd wish on anyone who values peace of mind over constant vigilance. But here you are, and here it is. Lev's world is not just one of boardrooms and stock exchanges alone; it's woven with loyalty, honor, and, at times, necessary brutality."

"I appreciate you filling me in. It helps a little, I guess."

"Lev is genuinely looking out for you. But, you know," he continues, his tone dipping into something a bit more solemn, "if you ever think this gig—or this crazy world—is too much, Lev would understand. He really would."

I let out a laugh, a bit sharper than I intend. "Bit late for that now," I say more to myself than to him.

He cocks an eyebrow, clearly intrigued by my offhand remark.

Realizing I might've let too much slip, I quickly add, "I just mean, I'm already in deep; I might as well see how the whole story unfolds, right?"

Vlad nods, though it's clear he's not totally buying it. "Well, if you need an out, remember you've got options," he says earnestly.

I stand up, feeling the need to escape before I really spill the beans. "Thanks for the tea and the ear, Vlad. It helped more than you know," I say, putting on my best smile.

He returns the smile, warm yet tinged with a bit of concern. "Anytime, Dalia. Take care of yourself."

I make my way out, my thoughts racing faster than my heels can carry me.

Two things are crystal clear: my feelings for Lev are as messed up and complicated as ever, and there's a new life on board for this wild ride I've found myself on.

CHAPTER 15

"Oh, this is them. No doubt about it," Vanya says.

I'm in a dimly lit alley on Chicago's South Side, riveted by a trio of scorched motorcycles. Beside me, Vanya keeps a watchful eye on our surroundings.

I step closer to one of the bikes, noting the deep scratches on its charred metal. This was the same bike that had nearly ended Dalia's life, and the realization makes my jaw tighten with anger. As I examine the wreckage, memories of that night flash through my mind. I had planned to subdue the rider, to extract every piece of information about who wanted to hurt us.

But when it comes down to it, my focus has shifted instinctively to Dalia's safety. Protecting her has overridden every other concern, pushing my need for interrogation aside.

Now, standing here among the remnants of that night's terror, I feel a twinge of frustration for the lost opportunity to learn about the assailant. Yet there's no real regret—

ensuring Dalia's safety was the only choice that mattered at the moment.

In the gloom of the alley, a jittery voice breaks the silence. "Is this what you guys were looking for?"

I spin around to see Sam, the skinny informant who tipped us off about the location. His eyes dart around nervously.

"You look spooked, Sam. Talk to me."

"Yeah, hell, yeah, I'm nervous," he blurts out, wiping sweat from his brow. "You'd be too if you saw what I did."

I narrow my eyes at him, stepping closer. "There's more cash in it for you if you prove yourself useful. And let's not forget, staying on my good side is beneficial to you."

Sam swallows hard, then nods, his resolve firming. "All right. I didn't just find these bikes. I saw three guys ditch 'em here. They were dressed all in black, real tactical-like. One of 'em was holding his shoulder. After they ditched them, these things went up like a damn bonfire."

Vanya, standing a few steps behind me, chimes in with his sharp analysis. "Gear like that isn't cheap, and neither are these bikes—there's serious money behind this."

Sam nods vigorously. "Exactly, man. Whoever's behind this ain't messing around."

I consider the information, my mind racing through potential adversaries with the resources to orchestrate such a move. "Thanks, Sam," I say. "Keep your eyes open and your mouth shut."

Sam nods again, eager to escape the chilling atmosphere.

Before he can disappear into the shadows of the alley, a thought occurs to me. "Sam, you got family out of town?" I ask.

"Yeah, got some folks down in St. Louis," he replies, a flicker of confusion crossing his face. "Why?"

I pull out a thick stack of crisp hundreds from my jacket. Handing them over, I fix my gaze on him. "There's extra in there for a little trip. Why don't you visit them for a while?"

Sam's confusion shifts to a dawning realization. "Why should I?" he asks, his fingers tightening around the cash.

I let out a slow breath, the weight of impending conflict heavy on my shoulders. "I've got a feeling a storm's brewing, possibly even a war. I don't want you caught in the crossfire. Better safe than sorry."

Gratitude washes over Sam's face as he clutches the money closer. "Thanks, Mr. Ivanov. Really, thank you," he stutters, the sincerity in his voice clear. He turns and nearly runs from the alley, the urgency of my warning fueling his swift departure.

I watch him go, the gravity of the situation settling in. If trouble is coming, it's not just the immediate players in the game who are at risk—it's anyone connected to us.

Vanya watches me closely, a trace of concern etching his features. "Do you really think war is on the horizon?"

I nod without hesitation. "That attack was calculated, a decapitation strike aimed at throwing us into chaos. Going after Maura and Luk like that and making them dual targets... It was designed to maximize damage and disarray."

Vanya shakes his head, his expression grim. "Nasty business, but we'll even the score."

I stride over to one of the charred motorcycles, spotting a small compartment that appears to have been sealed shut by the fire. My instincts kick in. Pulling out the Leatherman I always carry, I wedge it into the tiny gap and pry. The compartment creaks, resisting at first, but with a firm twist, it pops open.

Inside, amidst the soot and debris, something gleams. I reach in, and my fingers brush against something metallic. Pulling it out, I examine the item. It's a clue that might lead us closer to those responsible for the attack.

Vanya steps closer, his eyes narrowing as he takes in the find. "This could be what we need to start unraveling this mess," I mutter, turning the object over in my hands. I carefully lift the lid of the metal container, revealing scraps of paper. Vanya leans in for a closer look.

"What's that?" he asks, reaching out a hand.

"Wait, don't touch," I snap, pulling the container back sharply. "This could be forensic evidence."

I take another look around at the charred bikes, my anger simmering just beneath the surface. The thought of the men who dared attack my family fuels a violent urge to exact vengeance.

Vanya, perceptive as ever, places a calming hand on my shoulder. "Lev, keep your head. There's a time for revenge, but we need to be smart about this."

I stand up, my gaze fixed on the horizon as I consider our next move. "You're right," I concede, "but understand this—

every moment we don't act, word spreads. Our enemies are watching and wondering if the Ivanovs are weak and ripe for the taking."

Vanya nods in agreeance, a serious glint in his eye. "We won't let that happen. We'll strike back, but only when we have everything we need to crush them completely."

Turning the container in my hands, I make a decision. "I'll call my contacts at Chicago PD about this. They can run it through their labs." Securing the container in my bag, I'm ready to take action. "Let's get this to the police. The sooner we know more, the sooner we can end this threat."

We exit the alley, making our way to the car parked discreetly nearby. Vanya slides into the driver's seat while I settle into the back, pulling out my phone to make a crucial call. "Diaz, it's Lev Ivanov," I say, then wait for the Chicago PD detective to respond.

"Lev, to what do I owe the pleasure?" Detective Diaz's voice is steady and professional.

"I need a favor. Forensic analysis, and I need it ASAP. Found something that could help us on a case—burnt bikes, possible clues to who's behind a recent attack."

"Understood. Meet me in an hour at the usual spot; bring whatever you've got."

"Thanks, Diaz. I appreciate it."

Vanya glances at me through the rearview mirror, his eyes serious yet supportive. "Well, that's a start, right? At least we have something that might lead us to these bastards."

"Yeah," I agree, leaning back against the seat. "It's a start. But there's a long road ahead. We can't let our guard down, not until every one of them pays for what they tried to do."

Vanya smoothly pulls the car into traffic as we head toward our next move. "We'll get them, Lev. One step at a time."

We merge onto the Kennedy Expressway, the early fall sky heavy with threatening rain clouds. I lean back, my mind churning with more than just Bratva business.

As Vanya handles the traffic, I can't help but think about Dalia. The worry about her safety intertwines with excitement at the unexpected news of the baby. I've always wanted a family, something to ground me beyond the shadows of my Bratva life, but Dalia isn't just any woman, and our path to this point has been anything but typical.

We've catapulted past the stages that most couples slowly meander through. The intensity of our connection, both in private moments and in the madness of our lives, has left little room for traditional courtship, and I find myself unsure how to navigate these deeper waters.

I want her—more than just physically, but as a partner, as the mother of my child. I want to provide for her, protect her, and build something lasting.

But how do I bridge the gap between being the commanding Bratva COO and a man she can love and rely on, not just fear or desire in the shadow of power?

Rain begins to speckle the windshield. I need to find a way to show her that despite the control and demands, there's a man who values her beyond the roles she plays in my life, a man who needs her not just in his bed but by his side throughout all of life's storms.

CHAPTER 16

DALIA

I slump against the cool tile, the relief from the nausea short-lived as reality sets back in.

Here I am, hunched over the porcelain throne, grateful for my private office bathroom despite the circumstances.

Lev, the father of my soon-to-be child, has been practically a ghost. Our interactions are strictly professional, limited to emails about his endless meetings and travel schedules.

I rinse my mouth and stare at my reflection, trying to find that resilient woman who's used to tackling life head-on. Right now, she looks a bit pale and frazzled.

What if Lev decides he doesn't want this baby, doesn't want *us*? The thought twists a knot in my stomach that has nothing to do with morning sickness. I'm genuinely scared about facing this alone.

I think of my dad back home, the man with the strictest of morals. The news of his daughter, unwed and pregnant by a man who has both experienced and doled out brutality, would just about give him a heart attack.

Stepping out of the bathroom, I straighten my blouse and head toward the break room, my thoughts swirling. Just as I round the corner, I almost bump straight into Maura. Her face lights up immediately, her smile warm and welcoming.

"Maura!" I exclaim, both surprised and relieved to see a friendly face.

"Dalia!" she responds, her arms opening wide as we hug.

"It's so good to see you."

"Likewise."

"What brings you here?" I ask, stepping back with a curious tilt of my head.

"Just dropping off some lunch for Luk," Maura responds, holding up a small, insulated bag. She studies me for a moment, her eyes narrowing slightly as if she's trying to read something in my face.

"Hey, would you like to grab a quick coffee with me?" she suddenly suggests.

I laugh softly, the sound more nervous than I intend. "Sure. With Lev barely being here, I've got nothing but time."

Maura's smile doesn't waver as she nods. "Great, let's get out of here for a bit. A change of scenery might do us both some good."

Grateful for the distraction and the company, I agree, following her out of the office and into the crisp air outside.

We settle into a quaint little coffee shop just a block away from the office. It's a cozy spot with mismatched chairs and small bistro tables. The smell of freshly ground coffee beans fills the air, mixing with the sweet scent of pastries.

Maura has a steaming latte in front of her, the foam artfully swirled on top, while I nurse a cup of chamomile, my new go-to.

"So," Maura begins, her voice gentle, "how are you holding up after that night at the gala?"

I stir my tea, looking up. "I'm managing. But what about you? That attempt was aimed at your life. How are *you* feeling?"

Maura exhales deeply, a wry smile touching her lips. "Believe it or not, it's not the first time someone's tried to take me out. It's unsettling, sure, but I'm hanging in there. Luk's been incredible through it all. He's on the case, you know? I trust him completely with my life."

I nod, sipping my tea. The warmth from the cup spreads through my hands. "You two seem to really have a solid thing going."

She smiles, looking down at her latte. "We've been through a lot together, that's for sure." Her eyes meet mine again, and there's a flash of something strong and resolute in them. "How about you, Dalia? How's your relationship with Lev?"

My surprise at Maura's question causes my hands to shake, and I nearly knock my teacup off the table.

"What do you know?" I blurt out, a bit sharper than intended. I quickly wave my hand, apologizing. "Sorry, I didn't mean to come at you like that. It's just... a lot's going on right now. Well, I mean, *not* a lot's going on right now, and that's part of the problem."

Maura laughs it off with an easy grace. "Hey, no worries. I get it. Bratva men can be a handful."

I lean in, intrigued despite myself. "But you and Luk seem pretty stable to me."

Maura stirs her latte, her gaze drifting past me for a moment. "Well, our marriage wasn't your run-of-the-mill romance tale. I was more or less a peace offering to Luk from my stepmother."

My eyes widen, and I nearly choke on my tea.

"Yeah," Maura nods, her smile rueful. "Sounds a bit old-world, doesn't it? But thankfully, Luk turned out to be a dream. There's something about these Ivanov men," she muses, her eyes sparkling with mischief.

I set my tea down, my mind racing. "I can't even imagine."

Maura reaches across the table, giving my hand a reassuring squeeze. "It was definitely a wild ride, but here we are. And honestly," she lowers her voice, drawing me into her confidence, "once an Ivanov man decides you're the one, they're fiercely loyal. Just give Lev some time to sort himself out."

She's making me feel better by the second.

"Now it's your turn, Dalia. I'd love to hear a bit about you. What brought you into our little world?"

"God, where to begin?"

"Wherever you'd like."

With that, I go into it, giving her the full lowdown on Chad and his secretary, how I walked in on them, how our marriage turned out to be a sham. Maura hangs on my every word, her green eyes flashing with surprise with each twist and turn.

When I'm done, she sits back and blinks.

"Dalia, that's awful. No one deserves that kind of betrayal. What a sleaze."

"Yeah, it was a mess. But hey, I learned from it." I try to chuckle, but it's hollow. Maura reaches out, squeezing my hand in a silent show of support.

Her fiery spirit flares as she demands, half-jokingly, "Let me see this guy. Was he even worth the drama?"

Laughing, I pull out my phone. "Prepare yourself—he had charm, at least at first glance."

I scroll through my phone, find the picture of Chad I dreaded revisiting, and hand it over to Maura. Her reaction is instant; her eyes widen, and she lets out a sharp gasp.

"Oh, wow," she says, staring at the screen. "Oh, my God."

"What? What's wrong?" I lean closer, a knot forming in my stomach.

Maura looks up at me, her eyes serious. "This guy, he's the same one who got my cousin pregnant, then bailed on her."

My mouth falls open in shock. "You're kidding?"

"Completely serious. Mary was heartbroken," Maura says, shaking her head and handing the phone back.

I take it, my thoughts swirling. "Maura, please don't tell anyone about this. It's such a weird coincidence, and I really don't want Lev to find out and do something drastic."

"Well, if Lev doesn't find him first, my uncle Liam might. He's been on the lookout for that scumbag ever since he disappeared."

I force a nervous laugh. "Let's hope it doesn't get to that. Chad has already made enough trouble."

"Absolutely," Maura agrees, taking another sip of her coffee. "Don't worry, Dalia, your secret's safe with me. Let's just hope we don't run into him anytime soon." She glances behind her. "Can you excuse me for a moment? I need to use the little girls' room."

"Sure."

Alone at my table, I'm left with my thoughts again. The world feels ridiculously small, and the connection between Maura and me is surreal. As I stir my tea, I realize I've been so caught up in the whirlwind of the Bratva life and the unexpected pregnancy that I haven't fully processed my anger toward Chad or the open wounds he left behind.

I've never been one to back down from challenges, but figuring out my path with Lev and navigating this tangled web feels daunting. Yet, as I sit here, a part of me yearns for him to reignite our connection sooner rather than later. I want him, and I need that part of my life to settle, to become something real and tangible.

The buzz of my phone drags me back to reality. Still wrapped up in my own turbulent thoughts, I glance at the screen. It's a text from Lev. Despite the maelstrom of emotions he's caused, a part of me can't help but feel a flutter of anticipation.

The message is simple and direct.

Come over for dinner tonight? I'd like to talk.

I stare at the words for a moment, torn. I'm irked by his recent radio silence, followed by this casual invitation as if nothing happened. Yet the desire to see him, to confront and perhaps resolve the tangled feelings I have, is too strong to dismiss.

CHAPTER 17

M y stomach twists with nerves as the car pulls up to Lev's place.

It's not just about seeing him again; it's the whole situation. As I step out of the car, two guards are right there to greet me.

Lev's concern for my safety is both suffocating and comforting. Guards have been stationed at my place since I returned after staying with Lev the night of the shooting, which is part reassuring, part overwhelming.

The guards are silent sentinels, escorting me into the building. As we pass through the opulent lobby, I can't help but feel out of place—a small-town girl thrust into a world that's far too grand to feel like mine.

We reach the private elevator. As we ascend to the penthouse, my heart races faster with each passing floor.

"Hey, there."

Lev is waiting right at the door when I arrive. He looks impossibly good, dressed in a crisp white button-up that's casually rolled up to his forearms.

He thanks the guards, who nod and take the elevator back down, leaving us alone. He steps forward and greets me with a kiss on the cheek. Still stung by the recent distance between us, I want to pull back, but the warmth of his lips against my skin sparks something inside me.

My body reacts instinctively, a flush of heat surging through, tightening in places I wish weren't so traitorous.

"Glad you could make it," Lev says softly.

Jazz music floats throughout the place, giving off those chill vibes that make everything feel a bit smoother. "Nice music," I say, trying to keep things light.

"It's Chet Baker. A personal favorite of mine."

He helps me off with my coat, and I can't help but shiver a little when his fingers accidentally graze my shoulders. A warmth spreads through me, my pussy clenching.

"Want some sparkling wine or something else?" he asks, his tone casual.

"Just water, thanks," I respond, keeping it simple.

He nods and leads me through his sprawling place to a table set up on the patio that's got one killer view of the city. The table is beautifully set, candles flickering in the twilight, turning the penthouse patio into our own private little peaceful spot above the city's buzz.

He guides me into my chair with an attentiveness that, while sweet, is a bit much. I can't help but chuckle. "I'm only a month or so in, Lev. I can still sit down by myself."

He doesn't respond immediately, instead pulling out his phone and swiftly making a call. "We're ready for dinner," he says into the receiver, then hangs up and turns back to me.

"I just wanted to give you a break, a night just to relax."

I raise an eyebrow, unable to resist a jab. "Relax? Funny, I didn't know your vanishing off the face of the earth was part of your relaxation package."

He pauses, caught off guard, clearly not expecting that. Before he can muster a reply, the elevator dings, and a pair of chefs emerge, bustling over with dishes in hand. They quickly set our meals in front of us, giving Lev a convenient escape from having to respond.

The chefs skillfully remove the cloches from our plates, unveiling culinary masterpieces.

Lev raises his glass, catching the soft light of the setting sun. "To being more open," he declares, his gaze locking with mine.

"I'll drink to that," I reply, clinking my glass against his. The first bite is divine, and I savor the rich, buttery flavor of the fish. Lev watches me enjoy a few more bites before his expression turns serious.

"I'm sorry," he begins, causing me to pause mid-chew. I set down my fork and meet his eyes, noticing a rare hint of regret in them. "I know I have my reasons for being so elusive, but it wasn't right for me to just disappear on you like that."

I nod slowly, absorbing his apology with skepticism. "Thank you for saying that," I start, my voice steady but cool. "But I'm not quite ready to forgive you. You left me alone right when I needed you the most, right after I found out I was pregnant."

Lev's expression softens, and he reaches across the table, an apologetic look in his eyes. "I'm truly sorry for that. It was wrong of me to disappear when you were dealing with so much," he admits, his voice heavy with regret. "But you need to understand everything I did was to ensure your safety."

I raise an eyebrow, unconvinced.

He leans back, his jaw set as he prepares to explain. "After the attack at the gala, I've been working nonstop to uncover who was behind it, who dared to threaten you and my family." His fists clench at the thought, the anger evident in his eyes. "I couldn't stand the thought of you being in danger again. That's why I was gone. I needed to handle this threat."

Despite my frustration, the sincerity in his voice chips away at my steadfastness.

"And what have you learned?"

"I'm sorry to admit that I haven't found out much," he says, shaking his head in disappointment. "I have a small lead, but nothing concrete yet." His voice carries a weight of responsibility, and as he speaks with such passion, I feel my anger starting to dissolve.

"The thought of losing you that night at the gallery has haunted me."

Then, in a move that catches me completely off guard, he rises from his seat, steps around the table, and kneels before me, taking my hand gently in his.

"I swear to you, Dalia, I will never let any harm come to you or our child," he vows, his eyes burning with determination. "And I will personally deal with anyone who tries to put either of you in danger."

His words, so fierce and protective, wash over me.

As he kneels before me, the raw intensity in his eyes kindles a wild heat within me. His pledge leaves me breathless— this man is truly unlike any other.

"Will you trust me to keep you safe?" he asks, a fiery passion and a promise of wrath against my would-be harmers flickering in his gaze.

I nod, the words escaping me in a whisper, "Yes, I'll trust you."

CHAPTER 18

"You have no idea how much I've missed this," he murmurs against my ear, his breath hot and heavy.

After his declaration, we finished dinner quickly and soon sought a special kind of dessert.

We crash into his sprawling bedroom, our kisses wild and desperate. His hands roam across my body, reigniting a hunger that's been smoldering between us.

He grips my hips firmly, squeezing my ass with a possessiveness that sets my blood on fire. His fingers trace upward, teasing my nipples through the fabric of my dress, pulling soft moans from deep within me.

I tilt my head back, giving him better access as I reply breathlessly, "Then show me. Show me just how much."

His chuckle vibrates through me, deep and resonant, as he backs me toward the bed, his eyes dark with desire.

"I plan to," he says, his fingers deftly unzipping my dress.

His voice is a deep growl that sends a thrill through me. "I'm going to make you mine all over again," he murmurs, his fingers tracing the bare skin exposed by the slipping dress. "I'll explore every inch of you, taste you until you're shaking, begging for more."

He nips at my earlobe, pulling a gasp from my lips before continuing, "And when you think you can't take any more, that's when I'll slide into you, hard and deep. I'll fuck you so good, so hard, you'll forget your own name. Only mine will matter."

His hands find my waist, gripping tight. "You'll scream for me so loudly they'll hear you down on the street."

His words, dark and promising, are exactly what I crave, what I've missed.

He slides my dress down, the fabric pooling at my feet, leaving me standing in just my bra and panties. His eyes rake over me, devouring every inch.

"God, you're so fucking sexy," he murmurs, the intensity in his gaze making me feel like the most desirable woman on earth.

I give him a playful, challenging smile. "Less talk, more action," I tease.

His grin widens, mischievous and full of promise. In a swift motion, he closes the gap between us, his hand slipping between my thighs. Through the thin fabric of my panties, he begins to rub, the pressure just right, making me gasp and squirm with the building pleasure. I'm quickly becoming soaked under his expert touch.

He peels aside the flimsy fabric, and a shiver races through me as the cool air hits my heated skin. His fingers brush against me, gently at first, exploring the slick, sensitive folds before plunging deep.

The slow penetration shifts to a deliberate, rhythmic thrusting that sends waves of desire radiating through my body. His eyes lock onto mine, watching every flicker of intensity, every bitten lip, every needy whimper. I grasp his shoulders, nails digging in slightly, barely able to stand as my legs tremble under the relentless pleasure he orchestrates with his skilled fingers.

As his fingers delve deeper, his thumb finds its way to my clit, circling with a deliberate, teasing pressure that makes me moan. He varies the pace, quick flicks interspersed with slow, pressing movements that build a deep, aching need within me.

Meanwhile, his fingers curl inside, stroking the tender, ridged texture of my g-spot in a come-hither motion that sends jolts of electricity surging through me.

Just as I'm teetering on the edge, breathless and desperate, he stops. A groan escapes me as he scoops me up in his strong arms and carries me to the bed. Gently, he sets me down, his hands quickly working to slide my panties off and toss them aside.

His breath is hot on my skin as he kisses his way down my body, lingering on the sensitive skin of my inner thighs, his lips teasing closer and closer to where I need him most.

When his mouth finally meets my pussy, I almost leap off the bed. His tongue is relentless, exploring every fold and crevice. He licks up and down, then circles my clit, each movement more tantalizing than the last. I'm moaning and writhing, my hands fisting the bed sheets, as he brings me back to the brink.

"I'm going to come," I gasp out, barely able to get the words out.

"Now," he commands, his voice rough with his own arousal. He intensifies his efforts, his tongue flicking faster. It's all the encouragement I need. My entire body tenses, and then I'm tumbling over the edge into a blinding orgasm, crying out his name.

The waves of pleasure are prolonged and intense, leaving me shivering and spent under his skilled touch.

He rises from the bed, his erection clearly outlined against the fabric of his slacks. He looks down at me with a stern expression. "You've been a bad girl," he says, his voice low and commanding.

I furrow my brows, puzzled. "What did I do?"

He steps closer, the intensity in his eyes almost palpable. "You forgot to call me sir," he states.

I swallow hard, a thrill running through me. "What's my punishment?" I ask sweetly, my voice mischievous.

He pauses, a sly grin spreading across his face. "I'll need to think about it," he muses. "But for now, I want you to suck me off."

I can't help but grin back; that sounds more like a treat than a punishment.

I reach for his belt, unbuckling it with nimble fingers. Sliding down his zipper, I free his erection from the confines of his slacks. My pulse races as I take in the sight of his long thickness, my body responding with a familiar ache.

I start by kissing the tip, my tongue darting out to taste the bead of precum that has formed. The salty-sweet flavor makes me eager for more.

Slowly, I take him into my mouth, savoring the weight and heat of him as I begin to suck. My hands roam up his thighs as I work, my actions deliberate and eager, fully intent on showing him just how much I enjoy this.

I indulge him fully, taking him deep into my mouth, relishing the way he fills me. My hand wraps around the base of his shaft, stroking in rhythm with the movements of my lips. Occasionally, I shift my focus, descending to tenderly suck and lick his balls, drawing a deep, approving growl from him.

The taste of him is intoxicating, a mixture of man and arousal that drives me wild. I can feel his pleasure building, his body tensing under my touch. My own desire increases with every moan he emits, pushing me to take him in even deeper, to give him as much pleasure as he gives me.

Eager for the climax, for the warm burst of his release in my mouth, I double my efforts, sucking him with a fervent intensity. But just as he nears the edge, as I anticipate the reward of his seed, he firmly pulls me away from his cock.

Confused but still caught in the heat of the moment, I look up at him, my breath heavy, my lips swollen from my exertions.

I'm ready to protest, to ask why he stopped, but the commanding look in his eyes tells me this is just another part of his control, another element of our play. And so, I wait, breathless and eager, for what comes next.

I can't resist a cheeky grin as he looks up at me, the lines of his face softened with desire. "Was that my punishment?" I tease, "Because if so, I'm going to have to be bad more often."

His fingers deftly unhook my bra, sending it fluttering to the floor. He pulls me to my feet, and his mouth finds my breasts, kissing and suckling with a heat that stirs deep arousal within me. I can't help but sigh, my body responding intensely, almost enough to bring me to the brink of another climax just from his attention to my nipples.

"No," he replies, his eyes sparkling with mischief. "That was just the beginning of it. Get on all fours."

"Yes, sir," I respond instantly, the title slipping out naturally now. I turn and assume the position he requested, aware of his gaze devouring the view of me presented to him.

I revel in the thought of how much he enjoys watching me, and I wonder what he plans to do next.

His command is firm, tinged with an edge of control that sends a shiver of anticipation down my spine. "I'm going to spank you," he states clearly, "and I want you to ask for it."

Nervously excited, I comply. "Please spank me," I breathe out.

"Please, sir," he corrects.

"Please spank me, *sir*."

He delivers each spank with precision, the sharp slaps echoing in the room, each one sending a shockwave of pleasure through me. The stings blur into a warm, arousing heat that pools low in my belly, and I find myself on the edge of climax, breathless from the intensity.

"What do you want now?" he asks.

I'm nearly panting, lost in the haze of my arousal. "I want you inside me," I manage to say.

"Beg for it," he commands.

My plea spills out, desperate and raw. "Please, sir."

"Please, sir, I want it."

"Want what?"

"I want you to fuck me."

"Just want?"

"I *need* you to fuck me."

Satisfied, he aligns himself at my entrance, and I feel the head of his cock pressing against me. With a firm push, he slides inside, stretching me perfectly. The feeling of him entering me is intense—his size filling me completely, each inch he pushes in sending a ripple of pleasure through my body.

I moan loudly, the sensation of being so intimately connected overwhelming as he begins to move, setting a rhythm that promises nothing but raw, deep pleasure.

He takes me hard from behind, his hands gripping my hips firmly as he thrusts into me with a rhythm that's both relentless and perfectly measured.

His hands roam from my hips, one finding its way to my breast, squeezing gently then more firmly, enhancing the raw pleasure coursing through me.

My breasts sway rhythmically with his thrusts, the movement adding a sweet, tingling sensation that complements the deep, fulfilling strokes of his cock.

"I want to hear you beg for it," he growls as I teeter on the edge of climax. "Tell me you need to come."

"Please, sir, may I come?" I gasp out, desperate for release, my voice shaky with need.

"Yes, Dalia. Come for me."

The permission breaks the dam, and my orgasm crashes over me with overwhelming intensity. I shudder and cry out, my body tensing and then spasming in waves of pleasure so powerful that I collapse forward onto the bed.

The bed's covers muffle my cries as he continues to move, drawing out my climax until I'm limp and spent, utterly consumed by the intensity of the release.

He flips me over, and damn, he's a sight—sweaty, ripped, with a sprinkle of salt-and-pepper hair across his chest. He hovers over me, his hard cock ready at my entrance. I wrap my legs around him, pulling him closer, craving the feel of him deep inside me.

He slides into me, and it's electric. Every thrust hits just right, his cock filling me completely. We're in sync, moving together in a perfect rhythm.

Looking up at him, I catch something different in his gaze— a deep, almost tender connection. It's not just fucking anymore. There's something more here, something that feels a lot like love. His eyes lock onto mine, soft yet fiery, as he drives into me, slow and deep, then fast and urgent.

As we both edge closer to climax, his strokes become more desperate, his breathing ragged. I feel him swell inside me, and with a final deep thrust, he comes hard, and so do I. The hot rush of his cum fills me, the sensation all-consuming.

His moans mix with mine, a sound of pure satisfaction. He collapses next to me, our sweaty bodies clinging to each other as we come down from the high, wrapped up in a haze of passion and tender whispers.

He shifts to spoon me from behind, his strong arms wrapping around me, pulling me close. We bask in the afterglow in silence, the only sound the distant hum of the city below. The warmth of his body, the softness of the sheets, and the shimmering city lights create a cocoon of comfort.

He plants soft kisses on my shoulder, breaking the silence.

"I want you to move in with me," he murmurs, his voice tender. "I want you here. With me."

Turning to face him, I search his eyes, finding nothing but sincerity there. I lean in and kiss him, my heart swelling.

"I'd love that," I whisper back, sealing my answer with another kiss, feeling a future together beginning to take shape between us, uncertain though it may be.

CHAPTER 19

LEV

"...And if we adjust the projections based on last quarter's growth, we should see a 15 percent increase in revenue compared to..." Yuri's voice becomes a backdrop to my scattered thoughts.

I'm sitting across from Luk and Yuri, the conference table cluttered with charts and financial figures. I lean back, rubbing the bridge of my nose as Yuri drones on.

As I scan the figures, they blur into lines and numbers, none of which I'm truly seeing.

"You seem distracted today, Lev. Something on your mind?" Luk's eyes are sharp, missing nothing.

I exhale slowly, nodding. "It has nothing to do with the numbers."

Yuri leans forward, interest piqued. "What is it then? If it's affecting you this much, maybe we can help."

I hesitate, my fingers tapping a steady rhythm on the leather of my chair. "It's a personal matter," I finally say.

Luk presses, a knowing smirk playing across his lips. "We can sideline the business talk for a bit. Whatever's on your mind seems to need airing out more than these figures."

Yuri chuckles, the sound echoing lightly in the spacious room. "Since when does Lev put personal matters on the table? This must be serious."

I exhale slowly, the weight of the topic pressing down. "You're right, Yuri. Normally, I wouldn't bring personal issues here, but this affects us all."

Both men lean in, their previous amusement shifting to seriousness as they sense the gravity in my tone.

"It's about Dalia," I start. "She's pregnant."

Luk and Yuri exchange a brief glance before erupting into congratulations. Luk, animated by the news, jumps from his seat and heads straight for my hidden stash of scotch, usually reserved for closing monumental deals. Meanwhile, Yuri grabs a set of glasses, setting the stage for celebration.

I remain seated, a silent observer of their jubilation. Yuri, noticing my reserved demeanor, approaches with a filled glass, his expression curious.

"Why the long face, Lev? This is great news," he says as he hands me the scotch.

Accepting the glass, I take a slow sip, the rich warmth of the aged liquor doing little to ease my concerns. "I appreciate the celebration, but it's not just about becoming a father," I admit. "It's the danger that's lurking around us. Things in the city are getting more volatile, and it's my responsibility to ensure Dalia and our child are safe."

The room grows quiet, my words tempering the initial excitement. The reality of our situation and the threats we face begin to settle around us.

Yuri chuckles, breaking the sudden solemnity. I frown, irritation flaring.

"What's so funny?" I'm not in the mood for levity.

He shakes his head, his laughter subsiding as he sees my serious expression. "It's not mockery, Lev," Yuri clarifies, still with a hint of amusement. "It's just so typical of you. Here you are, about to become a father, and all you can focus on is shielding Dalia and your unborn child from potential threats."

Luk chimes in with a nod, his own smirk playing at the corners of his mouth. "He's right. You need to realize the gift you're being given, brother."

Yuri claps a hand on my shoulder, his grip firm. "Look, you're doing the right thing by being vigilant, especially with everything that's going on," he says earnestly. "But don't forget to take a moment to just celebrate. You're going to be a dad. That's worth a smile, at least."

The lightness in their voices and the sincerity behind their words gradually ease the tension on my shoulders.

"Maybe you're right," I admit. "A toast then, for what it's worth."

Yuri raises his glass. "To Lev and Dalia."

We clink our glasses, the sound leaving a lasting echo. I take a measured sip of the scotch, its rich, complex flavor grounding me for a moment.

Luk eyes me intently. "So, what's next, Lev?"

I place my glass down. "She's moving in with me."

Yuri's eyebrow quirks up. "Is that what she wants?"

I fix him with a look, my voice flat and direct. "It's a security measure," I answer sharply.

Luk and Yuri share another look, the kind that says they know more than they're letting on, and this time, I'm quick to cut them off.

"Things are fine with Dalia," I state firmly, "but don't start planning the wedding just yet. For all I know, she might want her independence, even prefer being a single mother—with my support, naturally."

I'm adamant about respecting her choices and making them clear. "If that's what she decides, then that's how we'll play it."

Yuri, undeterred by my stern front, pours another round of scotch. "And what's this one for?" I ask, eyeing the golden liquid.

"To love," Yuri declares with a flourish, "or at least the prospect of it."

Their laughter fills the room, but the weight of my responsibility—and my hidden hopes—settles deeper in my chest as I sip the scotch.

An hour later, I make my way down to the IT department located in the basement. The high-tech hum of the server room fills the air as I navigate through the rows of flashing lights and humming machinery. At the end of the corridor, I reach Elena's office.

I knock briefly, and her voice, crisp and clear, invites me in. The room is a fortress of technology—dark, windowless, cluttered with high-end gear—an entire wall obscured by monitors displaying streams of data.

Elena, our head of IT and the youngest of my siblings, doesn't look up as she types away furiously, code filling the screen in front of her.

"Lev," she finally acknowledges without turning. "Come in, sit down."

I pull up a chair across from her, taking in the organized chaos of her domain. This place is her battleground, where she wages wars on digital fronts with a cool, commanding presence. She pauses for a moment, fixing me with a look that's all business.

"What brings you down here?" she asks, her fingers poised above the keyboard. She stops, her nose twitching slightly. "Is that thirty-year-old Glenfiddich I smell?"

I nod. "Guilty as charged. Want a glass? It's one elevator trip to the C-suite away."

She shakes her head, a wry smile playing on her lips. "Thanks, but no. I never drink on the clock; it dulls my edge."

She swivels her chair to face me fully, her eyes narrowing slightly. "But neither do you, big brother, unless there's a reason to celebrate." Her gaze is penetrating, expecting.

I exhale slowly, guilty as charged. "Nothing gets by you, does it?"

"That's right," she confirms, her arms crossing over her chest. "And I'm going to keep pestering you until you spill, so you might as well lay it out now."

I meet her gaze, the gravity of the news weighing on me as I prepare to share. "All right," I relent, leaning forward slightly. "Dalia's pregnant."

Elena's eyes widen dramatically before she lets out a delighted squeal, springing from her chair to throw her arms around me, her embrace surprisingly strong for her tiny frame.

"Oh, my God, Lev! That's amazing!" she exclaims, her voice bubbling with excitement.

She pulls back, her energy palpable as she bombards me with questions. "When's the baby due? Are you ready to be a dad? How's Dalia feeling?" Her questions fire off like rounds from a gun.

I raise my hands, trying to slow the barrage. "Hold on, I haven't got all those answers yet. Truth be told, I feel a little guilty for not letting Dalia be the one to share the news."

Elena pauses, a thoughtful frown crossing her face. "Wait a minute," she murmurs, "I just tried to call Yuri and Luk, but they were busy in a meeting with you." Her eyes narrow as the pieces fall into place, and a flush of realization colors her cheeks.

Suddenly, she punches my shoulder, her annoyance clear. "You told them before me?"

"Easy, Elena," I say, raising a hand to temper another strike. "I didn't exactly plan to spill the beans to them either—they wrangled it out of me."

I chuckle softly, leaning back in the chair across from her cluttered desk. "Seems like everyone's got a knack for reading my mind these days," I muse, shaking my head. "Sorry I didn't tell you first. You know now, and I promise to keep you in the loop. Within reason, of course."

She nods, her earlier flare of annoyance softening into a satisfied smile. "You're damn right you will," she asserts. Her face brightens into a broad grin, the earlier excitement returning. "And I'm so happy to know I'm going to be an aunt again!"

I smile, appreciating her quick recovery and boundless energy. "There'll be plenty of time for celebrations," I say, my voice turning serious again as I stand to pace a little in the cramped space. "But right now, there are more pressing matters we need to discuss. And I think you know what they are."

She nods. "I've been deep diving into the bike situation," she says, her fingers flying over the keyboard as she pulls up several windows on her monitors. "I managed to track the VINs through some back door channels, then hacked into the DMV database to pin down the registered owners."

I watch her work, impressed as always by her technical prowess. She turns to me, a slight smile playing on her lips as she simplifies. "I found out who owns those bikes using the evidence you tracked down using some less-than-legal means, but I got the names we need. Let's just say those bikes weren't exactly bought from a dealership."

She clicks a few times, and a photo of a chubby, middle-aged man sporting a big, dopey smile pops up on the screen. "Meet John Willard," Elena announces, "an 'accountant' from Omaha."

I chuckle, piecing it together instantly. "Stolen motorcycles, then?" I confirm, leaning in for a closer look.

"Not exactly," she corrects with a slight shake of her head. "John Willard doesn't actually exist. He's an AI-generated identity inserted into the DMV database to cover tracks. The owner of this bike is a ghost."

I raise my eyebrows. "An AI façade? That's clever."

She nods, her eyes flickering back to the screen as she continues to dig through data. "Whoever's behind this has more tricks up their sleeve than your average street thug. This isn't just savvy; it's sophisticated, organized."

"Impressive," I admit, "and troubling. We're obviously not dealing with amateurs here."

She nods firmly, her gaze returning to her monitors. "I'll keep digging and see what more I can unearth," she promises, her fingers poised above her keyboard, ready to dive back into the digital trenches.

"Thanks, Elena. I appreciate it."

She pauses, then points a stern finger at me. "But remember —next time you decide to expand the family, if I'm not the first to know, it'll be more than a punch, brother."

"Duly noted."

Changing gears, she asks, "Mind if I take Dalia out for a meal to celebrate?"

"That sounds like a great idea," I agree, pulling out my phone to give her Dalia's number. "I'm sure she'll appreciate that."

We exchange a final nod, and I leave her office, the weight of the situation settling back on my shoulders as I make my way through the dimly lit corridors back to my office. The details about the bikes, the artificial identities... everything points to a cunning and formidable adversary.

CHAPTER 20

DALIA

I step out of my apartment, suitcase in hand, and pause for one last look around.

This place hasn't been mine for long, but it was *mine*. Now, I'm about to move in with Lev, a man who's as enigmatic as he is intense.

With a deep, settling sigh, I flick off the lights, the final click echoing slightly, marking the end of an era, however brief it might've been.

Downstairs, the lobby is unusually quiet—eerily so. Normally, the friendly doorman would give me a wave, but today, there's no one there. My footsteps echo off the polished marble as I approach the exit, but before I can reach the door, a man emerges from a side hallway. His presence startles me, and his next words stop me cold.

"We need to talk."

He stands there stoically, a striking figure with long blonde hair and sharp, Slavic features that could have walked straight out of a Cold War spy novel. His blue eyes burn with an intensity that pins me in place, unsettling yet magnetic.

Tall and undeniably commanding, he carries himself with a calm assurance.

"I'm Alexei Plushenko," he declares, making the silence of the lobby even more profound. "We need to talk—it's a matter of life and death."

His melodramatic flair makes me arch an eyebrow. "Life and death? That's quite the entrance line. Planning on auditioning for a spy thriller anytime soon?"

He cracks a smirk but remains earnest. "Believe me, I'd prefer a less cliché circumstance myself, but here we are." Alexei opens his hands, palms out. "I come in peace."

Stepping back, I cross my arms, not ready to drop my guard or buy into his apparent truce. "All right, peace emissary, let's hear it then. What brings you to my soon-to-be-former doorstep?"

His eyes flicker with a hint of admiration—or is it amusement—at my standoffishness. "It's about Lev Ivanov," he begins.

With those four words, all traces of my mocking tone fade, and I'm instantly on edge.

"I'm here alone, Dalia, and there are security cameras all around. You're in no danger from me."

I sigh, his assuring words not quite dispelling the sense of exposure that prickles my skin. There's something about

Alexei, though, a sincerity beneath his measured calm that nudges my instincts toward trust.

"Go on," I prompt, more intrigued than I care to admit.

His smile is slight, evidently pleased with my guarded acceptance. "As I said, it's about Lev, or rather, all of the Ivanovs. Each one of you has a target on your back."

I frown, my heart tightening. "What do you mean? I'm not an Ivanov."

He leans closer, lowering his voice as if the walls themselves might be listening. "There are forces at work, powerful ones, aiming to take down the top family in Chicago. And since you're associated with them," he pauses, his gaze locking onto mine with an intensity that sends a shiver down my spine, "you're now at risk, too."

The revelation hits hard, the air around me feeling suddenly thick. I've only just begun to know the Ivanovs and already the shadows of their world are creeping in to affect my life.

I stare at him, frustration mounting. "I need clarity, Alexei. No more riddles or half-truths. Tell me what you know."

He sighs wearily. "I understand your need for clear answers, Dalia. My people are still trying to piece everything together. It's a tangled web, and I don't want to mislead you with incomplete information. But this much is clear—you are in danger."

"Why are you telling me this?"

He steps closer, his presence imposing yet oddly reassuring. "I am, in many ways, like the Ivanovs. I adhere to the Bratva code. I have no interest in seeing an innocent caught in the crossfire. It goes against everything I stand for."

His words, sincere and firm, carve through my defenses. There's an earnestness in his eyes that softens the harsh lines of his serious expression.

"I can protect you," he adds.

As Alexei steps forward, a sudden instinctual alertness flares within me, compelling me to recoil. I raise my hands defensively, creating space between us.

"Don't come any closer."

His lips purse, and he halts, respecting my boundary. "I understand you're already under the Ivanovs' protection," he acknowledges. "But in times like these, you can never be too careful."

He pauses, his gaze intensifying. "Big changes are coming to Chicago, and sometimes with change comes danger."

As he speaks, his hand rises slowly, moving toward his inner coat pocket. My heart hitches, fear prickling at the base of my neck as I brace for the worst. Is he going to pull out a gun? Is threatening me his true intention?

But then, his hand emerges, holding not a weapon but a small, white business card. He holds it out toward me; his movements are deliberate and open, designed to show no threat.

"My information is on this card, including a direct line. If you need anything—anything at all—please don't hesitate to call me."

Despite my initial hesitance, something in his earnest tone compels me to take the card. My fingers brush against his as I accept it, and a slight jolt of tension passes between us.

I glance at the card, confirming it holds his contact details, and quickly tuck it away into the inner pocket of my purse.

He nods. "I'll take my leave now, but please, stay safe," he urges before turning and walking away, leaving me alone in the lobby once more.

As soon as he disappears, I let out a massive rush of air, not realizing I had been holding my breath. Tension slowly drains from my shoulders.

Just then, my phone buzzes with a new message. It's Elena telling me she's on her way to the tapas place. I type a quick reply, telling her I'll be there as soon as I drop off my bag at Lev's.

With a renewed sense of urgency, I adjust my grip on my suitcase and head toward the door. The weight of the card presses against my side, a reminder of the web of danger slowly tightening around my new life.

CHAPTER 21

DALIA

"I was wondering when you'd show up," Elena quips as I approach La Esquina Roja, a cozy tapas bar nestled in the bustling River North neighborhood of Chicago. She had been waiting for me on the bench outside the door.

"Sorry, something came up," I reply, the encounter with Alexei still pressing on my mind.

"Anything you want to talk about?" she asks.

"No, just business as usual."

Elena gives me a look that pierces right through me as if she doesn't quite believe my casual dismissal, but she drops it with a shrug.

As we head inside, I notice that she's not alone—Yuri is with her. He stands up to greet me, his presence a familiar comfort, and plants a warm, brotherly kiss on my cheek. "Good to see you, Dalia."

Elena speaks up. "Lev insisted that Yuri come with me as if I can't handle myself." She rolls her eyes.

Yuri chuckles softly, his demeanor relaxed. "Don't worry, I wouldn't dream of ruining girls' night. I'll be over at the bar, still keeping an eye out, but out of your hair."

His assurance does little to ease the knot of anxiety in my stomach, but I smile appreciatively.

Yuri saunters off to the bar as Elena and I find a quiet table near the back, the hum of conversation and clinking glasses filling the air.

Yuri gives us a wave when he's seated, letting us see that he's nearby if we need anything. I watch as he slips out his phone and orders a cocktail.

Elena's eyes light up with enthusiasm. "You have to try some of my favorite dishes here," she says, her eyes scanning the menu with practiced familiarity. "The patatas bravas are divine, and the gambas al ajillo are to die for."

A memory tugs at me. "This kind of reminds me of the Egyptian food that my dad likes."

Elena perks up at this. "Oh, that's no coincidence. There's a strong Egyptian influence in Spanish cuisine, dating back to when the Umayyad Caliphate controlled the Andalusian Peninsula." She catches herself with a sheepish grin. "Sorry, I'm kind of a history nerd."

I laugh, waving off her apology. "I'm always down for learning new things. Why don't you order for us since you know what's good?"

Elena beams, pleased, and waves over the waiter. She dives into ordering with confidence. "We'll have the patatas bravas, gambas al ajillo, and let's also go for the chorizo al vino. Oh, and we must try the pulpo a la gallega."

As the waiter jots down our order, Elena then turns to the drinks menu. "And for the drinks, a glass of your finest Rioja for me, please, and a passion fruit mocktail for my friend here."

I pause when Elena orders the mocktail, suspicion flickering. As soon as the waiter's out of earshot, I fix her with a look.

"A mocktail? So, does that mean you know?"

Elena laughs, her delight unmistakable, and claps her hands together.

"Yes!" she exclaims, then quickly turns serious. "But don't worry, I practically had to interrogate Lev to tell me. He's usually locked up tighter than Fort Knox."

The news that my secret is out sends a twinge of anxiety through me, but Elena's warm grasp on my hand eases the sting. "We're all thrilled, really."

"We?" I raise an eyebrow, a mix of surprise and a hint of annoyance flaring up.

"Well, it seems Yuri and Luk might have caught wind of it, too." Elena's casual shrug tries to downplay the revelation, but it doesn't quite reach her eyes.

Feeling as exposed as a celebrity caught by paparazzi, I let out a low groan. "Great, so I'm basically naked here."

Elena's smile is sympathetic. "In the Ivanov family, secrets don't stay secrets for long. But think of it this way—you have a lot of support around you."

Her sincerity cuts through my irritation, melting it away as she squeezes my hand. "Congratulations, Dalia," she beams, and I can't help but feel a little flutter of excitement.

Elena gives me a knowing look, her voice softening. "I know this might not be how you would've wanted your pregnancy news to get out, but you're in a family now that will give your baby so much love and both of you so much protection."

I give a small smile, a mix of emotions swirling inside me. "I know, and I'm grateful for that."

Just then, the waiter arrives with our drinks, and Elena raises her glass. "To the baby," she smiles warmly.

We toast, the clink of our glasses marking a tiny, perfect moment of solidarity.

After taking a sip of her cocktail, Elana leans in, curiosity dancing in her eyes.

"So, what does this mean for you and Lev?"

I sigh. "The truth of the matter is, I'm not sure."

"You're not sure?" Elena watches me closely, then presses, "What has Lev said about it all?"

I exhale, the truth itching to spill. "He said he thought we should get married, but he hasn't brought it up again. It's not like I'm desperate to get hitched or anything, but..." I shrug. "It would relieve some stress about the baby being taken care of."

Elena sighs, her frustration evident. "That's just like my brother, always spacing on important details. His mind's on work ninety percent of the time."

Her words echo my own thoughts but hearing them from her somehow makes the situation feel more manageable and less isolating.

Elena raises her finger, her determination clear. "I'm going to make damn sure my brother doesn't leave you in a lurch. I'll talk to him, light a fire under his ass."

I smile, touched by her protectiveness. "Thank you, Elena, but we'll manage on our own."

She returns the smile, warmth radiating from her. "We're family now, which means we look out for each other."

Before we can delve deeper into our newfound sisterhood, a man approaches our table. He's in his late forties, with a graying beard and thoughtful eyes that hint at a depth of experience.

"I'm sorry to interrupt," he starts, his voice carrying a respectful urgency, "but I am certain that I reserved this table." His gaze lingers on the spot.

Elena looks up, her expression firm yet polite. "This is something you should take up with the hostess."

His lips form a tight line as he considers her words, then shifts his approach. "I'd rather work it out with you, if possible. You see," he says, his voice dropping to a softer, more heartfelt tone, "this is the table where my late wife and I had our first date years ago. It holds a lot of sentimental value to me."

At the man's heartfelt plea, I find myself softening. "I think it might be possible for us to move."

Before I can finish, Elena shoots me a strange look, her eyes darting to the bar, then back to the man.

She speaks, her tone firm. "Sorry, but we're in the middle of our meal, and we're actually celebrating something important."

The man nods, seemingly understanding, but then adds, "I understand, but perhaps a little financial incentive could sweeten the pot." He reaches into his coat, and my heart skips as he produces a gun, pointing it directly at us.

I scream, the sound tearing through the bustling noise of the bar.

Before the man can act further, a glass smashes across his head. The sudden impact sends him staggering, the gun clattering to the floor as he tries to regain his balance. Turning, I see Yuri.

The whole place goes nuts. As the man reels from the blow, Yuri is ready to hit him again. But the man is quick. He drops down, snags the gun off the floor, and points it straight at me. Just as he fires, Yuri brings his hand down on the guy's arm. The shot goes wild, blasting into the wall.

Everyone's screaming and trying to get away.

In the chaos, Elena yanks me under the table. We've barely caught our breath when we hear something land with a thud next to us. I glance over and nearly choke—it's a grenade. My heart's pounding like crazy, thinking we're done for.

But Yuri's on it. He ditches the attacker, grabs our table, and flips it over us like a shield. We're ducked behind it, waiting for a boom that never comes.

Peeking out, I see the attacker booking it through the crowd.

Yuri, still leaning hard against the table with us, finally lets up a bit. Elena, her voice a low murmur, says, "I'm not a firearms expert, but aren't grenades supposed to explode?"

"Normal ones do," Yuri answers, shoving the table off us with a solid push. He stands and walks over to the non-exploding grenade, picking it up cautiously. "But dummy ones don't."

I instantly connect the dots. "He threw it just to distract us."

"You got it," Yuri confirms with a nod, holding the dud in his hand. "And it seems," he adds, his face turning serious as he looks back at us, "we're in more danger than we thought."

CHAPTER 22

DALIA

We are silent in the private car as we weave through the streets of Chicago. Yuri is focused on the road. It's been a harrowing evening, with nervousness sitting heavy in the air around us.

Finally, Elena breaks the quiet, turning in her seat to face me.

"How are you holding up, Dalia?" Her voice is soft, concerned.

I let out a slow breath, the scene from the tapas bar still vivid in my mind. "Still shaken," I admit, my voice a bit unsteady. "I've never had a gun pointed directly at me before."

Elena nods, her expression sympathetic but with a wry twist to her lips. "You always remember your first time."

I can't help but arch my eyebrows. "Is that what it means to be an Ivanov?"

"It would seem so," she replies, her smile fading as she turns back to look out the window. "It would seem so."

I look at Yuri. "Where are we going?"

Yuri glances at me briefly in the rearview mirror. "Ivanov Holdings HQ," he responds. "Lev's called an emergency meeting."

His words settle over me with a heavyweight, the night's events clearly just the beginning of what's to come.

As we pull up to the looming facade of Ivanov Holdings HQ, the seriousness of the situation hits anew. Before the car even fully stops, guards rush toward us, their movements precise and alert. Doors are pulled open, and hands quickly reach in to assist Elena and me out of the vehicle.

We're ushered into the building, the guards surrounding us as if we're heads of state. Their presence is a solid wall of protection, and I find comfort in their efficiency as we're led to a private elevator.

With a smooth ascent, we reach the C-suite, the atmosphere charged, the quiet of the floor punctuated only by our footsteps.

The main conference room is up ahead, its lights spilling out into the hallway, the only signs of life on this otherwise deserted executive level.

Despite everything, a flutter of excitement stirs in my stomach at the thought of seeing Lev.

As we step inside, I'm struck by the sight of Lev's brothers, along with Vladimir, Vanya, and many other formidable-looking men who I assume are high-ranking Bratva soldiers, filling the room. Their faces are stern, their postures alert. I scan the room quickly for Lev, but he's notably absent.

Luk is the first to reach us, embracing his sister in a hug.

"Thank God you're both safe," he says as he lets go.

Then Vanya comes forward, his smile a mix of relief and worry as he turns to me. "Dalia, we're so glad you're okay," he says, drawing me into a warm, comforting embrace.

Yuri grins. "Don't forget your favorite driver made it out in one piece, too."

Vladimir's next, and his hug is intense—almost too much for me — but I go with it, knowing he means well.

It's clear everyone's running high on emotions.

Just as we're catching up, Lev walks into the room. He looks all business, his face set in a serious and grim expression.

Lev's presence immediately shifts the atmosphere. At first, he's silent, pacing slowly at the front of the room like a caged beast, each step measured and heavy. The uneasiness builds with his every move, drawing all eyes to him.

After a moment, he stops pacing and turns his attention toward Elena and me. His approach is slow and deliberate as he reaches out to take my hands. His gaze is intense, burning with barely restrained anger as he searches our faces.

"Are you both okay?" he asks.

"We're fine," I assure him, and I can feel the slight tremor of his hands, the controlled strength and fury in his grip.

He lets go of my hands and looks over to Yuri, his expression softening slightly. "He told me everything," Lev says. "Thank you, Yuri, for saving the lives of Dalia and my sister."

Yuri just nods, brushing it off with a slight smile. "All in a day's work," he replies, though the weight of the night is evident in his eyes.

I'm relieved to see Lev, to feel his concern, but there's a part of him that's frightening at this moment.

The rage simmering just beneath the surface is palpable, and it's clear he's struggling to keep it in check. This man, driven by fierce protectiveness, is both comforting and fearsome.

Lev strides back to the front of the room, turning to face the gathered men, his voice deep and growling with unrestrained anger.

"What the fuck happened?" he demands, letting the words echo ominously across the quiet room. Everyone's attention is fixed on him.

He continues, the fury in his voice building, "How did danger get so close to my sister and my woman?" He pauses, his gaze flickering to me for a brief moment.

A part of me thrills at the designation—it carries a possessive ring that, under the circumstances, feels strangely right.

"They were nearly killed tonight," he asserts, his tone hardening further. "I want to know how the hell two separate attempts on the lives of my people were nearly pulled off."

The raw rage in his voice sends a spike of adrenalin through my veins. It's a side of Lev I knew existed but have yet to see fully unleashed. The room remains silent, the gravity of his words settling heavily on all present.

Lev's voice cuts through the tension in the room like a blade. "It will *never* happen again. I promise you that."

He pauses, letting each word sink in before he continues, his voice growing darker, more ominous with each syllable. "I'm going to rip apart, piece by piece, whoever the fuck dared to come near my family with violent intent. I'll destroy them, their associates, and anyone who stands in my way."

Lev then turns to his lieutenants, his gaze fierce and commanding. "All attention is to be focused on this matter," he instructs them. His orders are clear, and his authority is absolute. "Prepare for war."

The lieutenants nod, their expressions resolute, as they begin to rally, understanding the gravity of his commands. Watching Lev in this moment, I can't help but feel an undeniable thrill, an awe at the lengths he's willing to go to protect his family, which now includes me.

He goes on. "Our work begins tonight. I will not accept failure." His voice resonates with a lethal calm.

He then dismisses the room, signaling for his family, Vladimir and Vanya, to stay. As the room clears out, leaving only the requested few, Lev's demeanor shifts slightly.

He addresses them. "I want extra protection on all of you."

Luk nods in agreement. "Maura and the kids are at home under heavy guard."

Elena chimes in next, her usual vibrant tone tempered with seriousness. "My apartment is like a fortress already, and I'll be working from there. No one's getting through."

"You know my head's always on a swivel," Yuri says.

Vanya adds, "I'll be watching my back; don't worry about me."

Lev nods at each of them, pleased with their arrangements, but his eyes betray a lingering concern.

Vladimir steps forward, his tone all business. "I'll be meeting with my people, putting them on information-gathering duty."

Lev thanks them, then turns to dismiss the group, pausing as he addresses Yuri.

"Make sure Elena gets home safely," he instructs.

One by one, they leave the room until only Lev and I remain. Alone with him, the atmosphere shifts. The intensity of his earlier commands lingers in the air, and I find myself both frightened and inexplicably drawn to the fierce protectiveness he exudes.

It's a disturbing realization, a mix of fear and attraction. His commanding presence has always affected me, but tonight, the stakes feel different, higher.

My heart races as I watch him, the earlier anxiety morphing into a different kind of beast now that we're alone.

I feel a flush of heat, my body reacting in ways that both confuse and excite me. I try to steady my breath, my gaze locked on Lev, aware of every move he makes in the quiet aftermath of the storm.

He rests his hand gently on my shoulder, and the simple touch sends a jolt through me, making my breath hitch. My heart pounds fiercely in my chest.

He looks into my eyes, his searching mine, and I'm caught, unsure of what he'll say next. The room suddenly feels too small, and every sound is amplified.

"I'm sorry for putting you in harm's way," he says, his voice low and sincere.

"It's not like you did it directly," I manage to say. "It's okay."

He shakes his head, his expression tightening. "It's not okay, not until the people who have done this pay," he insists. Then, shifting topics slightly, he asks, "Have you started moving in?"

"Just one suitcase," I reply, feeling a strange relief at the mundane question.

"Whatever else is still at your place, I'll have it sent over tomorrow. I don't want you going back there at all."

The tone of his voice doesn't leave room for argument, not that I would challenge him on it, especially not now.

Then, Lev surprises me again. He leans in and kisses me deeply, his arms pulling me close. The intensity of his kiss sends a rush through me. For a breathless moment, I wonder if he's going to take me right here, right now, and I realize, with a jolt of surprise, that I would let him.

But he doesn't. Instead, he pulls back slightly, his eyes locked on mine, heavy with unspoken words. "We're leaving for my place now," he says.

With those words, I know my old life is gone forever. A new chapter is beginning, one entwined irrevocably with Lev's, filled with danger and passion. As I stand there, held close by him, the reality of my situation settles in.

I'm stepping into a world far removed from anything I've known, protected, and claimed by a man who is both a sanctuary and a danger.

CHAPTER 23

DALIA

As the first rays of morning light filter through the curtains, I stir awake, feeling groggy and worn out from last night. When we arrived at Lev's place, exhaustion had overwhelmed me the instant I crossed the threshold—probably the combined effects of the evening's adrenaline rush and my pregnancy.

I find myself in the familiar surroundings of the guest room where I've stayed before. Glancing around, I notice a note placed on the table beside the bed.

Dalia,

I'm out investigating the attempts on your life.

Your belongings have been shipped over and are waiting in the living room. I ask that you not leave the building for your own safety. I understand this might feel confining, but it's necessary under the circumstances.

If you need anything to eat or drink, we have a chef at the restaurant in the lobby. Feel free to order whatever you like, and it will be brought up to you.

Your comfort and safety are my top priorities right now.

Take care,

Lev

I set the note down and roll out of bed, still feeling the drudge of sleep and pause to take in the spectacular view from the window.

Slipping into some comfy pants, I leave the bedroom and wander through Lev's sprawling penthouse. I get to the living room, and all of my things are already there, as mentioned. My boxes and belongings take up such a tiny part of this vast space, and I can't help but chuckle at the sight.

I head to the kitchen to make some decaf. As the rich aroma fills the air, I decide to treat myself to breakfast from the restaurant Lev mentioned. I grab the phone and call the chef, curious about the special.

"Good morning. What's on the menu today?" I ask.

"Today's special is a smoked salmon with eggs Benedict and a side of herb-roasted potatoes," the chef replies, his voice cheerful.

"That sounds amazing, I'll have that, thank you."

Order placed, I sip my coffee, feeling a bit more fortified to tackle the day. I glance over at the boxes waiting to be unpacked and the furniture that needs arranging.

It's a new beginning here in this large and luxurious space, and I'm ready to put my stamp on it.

I dive into the task of unpacking, slowly transforming the space into something that feels like it could be mine. Not long after, the food arrives, and I take a break to enjoy the delicious meal.

As the morning fades into the afternoon, I manage to make a significant dent in the unpacking. Just as I'm breaking down the last empty box, I hear the door open.

Lev steps through, dressed down in a white henley with black buttons that subtly accentuate his toned upper body, paired with gray jeans. He looks effortlessly handsome and seeing him like this in such a casual, domestic setting adds a new layer of intimacy to our relationship.

He greets me with a warm smile. "Making yourself comfortable?" he asks, his eyes scanning the progress I've made.

"Yes, I've managed to move most of my stuff into my room."

He cocks his head to the side, a look of confusion passing over his face. "We can share a room now unless you'd prefer your own space?" he says, making it clear the choice is mine.

I smile a little sheepishly. "I didn't want to assume."

Lev looks at me intently, his eyes searching mine. "Well, we *are* having a child together, but what do you want, Dalia?"

The sincerity in his question warms me, and I find myself responding without hesitation. "I'd love to share a bed with you." The words feel so right as they leave my lips.

He steps closer, taking my hands in his and gently kissing them. "Good."

His kiss sends a flutter through me.

As we share this small, tender moment, Lev breaks away to pour himself a glass of water. I lean against the counter, watching him move.

"You're looking pretty casual for a day at the office," I tease gently.

He sighs, filling his glass. "I've been out in the field mostly, trying to dig up some information about the attack."

"What have you learned?"

He takes a sip of his water, his gaze distant for a moment as he considers his words. "There are more questions than answers at this point," he admits, setting the glass down. "It's complicated. We're still piecing things together."

Lev's expression darkens with determination. "I'm not going to rest until I find out who's behind what happened."

I nod, touched by his protectiveness. "I believe you."

He pauses, his head tilting slightly as if he's pondering something else.

Curious, I prompt him, "What?"

Lev hesitates, then ventures cautiously, "I couldn't help noticing you only had a few boxes of clothes."

I purse my lips, a flood of memories from the past momentarily silencing me.

He picks up on my discomfort and gently prods, "What's wrong?"

"When I left Chad, I left most of them behind. He ended up throwing them out, and I haven't had the chance to get more."

Lev's brow furrows with concern. "That's no good. We'll have to do something about that."

His response warms me, filling me with a sense of being cared for in a way I hadn't realized I'd wanted.

As Lev's tenderness washes over me, something else nags at the back of my mind, a part of my past with which I haven't fully reconciled. But I hesitate, unsure if I want to dive into that just yet. However, Lev, keen as ever, picks up on my hesitance.

"There's something else."

I sigh. "It's silly."

He shakes his head firmly. "If it's important to you, it's not silly at all."

Encouraged by his support, I decide to share. "I used to work part-time for a man named Claude Pascal, a jeweler. Chad was friends with him."

"What did you do for him?"

"I made jewelry," I reply. "I had hopes to maybe open my own store someday."

Lev looks genuinely impressed. "That's amazing, Dalia."

My tone drops as I continue, "When I left Chad, I didn't bring my jewelry with me. Claude fired me due to his friendship with Chad, keeping all the jewelry I made and taking credit for it."

I watch as Lev's jaw clenches and his eyes darken, a storm brewing behind his previous calm demeanor.

"Most of my jewelry—pieces that I had personally crafted—are still at Claude's store, being sold as if he had created them. He basically stole them from me."

Lev's reaction is immediate. "That's unacceptable."

I laugh lightly, trying to ease the tension. "Yeah, it sucks. But we've got bigger matters on our plate right now."

"Perhaps," he says, but I can tell the issue has lodged itself in his mind, his sense of justice clearly ruffled. He seems lost in thought for a moment, mulling over something he's hesitant to say.

Then, unexpectedly, he closes the distance between us, taking my hands in his. His touch sends a familiar thrill through me, grounding and intense all at once.

"I know it's been a long and trying couple of days, but if I don't have you now, I'm going to lose my mind."

His words ignite something fierce and immediate within me, a rush of desire so potent it's almost overwhelming. I feel my body respond instinctively, my breath quickening.

"Then what are you waiting for?"

The heat between us is almost unbearable, and when he kisses me, it feels like a dam breaking. His lips are insistent and hungry, and I melt into him, returning the kiss with equal fervor.

He sweeps me up effortlessly, his arms strong and secure as he carries me down the hallway. Every step he takes makes my heart race, anticipation coiling inside me like a spring ready to snap.

As he lays me gently on the bed, his eyes never leave mine, a burning intensity in his gaze that sends sparks through my bloodstream. He strips off his shirt, revealing the taut muscles of his chest and arms, and I can't help but reach out to touch him, my fingers tracing the contours of his skin.

"You're so damn beautiful," he murmurs, leaning over me, his hands trailing down my sides with a delicious slowness that leaves me breathless.

I pull him down, my lips finding his once more. The kiss is deep and demanding; my body responds instantly to his touch. His hands are everywhere—gliding over my skin, caressing, exploring—as he maps every inch of me with a tenderness that belies the urgency of our desire.

I feel his weight pressing down on me, his body aligning perfectly with mine, and I arch against him, craving more of that intoxicating contact.

His lips travel down my neck, leaving a scorching trail that makes me gasp, my fingers threading through his hair as he continues his descent. I feel the rasp of his breath against my skin; each exhale igniting a fire that consumes us both.

"Lev," I moan, the sound low and throaty, as I feel his hands slide beneath my shirt, pushing it up and over my head.

He pauses to admire the view, his eyes dark with need, before leaning down to capture my mouth in another searing kiss. It's as if we're trying to pour all the unspoken emotions into this one moment, and I revel in the intensity of it all.

His fingers skillfully undo the clasp of my bra, and the cool air sends a shiver through me as the fabric falls away. His mouth follows, trailing kisses down my chest until he reaches my breasts. He teases my nipples with soft, deliberate strokes of his tongue, drawing a breathless sigh from my lips.

I tug at his jeans, desperate to feel the heat of his skin against mine, and he obliges, discarding them quickly along with the rest of his clothes. The sight of him naked and ready only heightens my desire, and I pull him back to me, eager to feel every inch of him. His skin is warm and smooth against mine as he presses me down into the mattress.

"God, I've been thinking about this all day," Lev murmurs against my ear, his voice low and rough with need. "You have no idea how much I want you and how fucking perfect you are."

He peels my pants and panties down my legs, leaving me completely exposed to him. A shiver of anticipation runs through me as he takes a moment to admire the view.

He grins wickedly, his hands gliding over my hips and thighs, spreading them wider to make room for himself. "I love seeing you like this, all spread out for me," he says, his words sending a delicious thrill straight to my core. "I want to taste every inch of you, make you scream my name."

His lips find my breasts again, his tongue flicking over one nipple before taking it fully into his mouth, sucking gently and then harder, drawing moans from deep within me. My fingers tangle in his hair as he lavishes attention on me, the sensation a perfect mix of pleasure and teasing.

Lev shifts lower, trailing kisses down my stomach, his stubble grazing my skin and leaving a trail of fire in its wake. My heart pounds in anticipation as he moves between my legs, settling himself there with a look of pure hunger in his eyes.

"You're already so wet for me," he murmurs, his voice filled with a mix of admiration and desire. His hands grip my thighs firmly, spreading them even wider as he lowers his mouth to my most sensitive spot.

His tongue is relentless, skillful, as it flicks over my clit with a precision that makes my back arch and my breath catch in my throat. He teases me, alternating between gentle licks and firmer strokes that have me gasping for air, my hands clutching the sheets beneath me.

"Lev, please," I moan, half in plea and half in praise, my body responding to his every move, my hips instinctively lifting to meet his mouth.

He chuckles, the vibration sending shockwaves through me. "You like that? Tell me what you want, Dalia. I want to hear you beg for it."

His words, combined with his tongue, are a potent combination, and I can't help but comply. "I want more, Lev," I gasp, my voice breathless with need. "Please, don't stop. I need you to make me come."

Encouraged by my words, he doubles his efforts, his tongue working magic against my clit as one hand slides up my thigh and two fingers enter me with a smooth, confident thrust. He finds my rhythm, his fingers curling inside me, hitting that perfect spot that makes my world shatter and rebuild with every stroke.

The combination of his mouth and fingers is devastating, a perfect symphony of sensation that sends me spiraling toward the edge. He doesn't let up, relentless in his mission to bring me to the peak, his fingers pumping steadily as his tongue circles my clit with unerring precision.

I can feel the tension coiling inside me, building with every touch, every flick of his tongue, every delicious thrust of his fingers. My body tenses, every nerve alight, as I teeter on the brink of something spectacular.

"That's it, Dalia," he murmurs against me, his voice filled with raw desire. "Come for me. I want to feel you fall apart."

His words are my undoing. With a cry, I shatter around him, pleasure crashing over me in waves so intense they leave me breathless and trembling. My world narrows to this moment, this feeling, as my pussy clenches around his fingers, every muscle quivering with the force of my release.

He doesn't stop until he's squeezed every last shudder of pleasure from me, only then easing his fingers from my body and pressing one last lingering kiss to my thigh. I lay there, boneless and blissfully spent, as he rises to kiss me softly, letting me taste the remnants of my own pleasure on his lips.

"I want to make you mine," he declares, his voice deep and unwavering, filled with a promise that sends shivers down my spine. "I want to claim you completely."

My heart pounds in response, my body already aching for his touch, his claim. "That's what I want, too," I confess, my voice a breathless whisper of longing. There's no hesitation, no doubt, just an undeniable need to be his in every possible way.

He positions himself above me, his body a force of nature poised to take me. His hands find my wrists, pinning them above my head with a firm, commanding grip that sends a thrill of submission coursing through my veins.

With a slow, deliberate motion, he pushes inside me, and I gasp at the sensation. He stretches me in the most exquisite way, every inch of him filling me completely. I moan softly, adjusting to the delicious fullness of him, my body surrendering to his possession.

"You're still so tight," he groans, his voice rough with pleasure as he begins to move, igniting a fire that spreads through me with every powerful stroke. His hips drive forward with an intensity that leaves me breathless; each thrust is perfectly aimed to hit that spot that makes stars explode behind my eyes.

The bed moves beneath us, matching the rhythm of our passion, as he claims me with a raw, animalistic need that mirrors my own. I arch against him, meeting him thrust for thrust, feeling every delicious inch of him as if we were dancing on the edge of oblivion together.

The room fills with the sound of our bodies meeting, the ragged gasps of our shared pleasure echoing in the air. His hands maintain their grip on my wrists, holding me captive beneath him as he drives into me with unrelenting force, every movement drawing me closer to the edge of something profound.

"Lev," I gasp, lost in the overwhelming sensation of him inside me, the friction and heat building into a crescendo that I can no longer control. I feel myself spiraling, the world blurring as he pushes me ever closer to that precipice.

He leans down, his lips grazing my ear as he whispers, "I want to feel you come all over my cock, Dalia."

His pace quickens, his grip on my wrists tightening as he nears his own release. I feel him swell inside me, his thrusts becoming more erratic, each one sending shockwaves of pleasure through my oversensitive body as I reach a blinding climax.

"That's it," he groans, his voice a guttural growl as he reaches his own end. With a final, powerful thrust, he spills inside me, the warmth of his release lighting me up. He holds himself deep, the sensation of him draining into me a perfect counterpoint to the throbbing aftershocks of my orgasm.

We collapse together, our bodies slick with sweat and trembling from the force of our shared ecstasy. The world slowly comes back into focus, our breathing gradually steadying as we lie entwined, the afterglow of our passion enveloping us in a cocoon of bliss.

Lev releases my wrists, his touch now gentle and soothing as he pulls me into his arms, holding me close. I nestle against him, savoring the warmth of his body and the steady beat of his heart beneath my ear.

"You're incredible," he murmurs, pressing a soft kiss to my forehead, and I smile, feeling a deep, abiding sense of contentment.

In this moment, wrapped in his embrace, I know I'm exactly where I'm meant to be.

CHAPTER 24

"Any leads on Plushenko?" I ask, steering through an intersection with practiced ease.

As I navigate through the bustling streets of downtown Chicago, I'm deep in conversation with Yuri. We're unraveling the threads of our current predicament—specifically, the role Alexei Plushenko might have played in the recent attacks.

Yuri's voice comes through the Bluetooth, tinged with the same frustration I feel. "I've had the lieutenants digging everywhere, asking around. But nothing substantial, nothing that directly points to Alexei, at least."

I grip the steering wheel a bit tighter, my gaze fixed on the road ahead but my mind racing with possibilities. Alexei's a cunning player, his motives as murky as the waters we find ourselves wading through. If he's involved, he's covered his tracks well.

"Keep pressing. He's got to slip up somewhere," I insist, my voice firm, the city lights streaking past.

Yuri assures me they're on it, but the uncertainty gnaws at me.

I let out a sigh of frustration, the sound lost amidst the hum of the engine and the faint crackle of the call. Despite our efforts, we're no closer to clarity, and it grates on me, this not knowing, this strategic blindness that puts us all at risk.

Yuri's tone conveys his unease. "It's all so strange, Lev. It's clear this is the beginning of a war, and not just any war, but one with a formidable enemy. Yet it's so quiet."

I can't help but chuckle despite the gravity of our situation. "I wouldn't exactly call assassination attempts quiet," I retort, keeping my eyes on the road as I navigate through a particularly congested area.

"You have a point there," Yuri concedes with a sigh.

"Whoever's behind this, they're probably trying to weaken us, put us on the back foot before they launch the main push of their offensive."

"That means there's likely another assassination attempt on the way," Yuri adds.

"I agree. They're not going to let up until they're successful. We need to be vigilant, increase our defenses, and not give them another opening."

Yuri switches gears, bringing up a lighter subject. "What's your plan for tonight? It's Friday, after all."

I grip the steering wheel a bit tighter, my mind already on the evening ahead. "I'm taking Dalia out for a night on the town. She deserves a break from all this."

Yuri sounds concerned, his voice lowering slightly. "You worried about taking her out with everything that's going on?"

"I'm always vigilant," I assure him firmly. "But I refuse to let Dalia feel like she's trapped. We'll have a close perimeter, and Vanya will be with us."

"That's good to hear."

I grin. "I have a little something special planned for her."

"Is that right?"

"It is. A little resolution of the past."

He chuckles. "Cryptic as always. Just try not to scare the poor girl; she's already having a hard time easing into this new world of hers."

"I'll do my best."

As I pull up to the building, I spot Dalia in the lobby through the glass doors. She's dressed in a dark blue cocktail dress. The sight of her stops me in my tracks; she's stunning, her dress accentuating every curve with tantalizing precision. It sets off a raw pulse of desire through me. For a moment, the thought of skipping the night out and taking her straight upstairs crosses my mind.

I step out of the car, my attention immediately captured by Dalia emerging from the lobby.

As she approaches, a pair of guards follow closely behind her, a necessary precaution that I've insisted on. I catch a glimpse of Grigori's car parked nearby, a silent confirmation that everything's set for tonight.

When she reaches me, I place my hand on her hip, a familiar touch that brings a smile to both our faces. I lean in to greet her with a kiss, feeling the electric connection that always sparks between us.

"Are you ready?" I ask, filled with the anticipation of the evening ahead.

Her smile widens, eyes sparkling with excitement. "Yes, I am," she replies, her voice brimming with enthusiasm.

Tonight is about us, a brief escape from the looming threats and complications. As I lead her to the car, hand resting gently at the small of her back, I'm determined to make every moment count, for both our sakes.

I open the door for her, and she gracefully slides into the passenger seat. Once I'm settled behind the wheel, I place my hand on her thick, gorgeous thigh as I pull away from the curb. The contact is electrifying.

She turns to me with a mischievous smile. "What do you have in mind for tonight?"

"We're going to do a little shopping, grab some dinner, and then..." I let the words trail off suggestively, giving her leg a gentle squeeze as I say, "Who knows."

She catches the hint, her smile widening as she licks her lips in a tantalizingly playful response.

"I want to take you to get some new clothes," I continue, "but first, I've got a special surprise for you."

Her interest piqued, she asks, "What kind of surprise?"

I chuckle, glancing at her briefly before focusing back on the road. "Now, if I told you, it wouldn't be a surprise anymore, would it?"

The city lights pass by, a blur of illumination as we drive through the bustling streets, the night laid out before us like a promise.

We pull up in front of a jeweler's shop, the soft glow of its elegant storefront lighting up the early evening. Dalia looks out the window, her expression shifting from curiosity to shock as she recognizes the place.

She gasps, her eyes wide as she turns to me. "What are we doing here?"

I flash her a reassuring smile, my confidence unwavering. "I think it's time for Claude to make amends," I tell her. "He's got some things that rightfully belong to you, and we're here to get them back."

Dalia looks unsure, her gaze flickering back to the store. I reach over and take her hand, giving it a comforting squeeze.

"Trust me," I say, looking into her eyes. "I've taken care of everything."

After a moment's hesitation, she nods, placing her trust in me. Together, we step out of the car, our steps synchronized as we approach the entrance.

CHAPTER 25

"I'm not sure about this."

We pause just outside the store, the gleaming display windows inviting but daunting. I turn to Lev, the uncertainty clear in my voice.

He gives me a knowing smile. "I understand why you're nervous," he reassures me, "but trust me, when it's over, you'll be glad you did it."

Despite my reservations, something about his assurance makes me feel like I can indeed trust him.

"I've also arranged a private viewing of the latest from Claude's collection—some very rare pieces."

"OK," I reply, drawing a deep breath to steady my nerves. "Just... you're not going to kill him, are you?"

He laughs. "Not part of the plan. What I have in mind is a little more subtle than that."

He holds the door open for me, and together we step inside. The interior of the store is every bit as fancy as I remember, with luxurious displays of expensive jewelry that sparkle under the sophisticated lighting.

As I admire the pieces around us, I lean closer to Lev and whisper, "While Claude did steal some of my designs, it's not as though he doesn't have talent of his own."

As I wander through the aisles of glittering jewelry, my eyes are drawn to a particularly stunning diamond engagement ring.

It's a breathtaking piece, with a large, brilliant-cut diamond set in a delicate platinum band, encrusted with smaller pave diamonds that catch the light with every subtle movement.

The sight of the ring stirs something within me. Lev had mentioned that he was planning to propose, but for some reason, he hasn't yet.

Lev, noticing my lingering gaze, comes over and asks softly, "Is there anything that's caught your eye?"

I shake my head. "No," but the quick, knowing glance he gives me suggests he saw me staring at the ring.

As I take in all the glittering pieces, my stomach drops. Across the room sits an unmistakably familiar display. My steps quicken as I head over, my heart pounding. Laid out before me are my designs, my creations, showcased as if they belong to someone else and priced like treasures.

Lev comes over, his brow furrowed as he looks at the display.

"Are these yours?" he asks.

"They sure are. And look at the price tags. Claude always brushed them off, said they weren't worth much." I can't hide the bitterness in my voice.

Lev's jaw clenches as he takes it all in, his displeasure evident.

Before we can hash it out further, a voice calls out, overly cheerful and way too familiar.

"Welcome!" Claude says from the back of the store. "You must be my private customers. Can I get you anything to drink?"

We turn around to see Claude approaching, all smiles and hospitality. But the moment his eyes land on me, his smile falters, and he gasps. Clearly, he wasn't expecting to see me again, especially not like this.

Claude Pascal stands there, a picture of fashionable distress. He's trim, his hair perfectly styled, and his clothes scream designer chic—a look you might see on a celebrity at a New York fashion show. His mannerisms and sharp attire give him an air of theatricality reminiscent of those charismatic characters who own every room they enter.

His shock at seeing me is quite something.

"Dalia! What the hell are you doing here?" he sputters, his voice rising in panic. He takes his phone from his pocket as if to call security, but before his hand can even lift it, the front door swings open again.

Vanya enters confidently, swinging his cane, followed by three of Lev's men. They're calm and collected, an intimidating presence.

Vanya addresses the store staff with authority. "You're in no danger, but we will need you to stay in the break room for the duration of this showing."

The staff, picking up on the seriousness of his tone, quickly scurry to the back of the shop, Lev's men trailing behind them.

Vanya then turns to Claude, his voice firm but kind. "As long as you don't do anything stupid, you'll make it out of this no worse for wear."

Lev watches the scene unfold with a satisfied grin. Once the area is cleared, he turns to Claude, still smiling.

"I'm ready for my showing now," he announces.

Claude regards us with a wary eye. "Wait a minute, you're Lev Ivanov." There's a quiver of anxiety in his voice.

Lev smiles at him, both charming and chilling. "The one and only."

A visible wave of relief washes over Claude, and he manages a smile of his own, albeit a shaky one. "I've heard of your reputation. I'm told you're a gentleman."

From somewhere in the store, Vanya, who had been casually examining the jewelry, lets out a bark of a laugh at this description.

Lev doesn't miss a beat. "Perhaps you've been told correctly. But that doesn't mean I don't have my fair share of blood on my hands."

His tone is casual, but the underlying warning is clear.

The color drains from Claude's face as the implications sink in. He swallows hard before asking, "What do you want?"

Lev's expression turns stony. "I ought to smash every case in here, considering the way you robbed Dalia of her hard work and talent."

Claude tries to defend himself, his words coming out in a hurried rush. "Her pieces were left behind in the divorce. I was simply... ah, giving them a good home."

His feeble attempt at justification does nothing, and Lev is not amused.

"A good home," Lev echoes, his tone dripping with incredulity. "Bullshit—you're selling them and claiming that the designs are yours."

I jump in, unable to hold back my frustration. "Exactly, you've been making money off *my* hard work!"

Claude scoffs, waving a dismissive hand as if to brush away a pesky fly. "Nonsense. I taught you everything you know about making jewelry. If anything, *you* owe *me*."

From across the room, Vanya can't contain himself as he lets out another laugh. "You can't possibly think that line is going to work."

Lev doesn't miss a beat, pressing Claude further. "Tell me, Claude, how well have Dalia's pieces been selling?"

Claude hesitates but then, with a resigned sigh, admits, "Quite well, actually. Nearly half of them are sold, and I get constant requests for more."

Despite the tension and the less-than-ideal circumstances, I can't help but feel a surge of pride at his words. My work, my art, is desired and cherished by others.

Lev gives me a nod, all business. "Ready to start the private showing, Dalia?"

"Oh, yeah, I'm ready."

Claude, still looking jittery, motions us toward some fancy chairs. "Please, take a seat. Can I get you some champagne?"

I'm about to slip up about the pregnancy, but Lev's way ahead of me. "Sparkling water with lime will be fine," he cuts in quickly. Claude nods and scurries off, returning in no time with our drinks, which he pours with slightly shaky hands.

As we settle in, Lev leans closer and whispers, "What would you like to see? Anything at all."

Claude, lingering nearby, can't help but ask, "Seriously, you're not planning to kill me, are you?"

Lev shoots him a half-smile. "The night is still young."

I decide to steer us back to the purpose of our visit. "I'd love to see some tennis bracelets."

Claude quickly brings over a tray of glittering bracelets. "Here you go. This one here," he points to a particularly dazzling piece, "is set with a row of large, brilliant-cut diamonds, each one sculpted to perfection. And it's practically a steal at—"

Lev speaks up. "Let's skip the prices. Just show us what you've got."

Claude, a bit more at ease now, starts showcasing more tennis bracelets with an air of practiced flair.

Lev watches me, a slight smile on his lips. "Pick one," he urges quietly.

I scan the selection, and my eyes settle on a stunning bracelet with an elegant wave pattern, the diamonds set so they catch the light from every angle. "That one."

Claude nods, sliding the bracelet onto my wrist. The cool metal feels luxurious against my skin, and I can't help but be awestruck by how it sparkles.

"Now," Lev says, his voice firm but calm, "let's take a look at some diamond engagement rings."

My heart skips a beat, and I meet his gaze, excitement flickering in my eyes. Claude starts to offer, "We have many styles to—"

But I cut him off, already sure of my choice. "I already know which one I want. The one I was looking at earlier."

Lev tells Claude, "Bring it to me."

I show Claude which one, and he retrieves the ring, dutifully placing it in a box. Once he hands it over to Lev, the atmosphere shifts.

Lev casually pulls out a gun, and Claude's face blanches. "Oh, God!" he exclaims, stepping back.

Lev's voice is ice cold as he says, "Now, you're going to apologize."

Claude looks like he's about to faint, his face draining of color. "Apologize?" he sputters, shock written all over him.

"That's right," Lev replies, his voice cool and steady. "You stole Dalia's designs and passed them off as your own. You took advantage of her when she was down, then made money off it. You're both a thief and a liar."

Seeing Claude shake like a leaf, I feel a twist of nervousness. "Lev, I really don't want him to die."

Lev glances at me, then back at Claude. "His fate's in his own hands."

Claude practically falls over himself to apologize. "I'm sorry, Dalia, I'm so sorry."

Lev isn't having it. "You'll need to do better than that. First, get on your knees," he directs sharply.

Without much choice, Claude drops to his knees, his movements awkward and desperate.

Lev's voice is authoritative. "Now, Claude. Apologize specifically for what you did."

Claude nods quickly, turning to me with eyes wide. He clasps his hands together, almost as if he's praying. "Dalia, I am deeply sorry for taking your jewelry designs and passing them off as my own. It was wrong to profit from your creativity and hard work during a time when you were vulnerable. I regret my actions and the harm they caused you."

From across the room, Vanya chimes in, half-joking, half-serious. "You know, the Yakuza make people cut off a knuckle to show how sincere they are when they apologize."

Claude's face goes even whiter, and he lets out a shrill shriek at the suggestion. "No, please, no!"

Lev chuckles lightly, shaking his head. "I don't think we need to go that far," he says, dismissing the idea with a wave of his hand.

Turning to me, Lev's expression softens. "Is the apology sufficient?"

I pause, weighing the fear and remorse on Claude's face against the anger and betrayal I've felt. Finally, I say, "Yes."

His apology seemed genuine, and while it doesn't undo the past, it's a step. Lev nods in agreement, satisfied with the outcome.

Claude, still on his knees, looks up at Lev with a hopeful expression. "Have I done everything you want?"

"Not quite," Lev responds coolly. He glances around the luxurious interior of the store. "We still need to discuss the payment Dalia deserves for the sale of her designs." His gaze then fixes back on Claude. "A nice place like this must keep good records, right, Claude?"

Claude swallows hard, nodding. "Yes, indeed we do."

"Excellent," Lev says. "Where are they?"

"In the back," Claude responds quickly.

"Very good," Lev replies. He turns to Vanya, who's been quietly observing from the side. "I want you to go back with Claude and find all of the records for every piece of Dalia's that have been sold."

Lev then looks at Claude. "Do you understand what to do?"

"Yes, sir," Claude says, a bit of relief in his voice as he stands. He leads the way to the back of the store, Vanya following closely behind.

As they disappear into the back, I let out a breath I didn't realize I was holding.

Lev turns to me with a concerned expression. "You alright?"

"I'm fine. In fact, I'm enjoying this more than I would've guessed."

"Good," Lev replies with a hint of amusement.

"Just make sure not to shoot him," I add.

Just then, Vanya and Claude return, Claude clutching a manila envelope in his hands. He offers it to Lev dutifully. Lev takes the envelope, his expression turning serious again as he starts to sift through the contents. He lets out a low whistle, clearly impressed or perhaps shocked by the numbers. After a moment, he closes the folder decisively.

"Here's what we're going to do," he begins, laying out his plan. "The prices that these pieces sold at are what you owe Dalia. We'll subtract that amount from the combined cost of the tennis bracelet and the engagement ring."

He then turns to me, his eyes questioning. "Anything else catch your eye?"

Scanning the display, my gaze lands on a stunning pair of elegant diamond earrings, featuring a large teardrop central diamond surrounded by a halo of smaller stones set in white gold.

"Those earrings," I say, pointing them out.

Claude groans audibly, a sound of pure despair, as he sees where this is heading.

"Box them up," Lev instructs firmly, "then give me a total."

Claude is resigned and does as he's told. He boxes the earrings, then returns to his calculator. His face goes pale as he runs the numbers, the reality of the financial hit setting in.

"I owe you twelve thousand dollars," he announces, his voice barely above a whisper.

"Do you have that kind of cash on hand?"

Claude nods. "Yes, I haven't gone to the bank to make a deposit yet today."

"Give it to Vanya."

Claude again goes to the back, then returns with an envelope, handing it to Vanya. Lev turns to Vanya with a final instruction. "Confirm it's all there, then split the money among the staff for their trouble.

"Now," Lev shifts gears, still all business but with an undercurrent of support just for me. "There's still the matter of your pieces, Dalia. What would you like to do?"

I chew on the inside of my cheek for a second, mulling it over. "I'd like them back but I did make them to be sold, after all."

Lev's eyes light up with an idea. "How about this," he offers, turning back to Claude, "you keep these pieces here and sell them. You'll get a finder's fee of five percent for each sale."

Claude groans again, sounding like he's swallowed something sour. I have to press my lips tightly together to stop from laughing out loud.

Lev looks Claude square in the eye. "No funny business," he warns. "I'll be keeping an eye on you to make sure you're playing straight."

"Of course," Claude responds a little too quickly.

Vanya returns, grinning a bit. "The staff was more than happy with the cash."

"People always are," Lev replies as he stands, a hint of dry humor in his voice. He picks up the bag of jewelry we're taking with us. "Thank you for the private showing, Mr. Pascal," he says to Claude politely.

Stepping outside, I feel like I'm floating, the laughter and lightness between Lev, Vanya, and me making everything seem a little brighter.

For the first time in a long time, I feel like I've won.

CHAPTER 26

LEV

I wake up to the sight of Dalia next to me, her breathing even and calm as she sleeps.

It's a view that never fails to stir something deep inside me. The morning light spills across her bare skin, highlighted beneath the thin sheets.

I find myself thinking about the fun we had last night.

The way her hair fanned out on the pillow, the soft moans that filled the room, and the warmth of her touch flash through my mind, vivid and stirring. The joyous smile on her face as I slipped the engagement ring on her finger.

Part of me is tempted to wake her, to relive those moments, but I resist. She looks so peaceful, and I decide she needs the rest. Besides, today isn't a day for lingering in bed—there's too much to handle, and I can't afford to start late.

Quietly, I slip out from under the sheets, careful not to disturb her. I take a quick shower, letting the hot water stream down my body and wake me up fully.

Thoughts of what's on my agenda for the day begin to crowd my mind. The issues from yesterday haven't disappeared; they've just been temporarily compartmentalized.

I step out of the shower and dry off. Choosing my clothes for the day, I opt for something sharp yet practical—a well-fitted suit that's comfortable enough for a day that could stretch long into the night.

As I'm buttoning up my shirt, a voice floats from the bed, teasing and warm.

"Looking good, handsome."

I turn to see Dalia propped up on her elbows and her chocolate-brown hair tousled around her face in a way that sends my heart racing, a playful smile on her lips. I can't help but grin back and walk over to her.

"Were you watching me this whole time?"

She laughs lightly, her eyes twinkling with mischief. "Maybe a little. There's something sexy about watching you get dressed, almost as sexy as watching you get *un*dressed."

Climbing onto the bed, I lean in close. "Be careful; I have ways of dealing with spies," I tease, playing along with the flirtatious mood.

"Oh? Is that right?"

"That's right," I affirm as I gently pull down the sheet, revealing her perfect, round breasts. The sight stirs me, and I lean down, kissing her softly at first, then more insistently, my lips and tongue worshipping her skin, eliciting soft moans from her sweet lips.

Her sounds only fuel my desire, and I find myself getting lost in the moment. The feel of her warm skin, the taste of her, is intoxicating. I move down her body, kissing and licking every inch of her, savoring the way she responds to my touch.

"You know, watching you get dressed isn't the only thing I enjoy," she whispers, her voice breathy and filled with need.

"Is that so?" I murmur against her skin, my hands exploring her curves, feeling her shiver under my touch.

She arches her back, pressing her breasts closer to my mouth. I take one nipple between my lips, sucking gently, then harder, making her gasp. My hand moves lower, finding the heat between her legs, her wetness making me groan.

"I love watching your face when I touch you."

I slide my fingers inside her, finding her slick and ready. I pump them slowly, my thumb circling her clit, watching her face contort with pleasure.

"Don't stop," she pleads, her voice quivering as her hips move in rhythm with my fingers.

I press deeper, curling my fingers inside her, finding that perfect spot. My thumb circles her clit with increasing pressure, her breath coming in ragged bursts.

"Oh, Lev," she moans again, her body trembling with the buildup of her orgasm. Her back arches off the bed, and I can feel her tightening around my fingers, teetering on the edge.

"Come for me," I whisper against her ear.

Her body responds instantly, a cry of pleasure escaping her lips as she shatters around my hand. Her walls pulse and contract, her juices coating my fingers as she rides out the waves of her climax. I watch her face, the way her eyes flutter shut, her mouth open in a silent scream of ecstasy.

As she comes down from her high, her breathing slows, and she opens her eyes to meet mine, a satisfied smile spreading across her face.

"That was amazing," she murmurs, her hand reaching down to cover mine, still resting against her.

Before I can respond, she slides her hand down to my cock, her fingers brushing against the hard bulge straining against my slacks. She gives it a gentle squeeze, making me groan with pent-up desire.

"Your turn," she whispers.

Just as she's about to unbutton my slacks, a chime sounds from my phone on the nightstand, breaking up the moment. I let out a frustrated sigh, glancing over at the offending device.

"Ignore it," she urges, her hand continuing to caress me through the fabric.

I want nothing more than to heed her advice, but the persistent sound of another text chime draws my attention back.

"I can't," I say reluctantly, pulling away slightly. "It might be important."

She pouts but understanding flickers in her eyes as she releases me. I reach over to the nightstand, grab my phone, and unlock the screen. The message displayed makes my stomach knot.

"It's from the office," I explain. "I need to handle this."

She sits up, still looking disappointed, but nods in understanding. "Duty calls," she says softly, leaning in to kiss my cheek.

I'm jolted out of the moment by the shrill ring of my phone. It's Yuri. I step out of our room into the hallway to take the call.

"Talk to me."

Yuri's voice is abrupt. "We've finally made a connection with the motorcycles. Traced them back to an owner—a man named Nikolai Vetrov. Turns out, he's an associate of Plushenko."

A surge of rage flares up inside me, but I clamp it down, keeping my voice calm. "Good work. I'll be in soon to discuss. We need to move fast on this."

"Understood," Yuri replies, and I end the call.

When I return to the bedroom, Dalia is sitting up, her expression etched with concern. "Is everything okay?" she asks, watching me closely.

I nod, trying to reassure her while keeping the details sparse. "We may have a lead on the attacks."

"So, I'll be working from home as usual then."

I lean down and give her a deep, lingering kiss, a promise of my return.

"Stay safe," I murmur against her lips, then straighten and head out for the day, my mind already shifting gears to the day ahead.

~

Hours later, I find myself navigating through the streets with Vanya at the wheel.

We've got a lead on Plushenko's location—a Russian restaurant called Tsar's Table in the West Loop area. It's where Alexei holds biweekly meetings with his lieutenants, making it the perfect setting for an impromptu fact-finding operation.

Three other cars accompany us, all filled with men I trust. We pull up in front of the restaurant and confidently get out of the vehicle. Alongside me are Yuri, Vanya, Luk, Vladimir, and Grigori, plus a half-dozen of our most reliable enforcers.

I glance around at the group; everyone is alert and ready.

"Here's the plan," I begin. "We rush in, flash the guns, and force a meeting. No shooting unless I give the word. We're here to get answers, not to shed blood without reason."

The men nod, understanding the stakes and the need for precision.

We adjust our coats, check our weapons, and prepare to enter Tsar's Table. With a final nod from me, we move toward the entrance, ready to take control of the situation.

I slam the door open with a forceful kick, charging in with authority as my team swiftly files in behind me.

Instantly, the room transforms into a high-stakes standoff. Alexei, unmistakably in command, sits at a prominent table, a dozen of his men flanking him, their expressions stoic, hands reaching for their weapons.

As our presence disrupts the calm, guns are drawn in a heartbeat—Alexei's crew on one side, mine on the other.

The atmosphere crackles with the electricity of impending conflict, every man ready to spring into action.

Despite the sudden surge of adrenaline, Alexei remains seated, the picture of composure. He fixes me with a cool, assessing look, a wry smile forming on his lips.

"Lev Ivanov, to what do I owe the unexpected honor?" he asks calmly, sounding almost amused as if we're merely old acquaintances meeting by chance instead of on the verge of a showdown.

I take in the scene. Alexei's youthful and cocky confidence, along with his strategic poise, mark him as a formidable adversary. It's clear why he commands such loyalty and respect in this cutthroat world. There is also a strange spark of familiarity about him, though I've never met him before.

"Let's get one thing clear. I'm not here to fight. I want to talk."

Alexei chuckles. "Have you ever heard of a phone call? Or maybe a text? Perhaps we should add each other on Snapchat to avoid such dramatic entrances in the future."

Laughter ripples through the room from his men, a momentary lightness in the situation.

I remain unfazed, a slight smirk playing on my lips. "I've never been much for social media," I reply coolly. "Face to face always gets more immediate results."

"Indeed, it does." He then nods slightly, a signal understood by all. "Why don't we start by putting our guns away?"

"That's a good idea," I agree. The sound of firearms being holstered fills the room, and the atmosphere shifts slightly, moving from standoff to cautious negotiation.

With the immediate threat dialed down, Alexei gestures toward the empty seat at the other end of the table.

"Please, have a seat."

I walk over and take the offered seat directly across from him. The room settles, all eyes on us, waiting for the next move in this high-stakes chess game. Leaning forward, I lock eyes with him, ensuring I have his full attention before I speak.

"Nikolai Vetrov," I simply say. Those two words, loaded with implications, challenge Alexei to reveal his hand.

However, Alexei's reaction to the name Nikolai Vetrov isn't the shock or recognition I'd hoped for. Instead, he tilts his head slightly, a puzzled expression crossing his features as if he's genuinely trying to place the name.

"Am I supposed to know who that is?"

I narrow my eyes, skeptical of his reply. "Are you bullshitting me?"

Alexei holds my gaze. "I'm not playing games, Lev. I know about the attacks on your family, and frankly, they disgust me. That's not how I conduct business."

I study his face, searching for any telltale sign of deception. His demeanor seems genuine, but I know better.

"Vetrov was a low-level associate of yours," I state flatly.

"Was," interjects one of Alexei's lieutenants, a burly man with a keen eye. "He turned out to be a thief. We ran him out of the organization. He died a year ago."

My interest piques. "And did you have anything to do with his death?"

The lieutenant shakes his head, his expression unflinching. "No. He got himself killed over some petty drug bullshit. Nothing to do with us."

I sit back, processing this information. It's a dead end in more ways than one—a lead gone cold, and a suspect literally deceased.

Alexei seems interested as I explain the connection. "So, why do *you* know that name?"

I lean in slightly, making sure I have his full attention. "He was linked to a motorcycle used in the attack on my family."

Alexei's response is to drum his fingers thoughtfully on the table; his brow furrowed in concentration. "This is an odd development considering he'd been dead long before that incident occurred," he muses aloud, then adds with a hint of skepticism, "Sounds too convenient, doesn't it?"

I nod slightly, encouraging him to continue. "What's on your mind?"

He meets my gaze with a calculated look. "Someone might have purposely linked the bike to this man, knowing he was already dead as a way to connect him to the attack without risking anything."

I press for more clarity. "Are you suggesting this was a plot to frame your organization? To make it look like you were behind the attack?"

"I believe so," Alexei confirms. "Look, Lev, I may be competition, but I'm *civil* competition. There's more money to be made with deals than with bloodshed."

I sit back, considering his words. His rationale makes sense. Alexei's explanation feels sincere, and it fits the pattern of a setup designed to pit powerful players against each other.

This could mean there's another player in the game, one who stands to gain from our mutual destruction.

Alexei leans back, his expression turning more contemplative. "If you want my opinion," he begins, pausing for effect, "I think that 'the call is coming from inside the house,' as they say."

"A traitor?"

Alexei nods slowly, his gaze steady. "Indeed. It seems like only an internal job could stir such trouble within your organization," he asserts, his voice laced with a hint of disdain for such tactics.

He then shifts forward again, clasping his hands on the table, signaling a move toward a solution. "I have a proposal," he continues, "a truce between the Ivanov and Plushenko organizations until this unseemly matter is all sorted out. You now know we had nothing to do with the attack and with that, we need reassurance you won't try to retaliate.

Together, we can find out who is trying to pit us against each other."

I consider his words carefully. In the underworld, alliances are as fragile as they are necessary. Alexei, with his keen understanding and strategic mind, could indeed be a valuable ally in this tangled scenario. Having him on our side, even temporarily, might just give us the edge we need to root out the true culprit.

I rise from my seat, extending my hand across the table. Alexei reaches out his own.

"Truce it is," I say and seal it with a handshake.

CHAPTER 27

I t's the day of the wedding, and my nerves are practically dancing with anticipation. The room is alive with the buzz of excitement and activity, hair and makeup artists swirling around me, each brush stroke and hairpin transforming me into a breathtaking bride.

After Lev proposed, things moved very quickly as he didn't want to put off the marriage any longer.

I'm sitting in the middle of this beautiful chaos, trying to calm my jittery heart with deep breaths, feeling both elation and a hint of nervous anticipation.

Maura and Elena, looking absolutely stunning in their bridesmaid dresses, are providing much-needed laughter and lightheartedness. They're chatting away, their stories drifting over to where I'm sitting, making me smile.

A sudden wave of nausea sweeps through me, and despite my best efforts to hide it, it must show on my face because Elena and Maura are instantly at my side. Elena places a gentle hand on my shoulder.

"Are you okay?"

Maura, who's always had a knack for reading me like an open book, chimes in with a half-teasing, half-serious tone, "Is it just nerves or the baby stirring up trouble? Or maybe a little bit of both?"

"Hard to say," I reply. "The morning sickness has been killer this last week."

Their attention and care make me smile, easing the discomfort slightly as the hair and makeup team announce they're finished.

"Why don't you take a look?" one of them suggests, gesturing toward the full-length mirror.

I stand on shaky legs and make my way to the mirror. The reflection that greets me is almost unrecognizable. My dress is a stunning creation of soft lace and flowing fabric, the bodice intricately detailed with floral embroidery that cascades down into a full, graceful skirt.

My hair is swept up in an elegant updo, loose curls framing my face to soften the sophisticated style. The makeup is perfection—subtle smokey eyes that enhance my features and a soft, rosy hue on my cheeks, giving me a radiant glow.

Maura, catching sight of the sparkle in my ears, compliments, "Those diamond earrings are just dazzling, Dalia!"

Elena, her eyes sparkling with mischief, laughs. "You'll have to tell Maura the story behind those someday. It's quite the tale."

Maura perks up, intrigued. "Is that right?"

I can't help but grin, feeling even more woven into the fabric of this family. As I turn to admire the different angles in the mirror, I catch sight of my tiny baby bump, a sweet reminder of the new life joining today's celebration.

Maura leans in slightly. "So, are you going to find out the gender, or are you going to wait and be surprised?"

I pause, my hand instinctively resting on my bump. "I'd like to wait until the birth, but Lev, as you know, likes to have all the information as soon as possible. So, we'll see."

Elena and Maura step back to take a full look at me, their expressions both of awe. "You look absolutely stunning, Dal," Maura says.

Elena, who's usually the tough, composed one, has tears glistening in her eyes as she steps forward to hug me. "You're really part of the family now."

Their words and warmth wrap around me like a blanket, fortifying me against the nerves and filling me with gratitude.

As laughter and chatter fill the room, a twinge of sadness sneaks up on me. My face must give away my feelings because Maura suddenly comes close, her voice soft. "Hey, what's wrong?"

I let out a little sigh, caught between happiness and heartache. "It's all amazing, really, and I'm over the moon about joining the Ivanov family. I just wish my parents could be here, too."

Elena's eyebrows knit together in confusion. "Why aren't they?"

My heart tightens a bit as I explain. "My family's pretty old-school, especially my dad. He really pushed for me to let him pick my husband. I told him I wanted to find love myself. I thought he'd let it go, but when I called to tell him and my mom that I was getting married, he blew up, and I haven't heard from either of them since."

I recall the shocking conversation I had with my parents a few weeks before. Even though my dad has always been old-fashioned, I never expected him to shut me out. Or for my mother to go along with it. I've been gutted about it ever since.

Elena squeezes my hand, her presence comforting. "Look, there's always time for making up later," she says. "Today is about you and what you've got right here."

Her words, filled with warmth, help lift my spirits.

Just as we're soaking up the last bit of girl time, someone peeks their head through the door. It's Grigori, looking sharp and slightly amused by the buzz of activity in the bridal suite. His eyes sweep quickly over Elena before he speaks.

"Ladies, it's showtime," he announces with a grin, signaling that the ceremony is about to start.

Maura and Elena instantly wrap me in big, warm hugs, filling the room with even more love, if that's possible. "Go get 'em, beautiful," Maura whispers, giving me an encouraging squeeze.

Elena gives me a quick, strong hug and a bright smile. "You've got this."

Then they're off, leaving me in a moment of solitude. I wander over to the window, pulling back the curtain to take in the view. The day is gorgeous—sunny, with just a few fluffy clouds scattered across a brilliant blue sky. It's not exactly the wedding I daydreamed about when I was a little girl, but honestly, it's pretty darn close.

I'm about to marry an incredible man, I'm carrying our child, and I'm enveloped by a new family that's shown me what unconditional support looks like. What more could I possibly ask for?

With my heart brimming with joy, I take a deep breath, ready to step into this new chapter. I turn from the window, my dress swirling softly around me, and head toward the door.

CHAPTER 28

As the music begins, I take a deep breath, readying myself for the walk down the aisle.

The church, a gorgeous Orthodox structure in the heart of Chicago's historic district, couldn't be more perfect for our big day.

With my bouquet of flowers in hand—lush peonies and delicate roses—I step up to the aisle. The church is packed, every pew filled with the faces of friends and family, all smiles and teary eyes. The bridesmaids and groomsmen are already lined up at the altar.

And then there's Lev.

He's standing there, looking ridiculously handsome in his tuxedo, with that slight smirk that always makes my heart skip a beat. Seeing him so dapper and debonair, I can barely keep my thoughts straight. My big day has hardly started, and I'm already daydreaming about all the things I want to do with him once we're finally alone tonight.

The familiar strains of the wedding march fill the air, signaling my cue. I take a steadying breath, clutching my bouquet a little tighter. I'm standing alone at the start of the aisle, a bittersweet twinge in my heart.

Even though my father disapproved of every single detail of this day, a part of me still wishes he were here to walk me down the aisle.

But today, I walk alone by choice. Luk had kindly offered to accompany me, a gesture that meant the world. But I decided to go solo. There's something empowering about stepping into my future on my own terms and embracing a destiny I've chosen for myself.

When I finally reach Lev, he whispers just loud enough for me to hear, "You look so gorgeous; I can't believe my luck."

His words wash over me, igniting a warmth that radiates through my entire body. All I can do is smile back at him, my heart overflowing with love and joy.

The priest's deep voice resonates through the church, articulating the solemn rites of the Orthodox wedding. "And now we come together not only to witness but to celebrate the union of two hearts, two souls, in the sacred bond of marriage," he intones as the packed pews of family and friends listen intently.

Standing next to Lev, I beam with happiness, my heart racing with anticipation of the moment we seal our vows with a kiss. Luk, standing nearby as best man, catches my eye and smiles reassuringly. I try to focus on the priest's words, but my excitement about the kiss makes it difficult.

As the priest continues, "May this couple be blessed with health, happiness, and honesty..." the sudden smell of smoke infiltrates the church.

Whispers ripple through the congregation, the tranquil ceremony disrupted by growing concern. The priest pauses, his expression turning to one of confusion as he, too, smells the smoke.

"It seems there may be an urgent matter to attend to," he says, addressing the crowd. "Please remain calm but prepare to evacuate."

Bedlam erupts with a single, piercing cry from the back. "Fire!"

Instant panic seizes the congregation. Guests surge to their feet in a desperate scramble for safety, the serene atmosphere of our wedding violently ripped apart.

Lev, with his ever-commanding presence, stands tall, his voice cutting through the pandemonium.

"Stay calm! Move in an orderly fashion toward the exits!" His firm instructions allow a brief moment of order in the storm of panic.

But it's short-lived. A dense, choking smoke begins to flood the church, swirling around the ceiling and casting a sinister veil. Screams escalate into a frenzied cacophony, echoing off the walls, magnifying the terror.

Amidst the confusion, a chilling revelation cuts through the noise. A voice, shrill with terror, declares, "The doors are locked!" The words strike like a cold blade, sending shock-waves through the crowd.

Panic morphs into outright horror. My heart hammers against my ribs, fear gripping me with icy fingers. Locked doors and a fire? On our wedding day? This can't be happening.

I clutch Lev's hand, desperate for his calming effect, but even his face is etched with alarm.

The realization that we might be trapped, that this could be more than an accident sends a wave of dread crashing over me.

In the midst of the escalating chaos and thickening smoke, Lev remains a beacon of hope, his composure standing out starkly. I stay close to him, drawing some reassurance from his clear-headedness as he starts to take control of the situation once again.

Noticing a fire extinguisher nearby, I instinctively rush toward it, eager to do something, anything, to help. But Lev quickly calls out to me, halting me in my steps.

"You can't risk smoke inhalation, not with the baby. Stay low to the ground, away from the smoke."

I pause, the weight of his words hitting me. As much as I want to help, I know he's right. I can't put our baby at risk. I nod reluctantly and step back, staying low as he instructed.

Turning to Maura and Elena, he points them toward the fire extinguishers.

"You two, start on the fire. Quickly and be careful." Without a second's hesitation, they sprint to the fire extinguishers and get to work, their actions efficient and focused.

Lev then quickly organizes a group of able-bodied men to deal with the locked main doors. "We need to break through," he says, rallying the men into position.

They line up, ready to force the doors open, their expressions set with determination.

Lev and the group of determined men brace themselves, launching into the door with full force. The first attempt makes the door buckle, but it stubbornly holds. They regather themselves and slam into it again and again, their efforts marked by grunts of exertion and the loud bangs of impact.

Finally, after several intense tries, the towering doors give way, crashing off their hinges and landing with a resounding crash.

From somewhere amidst the chaos, Luk's voice rises, urging everyone to stay calm. I can feel the edge of panic nibbling at me, threatening to overwhelm me.

Reacting instinctively, I rush to Lev's side, keeping my body low to avoid the worst of the smoke. He puts an arm around me, steadying us both as we move.

Lev takes the lead, guiding us with a commanding voice through the smoke-filled entranceway. His presence is a reassuring, steady force as we navigate. Finally, we emerge into the safety of the outdoors, and I take a deep breath of fresh air, filling my lungs with it gratefully.

As the fire starts tearing through the church, the blaring sirens quickly follow. Firefighters jump into action, hoses in hand, battling the flames that dared to ruin our day.

"Are you okay?" Lev asks, scanning me from head to toe.

"My chest feels a bit tight from the smoke, but I think I'm okay."

Suddenly, a car pulls up fast into the lot, and out hop Vladimir and Vanya, both looking like they just dodged the apocalypse.

I watch their faces drop as they take in the chaotic scene— fire trucks, water hoses, ambulances, and us standing in the middle of it all.

Suddenly, an EMT is at my side. "Let's get you checked out," he insists, leading me away from the group.

As the EMT does his thing, checking my vitals and making sure I'm not in any immediate medical danger, I can't help but glance back at the church, the water dousing what's left of the flames.

CHAPTER 29

A s I watch the last of the flames being extinguished, rage courses through me.

The firefighters are reigning it in; their efficiency is a small comfort compared to the ruin of the church. The place that was supposed to witness our joy is now a charred and soaked mess.

I scan the crowd, my eyes darting from face to face. Relief tempers the anger slightly; everyone seems to have made it out, though not unscathed. EMTs are busy tending to burns and cases of smoke inhalation, their presence a grim reminder of how close we came to tragedy.

I rush over to Dalia, who's sitting on a gurney inside an ambulance. Her face is pale but composed, and seeing her there, seemingly unharmed, reignites my focus.

"Are you sure you're okay?"

She nods, giving me a small, reassuring smile. "I'm fine, Lev, really."

I turn to the EMT. "She's pregnant. Are you sure everything's fine?"

The EMT, a young guy with a calm demeanor, meets my gaze steadily.

"Her lungs sound clear," he says. "But she really should be checked out at the hospital, just to be certain."

I find Dalia's hand, squeezing it lightly. "Okay, let's go."

Dalia holds up her other hand. "You make sure everyone else is alright first then meet me at the hospital, okay? I need to know no one is seriously hurt."

I shake my head. "Are you sure?"

"Yes, I'm sure. The EMTs will take good care of me."

"Okay. I'll be right behind you."

I lean in and give Dalia a quick but intense kiss. "I'll see you soon," I promise as I reluctantly release her hand.

The remnants of the fire still hiss and steam around us as the firefighters wrap up, and I know I need to act fast to find out what happened before any evidence is lost in the cleanup. With a heavy heart, I turn back to the scene, my mind shifting back into high gear.

I spot Elena and Maura a short distance away, their beautiful bridesmaid dresses marred with soot and ash. Striding over, I check on them. "Are you two alright?"

They both shake their heads in the affirmative, brushing off their dresses with a resilience that's become characteristic. "We're fine," Maura assures me.

"Thanks for jumping in with the extinguishers," I say, clapping a hand on each of their shoulders gently. "Seriously, you two were incredible."

With reassurances exchanged, I turn my attention back to the church.

My gaze sweeps across the crowd, sharply assessing the situation as my mind races through the implications of today's disaster. I spot the officiant off to the side, looking dazed, and several children huddled together with EMTs attending to them. My jaw clenches at the sight, realizing what we came close to losing.

The sight of the kids, particularly my niece and nephew—Sasha and Michael, Maura and Luk now with them—stirs a fury within me like nothing else.

"Why were the doors locked?" I murmur under my breath, a question that's been gnawing at me since we broke them down. This wasn't just an accident.

As my anger simmers, threatening to boil over, I notice Vanya and Vladimir. They're standing by the car, their expressions grim. I stride over to them.

"Vanya, Vladimir," I call out as I approach, my voice carrying the sharp edge of my barely contained rage. They both turn, instantly alert to my tone.

"We need to talk. Now."

The gravity of the situation is etched deeply into their faces. Vanya looks particularly shaken, his eyes wide with concern.

"Lev, is everyone okay? Is there anything I can do to help?" Vanya's voice tremors slightly as he speaks.

"Everyone's accounted for. A few injuries here and there. Dalia's headed to the hospital to make sure the baby is okay." My words seem to bring a brief wave of relief to Vanya, though his hands continue to tremble.

Vladimir, who appears somewhat calmer, adds, "I was already running late when I got a call from Vanya about car trouble on my way over, so I went to pick him up."

I fix him with a sharp gaze. "And why were you running behind, Vladimir?"

He offers a weak smile, a rare break in his usually stoic demeanor. He reaches into his pocket, pulling out a pair of cufflinks.

"It's silly, really," he begins, holding them up for me to see. "These are my lucky cufflinks. They were a gift from my grandfather, who said they bless any wedding with good luck. Dumb, I know, but it's sentimental. Anyway, I couldn't find them this morning..."

His voice trails off.

The unease in my gut deepens as I process Vladimir's seemingly innocuous delay.

I cut off the conversation abruptly. "Come with me," I instruct them sternly. They follow without hesitation, sensing the urgency in my tone.

I nod sharply to Luk and Yuri, signaling them to join us. I briefly consider calling Elena over, but she's entrenched with Maura and the kids, soothing Michael and Sasha amidst their tears and confusion. She's needed there.

Once our group is huddled together, away from the crowd, I lay out the situation in no uncertain terms.

"It goes without saying that we're going to get to the bottom of what the fuck happened here today."

Luk crosses his arms, his mouth set in a grim line. "It's almost certain this was a plot."

Vladimir's face blanches as he catches up. "Are you saying this was intentional?"

Yuri steps in, his voice steady but grave. "The doors to the church were sealed. If we hadn't managed to get them open..." He lets the implication hang ominously in the air. The potential disaster we narrowly avoided looms large over us.

My jaw clenches.

"This is the third goddamn attempt on our lives," I declare, my expression hard as I scan the faces before me. "This time, they aimed to wipe out the entire Ivanov family in one fell swoop."

Luk nods gravely. "We've been lucky three times in a row—asking for a fourth is tempting the fates. It's only a matter of time before we're not so fortunate."

"I'm furious at this failure," I confess, the admission raw. "But I promise you, this will be rectified. We will find who's behind this, and we will make them pay dearly."

My tone leaves no room for doubt, my commitment to safe-guarding my family is absolute. We will turn this crisis into a catalyst for tightening our defenses and striking back with precision. The next move is ours.

I take a moment to survey the scene, noting that the firefighters and EMTs seem to have things under control. I turn to Luk. "I need you to take over here, ensure everyone is looked after."

"Of course," Luk replies.

With that responsibility handed off, I address the rest of my men. "I'm heading to the hospital to check on Dalia."

I stride to my car with purpose. Slipping behind the wheel, I roughly pull off my bow tie, the fabric suddenly irritating and feeling like a noose. As the engine springs to life, I press the accelerator, the car's power mirroring the surge of adrenaline through my veins.

As I race down the road, anger simmers within me, a lethal quiet storm. This was an attack not just on our wedding but on my family, on everything I stand to protect.

The thought of Dalia, scared and hurt, fuels a growing resolve.

This isn't just about retribution; it's about sending a message —no one threatens my family and lives to tell the tale.

CHAPTER 30

DALIA

I sit in a hospital room, feeling the sterile chill more than ever as doctors prepare to check for my baby's heartbeat.

I'm a bundle of nerves, desperately wishing Lev was here holding my hand.

The doctor and nurse start setting up the equipment for the ultrasound, trying to offer comforting smiles throughout the process.

Every second that ticks by feels like an hour as they move the ultrasound wand over my stomach. The cool gel on my skin and the soft hum of the machine are the only sounds before the room finally fills with the quick, rhythmic beat of the baby's heart. I hold my breath, my own heart caught in my throat.

Tears start streaming down my cheeks as I hear the steady, strong heartbeat of my baby echoing through the room.

The doctor gives me a reassuring smile. "Everything sounds great with the heartbeat. It looks like the smoke and stress didn't affect your little one at all. And you're measuring right around eight weeks."

I'm so overwhelmed with relief that my mind goes a bit fuzzy with gratitude. "Thank you."

"We want to make sure everything else is okay while you're here. If all's well, you'll be free to go soon," the doctor tells me.

They start by checking my lungs for any smoke damage. I feel the cold metal of the stethoscope as they press it against my back and chest, asking me to take deep breaths. Each inhale and exhale feel like a triumph.

Next, they look over my skin for any burns or signs of irritation that might've come from the heat or smoke. They're super thorough, making sure they don't miss anything that could cause trouble later on.

As they perform the exam, my mind can't stop replaying the day's scary moments—smoke filling the church, everyone scrambling, the doors jammed shut. I shiver thinking about how close it all came to turning into a tragedy.

I try to shake off the fear, focusing instead on the here and now, especially that little heartbeat that's still going strong, reassuring me that life keeps ticking on, no matter what.

The doctor wraps up his checkup, giving me a clean bill of health, at least physically. "Why don't you lie back and relax for a bit? Let the IV run through and make sure you're good and hydrated."

I nod and thank him as he walks out of the room.

I automatically rest my hand on my belly, a huge sigh of relief escaping me, knowing my little one is safe. But the silence soon lets my mind wander back to the fire, to the thick smoke that seemed to swallow everything in sight.

My thoughts start to spin out worse and worse scenarios. I imagine all of us trapped, the doors locked tight, the fire closing in.

Sitting here alone, those terrifying images just won't stop replaying in my head, and all I can think about is keeping my baby safe. The more I think about it, the more it feels like my life with Lev, despite all his efforts, is like balancing on a knife's edge.

It's not just the scare today that's got me so shaken; it's realizing how often danger seems to lurk around us. Being with Lev, in his world, comes with real risks, and now that I'm going to be a mom, those risks feel a thousand times more significant.

The fear is eating away at me, building with every moment I sit here alone, making me wonder if our future together is just one big, dangerous gamble.

I love Lev, I really do, and I know he'd do anything to protect us. But it's starting to feel like the only sure way to stay safe is to put as much distance between us as possible.

It's a heartbreaking thought, but with each attack, it feels more and more like it's only a matter of time before one of them succeeds. I can't let that happen. I need to get out, and I need to do it now before Lev gets here.

Just then, my phone lights up with a text from him.

On my way.

My heart sinks as I start to formulate a plan. Across the hall, I notice a staff room. I spot some scrubs and a few pairs of Crocs on the shelves. I keep my eyes on the door, waiting for the last person to leave. As soon as they do, I pull the IV from my arm and make my move.

I slip inside, quickly grabbing a pair of scrubs and Crocs in my size before darting into the bathroom to change.

Dressed in my new clothes, I take a deep breath, steeling myself. Then, I quietly slip out of the bathroom and dart back into the room, quickly grabbing my purse and rifling through it to pull out just my wallet and phone. My hands shake a little as I quickly disable the tracking on my phone. I can't risk Lev, or anyone else for that matter, following me right now. I call an Uber, my heart pounding as I realize I could run into Lev at any moment.

Keeping my head down, I weave through the crowded ER, my nerves on edge, every face I pass making me jumpy. I just need to make it out the door without being seen.

A notification buzzes—my Uber is outside. As I make my way to the exit, I spot Lev walking in. My breath catches in my throat as he scans the ER. For a split second, our paths almost align, but he doesn't notice me in the scrubs.

My heart aches as I see him, a part of me screaming to run to him, to explain everything about how I'm feeling. But the stronger part knows this is the right thing to do for the safety of our child.

With a heavy heart, I slip out the door, the cool air hitting my face as I spot the Uber. I hurry over and slide into the back seat. As the car pulls away, I allow myself a moment to look back. Lev is inside, and I'm out here, forging into the unknown.

As the hospital fades into the distance, I'm gripped by determination. I'm not sure what comes next, but I know I have to keep moving forward—for my baby's sake and mine.

Hours later, I'm tucked away in the corner of a dimly lit, upscale restaurant I've never set foot in before.

In my hand, I clutch the card Alexei gave me, my fingers brushing over the embossed letters nervously. I'm waiting for him to show up, and every second he's late cranks up my anxiety a notch.

My phone buzzes—a call from Lev. I let it go to voicemail, adding to the growing list of messages I haven't had the heart to listen to yet. It's been six hours since I slipped away from Lev and everything I knew. Now I'm down to the last bits of cash, the rest used to buy some nondescript clothes to replace the scrubs.

I'm utterly lost, with no clear plan, sitting here spending what little money I have on a meal I can't even enjoy. Alexei had texted to say he'd be running late and told me to order whatever I wanted, but my appetite is gone. I pick at the food, my stomach tight with nerves and guilt.

What am I going to do? The question whirls in my mind relentlessly. I left everything behind for the safety of my baby, stepping into uncertainty with nowhere to turn but to a man I barely know and can't fully trust.

As I wait for Alexei, I wonder if I've jumped out of the frying pan and into the fire.

Finally, he arrives. He's dressed in a sleek suit that fits his frame perfectly.

He approaches with a smooth confidence, greeting me with a gentlemanly kiss on the hand that feels more ceremonial than intimate. I don't sense any ulterior motives in his gesture. He slides into the seat across from me and signals the waiter to bring him a glass of wine.

"Eat up," he urges me gently, and oddly enough, his encouragement nudges my appetite back to life.

"I heard about the church; that's some nasty business." He pauses, giving me a moment. "Are you okay?"

"Physically, yes," I admit. "But everything else is a shitshow, and that's why I'm here."

As I say it, the reality of my situation sinks in even deeper. I'm here, sitting with a man who might just be as dangerous as the situation I fled, looking for protection and answers or maybe just a moment to catch my breath.

His wine arrives just as he's settling into the conversation, but Alexei barely glances at it, his focus entirely on me. He gestures slightly with his hand, encouraging me to continue.

"Go on," he prompts gently. "Tell me what happened."

I take a deep breath, the words feeling both liberating and terrifying as they leave my lips.

"I left Lev, at least for now. Truthfully, I don't know what I'm going to do."

The admission hangs between us, heavy and real.

He nods slowly, his expression serious. "Someone clearly has it out for the Ivanov family," he says, his tone grave. "Targeting a church filled with women and children is the coward's way of doing things."

There's a hardness in his eyes that suggests he's no stranger to violence, yet there seems to be genuine anger in his voice.

Part of me is wary, wondering if I can really trust him, but his reaction seems sincere. I find myself continuing, drawn in by his apparent sympathy for my situation.

"I'm just not sure I'm safe with Lev anymore."

He nods again, his gaze meeting mine with a depth that surprises me. "I understand," he says simply. There's an odd reassurance in his words that makes me feel slightly more at ease, at least for the moment.

Alexei finally takes a moment to sip his wine, his gaze wandering as he ponders our conversation. After a thoughtful pause, he refocuses on me, his eyes serious.

"This is a very complicated situation," he begins, setting down his glass. "I just reached a truce with Lev and the Ivanovs. It wouldn't be right for me to take you in without giving him a heads-up."

"Yeah, it's definitely a tough scenario," I agree, the reality of it all feeling increasingly heavy.

Then, a strange look comes over Alexei's face.

"There's more, Dalia," he says.

"More what?"

"More. The Ivanovs and I have a history they are unaware of."

"What do you mean?"

He taps his fingers on the table as if debating whether or not to tell me.

Then he shakes his head. "No. Not now. There's too much to take care of before I even begin unpacking all of that." He turns to me, intensity flashing in his eyes. "First things first, you need to be protected. I have a safe house here in the city. It's an apartment I set up for emergencies, secure as a bank vault. We can head there, and you can settle in to think things through. Then we'll figure out what to do next."

Alexei looks around the restaurant, a hint of urgency in his eyes, before turning back to me. "I hate to rush you, but we should probably get going soon," he says. "Don't worry, there's plenty of food at the safe house. Plus, I've got a doctor on standby just in case you need anything for the baby."

"Thanks," I manage to say.

"Anytime," he replies with a smile, dropping a couple of hundreds on the table as we get up to leave. I'm still on edge about trusting Alexei completely, but he hasn't done anything yet to make me doubt his intentions.

We head out to the parking lot and walk toward his sleek black car. It's starting to get dark, and a knot of anxiety tightens in my stomach.

Suddenly, a voice cuts through the evening air. "Hey!"

We both whip around. A guy dressed all in black, wearing a face mask, is standing right behind us. He wastes no time pulling out a gun and firing at Alexei.

The sound of the shot reverberates sharply in the quiet lot. Alexei groans and drops to the ground.

I let out a scream, frozen in shock for a split second. But before I can do anything, the masked man turns the gun on me. I feel the coldness of the weapon slam against my forehead before everything goes dark.

CHAPTER 31

LEV

"I swear, Vanya, I'll burn this whole damn town down if that's what it takes to find her and protect my child."

As I barrel down the road, fury courses through me like wildfire, Vanya beside me in the passenger seat; his presence barely registers. My grip on the steering wheel is iron-tight, my knuckles white, and every muscle in my body is tensed with unrestrained anger.

The information I received is fragmented but damning. One of Alexei's lieutenants messaged me that Alexei had been shot and, worse, that Dalia was with him at the time, and now she's missing.

Vanya attempts to offer some calming words, trying to pierce the veil of rage that's descended over me, but I'm beyond the reach of reason. I don't respond; my jaw is set, my mind racing through scenarios, each more violent than the last.

As we race back toward the hospital where I'd learned Dalia had left on her own hours before, my mind is a whirlwind of strategy and fury, plotting the downfall of those foolish enough to target what's mine.

I will do anything, cross any line, to ensure their safety. The entire city will feel my wrath if a single hair on Dalia's head has been touched.

We pull up to the hospital in full force, my guards fanning out as we hit the pavement.

There's a grim determination in the air as we storm through the doors; my presence is commanding enough that staff step aside rather than challenge us.

Vanya keeps pace behind me, updating as we go. "They're expecting us," he mutters, referring to the hospital staff briefed on our imminent arrival. "And Alexei is stable for now."

"For now," I echo darkly. If Alexei had any part in what went down today, his current condition would be the least of his worries. "If he's involved, I'll kill him with my bare hands."

Vanya tries to tamp down my fury. "Let's talk to him first, Lev. See what he knows before making any moves."

We navigate the hospital corridors with purpose, reaching the room where Alexei is being kept. Nurses at the door tense up as they see me approach, but one sharp look from me is enough to make them reconsider any attempts to block my path.

They know who I am and know better than to get in my way.

I push the door open, and there lies Alexei, propped up in bed, his shoulder swathed in bandages and held up by a sling. The sight of him, wounded yet alive, stirs a complex swirl of anger and relief in me.

I loom over him, and he looks up at me with a dazed, almost resigned expression. His face holds an accepting calm that almost seems out of place, as if he's bracing for the worst— like me pulling a gun and finishing what the assailant started.

"You have to admit, this looks bad," I state flatly, the underlying accusation hanging heavily in the air.

Alexei nods slowly, his placidity unshaken. "I know," he concedes. "It all happened so fast—one moment we were heading to my car, and the next, I'm on the ground, shot."

He pauses, the faintest trace of frustration crossing his features. "I guess the only reason the assassin didn't finish me off is because their mission was to take Dalia, not kill me."

His explanation does little to cool the fire in me. The mention of Dalia, kidnapped right from under our noses, reignites the fury and the fear, the mixture churning in my stomach. I lean in closer, my voice a low growl.

"Where is she, Alexei? And why the hell was she with you to begin with?"

Alexei shifts with a wince, using sheer will to sit up straighter in the bed. "I offered her protection, and she accepted."

Vanya interjects sharply, "So you were dealing with her behind Lev's back. So much for a truce."

Alexei shakes his head, his expression taut. "It's not like that," he insists. "She came to me in fear for her life, and I had already made a promise to protect her if she ever needed it. Of course, I was going to tell you," he says directly to me, trying to convey his sincerity.

"I was taking her to a safe house downtown," Alexei continues. "Once she was secure, I planned to call you and tell you what was going on. What, do you think I have a death wish?"

As much as I want to dismiss his explanation, the logic is there, cold and clear. Still, the gnawing suspicion and the raw fear for Dalia's safety overshadow any semblance of reason.

My voice is low and dangerous as I lean in closer, "If you're lying, Alexei, if any harm comes to her because of this— truce or no truce—you'll wish the assassin had finished the job."

"I understand trust is hard to come by in our line of work, but I'm willing to earn yours if you give me the chance." He pauses, measuring his next words carefully. "Whatever's going on, your organization is only the first target. If they succeed in taking you down, I'll be next. It's in my best interest to help you."

I stand there, my fury simmering just below the surface, analyzing his demeanor and his words. There's nothing in his demeanor that suggests deceit, and reluctantly, I have to consider the strategic implications of his position. It would indeed be a precarious situation, having the wife of a rival Bratva head seek refuge with him without informing the man himself.

After a moment of tense silence, I lay down my terms, my voice hard as steel.

"Here's how you're going to repay me—all your operations are paused, effective immediately. Every resource, every man you have, will be redirected to help me find her and take down those responsible."

Alexei meets my gaze, unflinching, and nods in agreement. "I'm happy to help."

This temporary alliance might just be the key to unraveling the threat looming over us. But I remain on guard, ready to act at the slightest hint of betrayal.

My phone buzzes in my pocket. I glance at the screen, then back at Alexei.

"Vanya, stay here. Work with him on how best to support our efforts."

I'm about to walk through the door when Alexei calls out, trying to catch my attention before I leave. I pause, turning back to face him. His expression is serious, almost apologetic.

"It's not any of my business, but for what it's worth, she's just worried about her baby."

The words hit hard, and I clench my jaw, holding back the storm of emotions threatening to break free. Without a word, I turn and leave the room, the heavy door closing behind me with a thud.

Once in the hallway, I pull out my phone again, expecting a strategic update from Luk or one of the others. Instead, my heart drops as I stare at what's displayed on the screen, an image that sends a cold wave of dread through me.

It's Dalia, bound to a chair, her eyes wide with fear.

Accompanying the image is a message from an unknown number, the words chillingly succinct.

Come now and come alone.

Whoever is behind this has just made the biggest mistake of their life. They've taken what's mine, and for that, they will pay.

CHAPTER 32

DALIA

My head is pounding like it's got its own heartbeat as I slowly come to.

Blinking open my eyes, I'm greeted with pitch-black darkness. I let out a scream, but it sounds muffled like I'm buried under layers of something thick.

"What the hell is going on? Where am I?" I ask out loud to no one.

I try to shift, to sit up, but I quickly realize I can't move much—I'm tied down. Panic flares up inside me, wild and uncontrollable. I feel like a trapped animal in a cage. I'm starkly aware there's no sign of anyone else around.

I force myself to take a few deep breaths—I have to keep it together for the baby. But staying calm is a monstrous task when you haven't the first clue about where you are or what's happening.

The last thing I remember before everything went black was the sound of a gunshot and Alexei dropping to the ground. Is this all my fault? Did I put him in the line of fire by going to him for help?

I strain my ears for any sound that might give me a clue as to where I'm at. But all I hear is my own ragged breathing and the echo of my heart beating fiercely in the dark, lonely silence.

There's something smothering my mouth; it feels like a rag, but I can't be sure. I bite down on it, tugging it into my mouth, chewing as ferociously as I can manage. It's a desperate move, but to my immense relief, the fabric starts to give way under the assault of my teeth, and I manage to rip it in half.

As soon as my mouth is free, I let out the loudest, most piercing scream I can muster. But I don't even get to enjoy a full second of rebellion. Almost immediately, there's a rumbling sound that spikes my adrenaline—it's the heavy, unmistakable thud of someone charging across the room.

Before I can react further, a huge hand clamps down over my mouth, silencing me. The smell of vodka hits me like a wave, almost choking me with its potency.

Then, a voice, thick with a heavy Russian accent and dripping with menace, growls right by my ear, "Shut the hell up, girl, if you know what's good for you."

The threat sends a chill down my spine, but it also lights a fire in me. I bite down hard on the hand over my mouth, ready to fight back with everything I've got.

The man lets out a yowl of pain as my teeth sink into his flesh, but his reaction is swift and brutal—a hard smack across my face that sends stars exploding across my vision.

Dazed, I blink rapidly, struggling to focus as he roughly yanks the cover off my head.

My eyes adjust to reveal a grim scene. I'm in a crummy, cheap motel room with the curtains drawn tight. A silent TV flickers ghostly images. I'm tied to a chair, and my company is a hulking man dressed in all black, his head shaved clean. The most distinct feature about him isn't his menacing presence but the silver pistol tucked into his belt —the very same one that smashed into my forehead.

As soon as my mouth is free, I take a deep breath to scream again, but he's faster. He grabs the cloth I'd been gagged with and stuffs it back into my mouth, silencing me once more. His actions are rough and practiced, like he's done this sort of thing before.

I glare at him, fury and defiance burning through the haze of pain. Despite the fear gnawing at my insides, my rebellious spirit isn't quite snuffed out. If looks could kill, the glare I'm leveling at him would have him on the floor.

I might be tied up and gagged, but I'm not beaten yet. No way I'm letting this guy think he's got the upper hand for even a second.

He inspects his hand where I bit him, noticing the blood I drew. Muttering curses in Russian that would probably make my grandma blush, he stomps off to the bathroom. He's so massive that every step he takes makes the tacky motel art on the walls shudder.

After a few moments, he comes back, hands washed but fury still on his face. I'm just gearing up to spit out the cloth he jammed back into my mouth when he pulls out that silver pistol again and points it straight at me.

The cold metal gleams under the flickering dim light of the motel room, and his next words chill me more than the weapon itself.

"You're going to keep that in your mouth," he growls, "unless you want to end up like poor Alexei."

The threat hangs heavy in the air, but I'm not about to let him see me sweat. Locked in a stare-down with him, I force my eyes to stay steely and defiant.

A risky thought darts through my mind—they're not going to kill me, not after going through all this trouble to kidnap me. Emboldened by this realization, I decide to push my luck. With a defiant flick of my tongue, I spit the gag out onto the grimy motel floor right at his feet.

The man groans in annoyance, his patience clearly wearing thin. "You're lucky you're needed," he snaps, his voice harsh. "If it were up to me, I'd have killed you in that parking lot."

Ignoring his threat, I shoot back with my own demands.

"Where am I? Who do you work for? Why am I here?"

He pauses, eyeing me like I'm some kind of curiosity that's both amusing and irritating. Then, to my frustration, he throws back his head and laughs—a deep, mocking sound that echoes off the cheap paneling of the room.

"You're a damn fool if you think I'm going to answer your questions." He shakes his head as if I'm a child throwing a tantrum.

I narrow my eyes at him, my heart racing but my voice steady. "If you don't start talking, I'm going to scream again," I threaten, hoping he'll take the bait.

He just laughs, a grating sound that echoes mockingly around the dingy room. "Go for it," he smirks, waving a dismissive hand. "This hotel is abandoned, owned by the guy who wanted you taken. None of the other rooms are occupied."

Frustrated but not deterred, I draw in a deep breath and let out a piercing scream just to test his claim. Sure enough, he doesn't even flinch, just rolls his eyes at my effort.

He sighs, clearly annoyed now. "You really should shut your mouth."

I shoot back quickly, "And what are you going to do to make me?"

The smirk fades from his face, replaced by a wicked look that makes my skin crawl. He strides over, yanks off my shoe, then peels off my sock. I try to pull away, but I'm tied too tightly. He then starts caressing my foot, and I feel the bile rise in my throat at his touch.

"You have lovely feet," he murmurs, his eyes fixed on them with an unsettling intensity.

He then looks up at me, his expression darkening. "Every time you scream, I'll take a toe as a souvenir," he says coldly. His twisted smile sends ice through my veins, the threat hanging heavy in the air between us.

"You're absolutely revolting."

He just shrugs off my disgust, grinning like he's in on some sick joke. "What's that American saying? Different strokes for different folks?" he laughs, obviously enjoying this far too much.

Desperate for anything that might tell me what the hell is going on, I push harder. "Come on, you've got to give me something. Throw me a bone here."

But he just nonchalantly waves his gun in my direction, dismissing my demand with a cocky smirk.

"No, I really don't have to give you anything," he taunts, then flops down onto the bed, which nearly buckles under his weight.

He pauses, a sly look crossing his face. "However, I'll give you one clue. What's happening now? It's been brewing for a while," he says cryptically before turning to change the channel on the TV. "A long, long time coming. Yes, indeed."

Then, with a menacing glance back at me, he adds, "And just remember, any noise from you means one less toe."

As he settles in to watch TV, ignoring me like I'm just part of the furniture, I'm left fuming and frightened in equal measure.

Is this really happening?

Trapped in this shabby motel room, tied to a chair, I can't help but wonder... will Lev and his crew make it in time?

CHAPTER 33

LEV

My grip on the steering wheel is iron-tight as I barrel toward the outskirts of Chicago, the destination of an abandoned motel complex just visible against the twilight. My phone rings, cutting through the silence of the car like a gunshot. It's Vanya.

"What?" I snap, my tone sharp as a blade.

"We're keeping tabs on your position," Vanya's voice is calm and collected. "I'll be close by. Whatever you need, just holler."

"Good. Keep your eyes peeled. I've got a damn strong feeling I'll need backup."

The motel is a relic, shadows clinging to the dark, broken windows, but one room breaks the pattern with a flicker of light. That has to be where they're holding her.

My mind churns with questions and possibilities as I slam the car to a stop and get out, gravel crunching underfoot.

As I approach the lone lit room, my heart pounds a relentless beat. Why drag her all the way out here? What's their endgame? The chill night air does nothing to cool my simmering rage. My hand instinctively rests on the gun at my side, ready for whatever might come.

I'm at the door, every nerve alight with a mix of fear and fury. Tonight, I'll face whoever thought they could use Dalia to get to me. They're going to regret waking this beast.

As I reach for the doorknob, ready to burst into the room and take control of the situation, a familiar voice stops me cold.

"Lev!"

It's Vladimir.

My mind reels as I spin around to face him.

"Vlad? How the hell did you get here? How did you know where to find this place?"

But I already know the answer.

Vladimir just grins, a smug, knowing smirk that makes my skin crawl.

"You?" I ask my once-trusted ally.

My gut tightens, the betrayal slicing through me like a knife. Without a second thought, my hand flies to my weapon, intent on ending this deceit here and now. But before my fingers can even brush the handle, I feel the cold, hard press of a gun barrel against the back of my head. I freeze, my heart hammering in my chest.

Turning slightly, I catch sight of a hulking hitman stepping out from the shadows of the room. He moves quickly, shutting the door behind him before I can catch a glimpse of Dalia inside.

"Be smart, Lev. Take your hand off the gun," Vladimir advises, his voice eerily calm. "After all, this won't be any fun if I have to kill you before I even get to explain my plan."

Rage swirls within me as I slowly raise my hands, the reality of the situation sinking in. I'm utterly powerless at the moment between these two men.

Shock courses through me, freezing me in place for a split second.

"Vladimir, how could you do this?" I manage, my voice low and incredulous. "How could you betray me like this? And for what?"

Vladimir's response is a harsh bark of laughter, cold and devoid of any comradeship we once shared.

"And for what?" he mocks, his eyes alight with a bitter fire. "Are you truly such a damn fool? Because your father killed my father, Lev. That's why."

The accusation hits like a physical blow, and I wince, the old family grievances resurfacing like a festering wound.

With my hands still raised in a forced gesture of surrender, I try to reason with him. "Vladimir, there were reasons for what happened to your father. You know this."

He laughs again, louder this time, and it's filled with scorn. "The arrogance of the Ivanovs will be your undoing."

I press on. It's clear he doesn't know the full story. "What did your brother tell you? What have you been led to believe?"

As Vladimir's face hardens, I realize that finding common ground might be farther out of reach than I thought.

Vladimir's face contorts with rage as he clenches his teeth, a muscle in his jaw twitching. "My brother told me everything," he spits out, his voice laced with bitterness. "He said your father killed ours out of jealousy. He saw my father as a threat, a rising star in the organization about to eclipse him. So, he took him out, executed him in cold blood, without any warning."

I wince at his words. "Vlad," I start, my voice steady despite the dismal situation, "your brother lied to you, or at the very least, he didn't tell you everything."

Confusion flickers in his expression, overtaking the anger for just a moment. "What the hell are you talking about?" he demands, his grip on his gun tightening as if preparing to brace for a blow.

Taking a slow, calculated breath, I choose my words carefully, knowing the next few moments are critical.

"Your father wasn't just a rising star; he was involved in dealings that would have destroyed the organization. My father acted to protect us all—not out of jealousy but necessity. It was never about personal power, it was about survival, about safeguarding the future for all of us, including you."

Vladimir snarls. "Lies!"

I stare him down, my voice low and unyielding, knowing the weight of the history I'm about to disclose. "Listen carefully, Vladimir. Your father once conspired with other Russian families to overthrow Ivanov Holdings. This was back when my brothers and I were just infants, vulnerable to any threat against our family."

I pause, letting the gravity of the truth sink in before continuing. "Our father picked up on Evgeny's treachery. He confronted him and offered him a chance to repent and swear loyalty again to our family. But your father chose a darker path."

My voice hardens with the pain of the next revelation. "He attempted to poison our mother with polonium. It was his betrayal that led to her death, a slow and painful one that tore our family apart."

Vladimir's eyes widen, his stance faltering as the narrative he's always known starts to crumble. "Our father had no choice but to act. It wasn't a simple act of jealousy or power; it was retribution, a protective father's response to a direct threat to his family. He had to discreetly execute Evgeny to protect all of us."

The air between us thickens as I wait for Vladimir's response, hoping he sees the truth in my words.

Vladimir stands there, visibly shaken, grappling with the revelations. His voice barely a whisper, he stammers, "Why would Igor lie to me about what our father did?"

I lock eyes with him; my expression is grim.

"Igor," I reply, "was ever the spiteful bastard. He never told you the true reason behind Evgeny's execution because he wanted to use you as his weapon. Igor wanted revenge but never had the courage to pursue it himself. Instead, he manipulated you, hoping you'd be the tool to avenge your father's death."

I pause again, giving him a moment to absorb the bitterness of the betrayal. "Then Igor died, leaving you without any real understanding of past events. And now, here you are," I finish, gesturing to the tense standoff around us.

The truth hits Vladimir like a sledgehammer, his posture slumping as he grasps the impact of his brother's manipulation.

"Vlad, you've been living a lie fashioned by a brother who cared more for revenge than for truth or family."

Vladimir is reeling, his face etched with conflict and denial. "I know what I know," he snaps back, his tone thick with defiance. "And besides, it's too late for me to turn back now."

I study him; my gaze is unflinching, the fire of resolve burning within me. Slowly, deliberately, I press him, needing to hear the confession from his own lips.

"Were you the one behind the attacks, Vladimir?"

His eyes meet mine, and after a tense moment, he nods. "Yes," he admits, his voice almost a whisper. "I wanted to make you suffer, to feel the pain your family caused mine."

With that, I realize the depth of his bitterness and the irreversible path he has chosen. There's no redemption here, not anymore. This isn't just about avenging past wrongs; it's about a cycle of hatred that won't end until one of us is destroyed.

Understanding that it has gone too far to turn back, I glance briefly in the direction where Vanya is parked, signaling subtly.

It's a small gesture but one loaded with consequence.

We're past talking now. Actions must speak for us, and I'm ready to end this, one way or another.

The moment I give the signal, it begins.

A car engine roars to life in the distance, its sound growing rapidly louder as Vanya accelerates toward us. The surprise attack catches Vladimir and the hitman off guard, their reactions a split second too slow.

Vanya, with practiced precision, pulls up and levels his gun at Vlad, ready to fire. But the hitman, a behemoth of a human, reacts with unexpected agility. He pulls his own trigger, the bullet slicing through the air and striking Vanya's arm. The impact throws off Vanya's aim, and his shot veers off wildly.

In the sudden frenzy, Vladimir seizes his chance. His face is a mask of desperation and rage, and he swings his gun up toward me. My heart pounds, adrenaline surging as I brace for the shot.

Before I can react, before Vladimir can squeeze the trigger, another gunshot pierces the air.

Time seems to freeze.

Vladimir's eyes widen in shock as a dark red stain blossoms on his shirt.

He touches the growing wetness, his expression one of disbelief and horror. Then, as if his strings have been cut, he collapses to the ground, lifeless.

Silence falls, heavy and suffocating. I stand there, stunned, scanning the area for the source of the shot that saved my life and ended Vladimir's.

I don't have time, however, to dwell on the confusion of who took that lifesaving shot. My instincts kick in, driving my next move. I spin around, my foot swinging and connecting hard with the hitman's gut. The force of the kick expels the air from him in a whoosh, his gun clattering to the ground as he doubles over.

In one fluid motion, I scoop up the fallen weapon, take aim, and fire two quick shots. Both hit their mark, dropping the hitman dead before he could recover or retaliate. Just like that, the immediate threat is neutralized.

I turn to Vanya, who's still in the car, clutching his arm but alive.

"I'm fine, just a flesh wound," he calls out. "Go check on Dalia."

I don't hesitate.

I rush to the door of the motel room. Heart pounding, I push it open and find her exactly as I feared: tied to a chair, eyes wide with terror, then relief as they meet mine.

Wasting no time, I stride over to her. My hands work quickly, untying the ropes that bind her and pulling the gag from her mouth. All that matters now is that she's safe, that she's alive.

As I free her, the weight of the night's events begins to settle in, but there's no time to process it—not yet.

I scan her quickly, my eyes probing for any sign of injury. "Are you okay?"

She nods, managing a shaky smile. "Yes, I'm okay, just shaken up." Her voice trembles as she adds, "They didn't hurt me, but they wanted to."

Seeing the tears welling up in her eyes, I pull her into a tight embrace, my arms a protective shield around her. "You're safe now."

But even as I say the words, a nagging doubt creeps in. The danger hasn't yet fully passed. There's another gunman out there, and I have no way of knowing where he is or what his intentions are.

Suddenly, a voice cuts through the air. "Lev! Dalia!"

Gun at the ready, I move cautiously toward the door, my senses heightened. As I peer out, I see a figure standing near Vladimir's body. It's Alexei, his shoulder still bandaged, a gun in the uninjured hand.

"It's good to see you alive," he calls out, a small smile on his lips. "Brother."

CHAPTER 34

DALIA

"**B**rother?"

The word bounces off the dingy motel walls like a bad joke.

Lev and I share a wide-eyed look—has the world gone topsy-turvy tonight?

Lev puts up a hand like a traffic cop as Alexei steps closer.

Alexei, unfazed, whips out his phone and calmly dials like he's ordering pizza.

"Come now," he barks into the device. Turning to me, he says, "My top-notch cleaners will take care of this mess. I have a medic coming with them. I figured tonight would get messy."

Speaking of messy, Vanya limps over, his hand clamped on his arm, blood seeping through his fingers. His face is stoic, like he's simply stubbed a toe.

"It's not that bad," he tries to assure us. "Let me just sit for a moment."

"You've been shot," Lev says. "Sit and keep pressure on it."

"It's fine, it's fine," Vanya says. "I've had worse."

Alexei begins to stride over with that gangster swagger of his, then pauses mid-step. He drops the duffel bag that's been hanging off his good shoulder, rummages through it, and pulls out a bottle of vodka.

"Got this from my private stash." He presents the bottle to Lev like he's unveiling a rare treasure. "Figured we'd need something strong to celebrate our survival and to brace ourselves for the chat we're about to have."

As if on cue, a big white van pulls up, and out tumble a bunch of guys in janitor uniforms. They get straight to work, cleaning up the night's mess with a precision that's slightly disturbing.

Meanwhile, a medic finally gives Vanya some much-needed attention, patching up his arm with a professionalism that suggests he's used to bullet wounds more than bruises.

Alexei gestures grandly toward the motel lobby. "Shall we?" he says, and we head in.

Lev and I take a seat on the kind of tacky sofa you'd expect in a place like this, bracing ourselves for whatever Alexei's about to drop. With a deep breath and a not-so-quiet prayer for patience, I prepare for another round of Russian roulette —this time with words and vodka.

Alexei starts playing bartender, pouring shots with the casual flair of a man who's done this many times before.

Lev cuts to the chase. "Get to the point, Alexei."

Alexei responds by knocking back his shot like it's water and quickly pouring another. "You and I are brothers, Lev. Well, half-brothers. We share the same father."

Lev leans forward, his face a mask of disbelief. "You're bull-shitting me."

I study Alexei more closely, and suddenly it's like one of those family resemblance charts pops up before my eyes. Lev's all rough edges and raw power, while Alexei's got that sleek, polished look about him. Lev's handsome, but Alexei's *pretty*. In many ways, they couldn't be more different.

But those intense gray eyes, that imposing height, and the way they both carry themselves—like chess masters always three moves ahead—are identical.

I blurt out before I can stop myself, "Wow, you two *are* related."

Lev narrows his eyes, clearly wrestling with the bombshell Alexei just dropped. After a moment, he reaches for the vodka, throwing it back like he's trying to swallow the truth along with it.

"Let me tell you how it all started. Our father had a bit of a wild streak. He met a woman, Marina Plushenko, at a gala in Moscow. She was a ballet dancer, stunning and completely outside of his world of Bratva and bullets. They had an affair." Alexei's eyes are distant, as if he's visualizing the past.

"He kept her paid and quiet, a classic Ivanov move, while she raised me away from the family spotlight. I've known about my lineage all my life, and when our father passed, I saw my chance to step into the Ivanov Bratva to claim my birthright, albeit from the shadows."

Lev listens intently, his expression unreadable, absorbing every detail of the story that rewrote his family history without his consent.

"And now here you are," Lev says when Alexei finishes.

"That's right," Alexei replies, cool as a cucumber with that knowing smirk of his. "I've been watching everything unfold, waiting for just the right moment to make my grand entrance. Couldn't resist a little drama."

Lev squints at him, obviously not buying the whole casual act. "What do you want, Alexei?"

Alexei chuckles, light and breezy, which feels a bit out of place given the story he just told.

"I get it. Skepticism suits you, Lev, but really, what more can I do to prove I'm on the up and up?" He leans in. "I want to be a part of the family. Running my own little empire is fun and all, but joining forces with the most formidable Bratva in the city?" He spreads his hands wide like he's ready to embrace the future he imagines. "Think about it—the chance to help it grow, to take it beyond our city limits— how could I possibly pass that up?"

His pitch is slick, and I can't help but admire his boldness.

Lev kicks back in his chair, an eyebrow raised as if he's just been pitched a dodgy business deal. He grabs the vodka bottle, giving it a contemplative look.

"So, are we negotiating here?"

"Sure, why not?" Alexei shoots back.

Lev nods, a sly grin playing on his lips. "All right. If we're wheeling and dealing, I'm going to need a case of this stuff."

Alexei laughs heartily, the sound echoing in the sparse room. "Of course, of course."

Lev sobers up, the gravity of the night reclaiming its hold on him. "This is a lot to process, especially since tonight I almost lost the love of my life and the mother of my future kids."

The way he says it sends a flutter through my heart, and tears prick my eyes.

I squeeze his hand, feeling a rush of emotion as he returns the gesture with a reassuring smile that manages to ease some of the tension in my shoulders.

Turning his attention back to Alexei, Lev's voice firms up. "But first things first. I'm going to need a DNA test to confirm your story."

"Naturally," Alexei agrees smoothly like he expected to hear that all along. "And if it all checks out, perhaps a seat at the table is in the cards."

Lev stands, vodka in hand.

Alexei extends a hand to Lev, a sincere gesture filled with newfound ties and unspoken promises. Lev pauses, eyeing the hand as if it might be a trap, but after a moment, he grabs it firmly. "Appreciate the assist, Alexei. Owe you one."

"No worries," Alexei responds with a half-smile. "I sincerely hope this is just the first of many times I can lend a hand to the Ivanov family—*my* family."

We exit to see Vanya patched up but still looking like he's been through a war zone. Lev hands him the vodka with a stern look. "I'm not suggesting; I'm ordering—take the week off."

Vanya laughs, a rough sound that's more relief than humor. "Think I've earned that, boss." He pops the top off the vodka and takes a long, deep pull.

As the cleaners wrap up their eerie efficiency, Lev turns to me, something soft in his gaze that's usually reserved for quiet moments far from danger. He takes my hands, pressing them against his chest where his heart beats a steady promise.

In that quiet gesture, the night's madness fades for a moment, replaced by the silent strength of his presence.

Lev's gaze is intense, almost burning a hole right through me as he blurts out, "I'm a damn fool."

I blink, taken aback by his sudden confession. "What are you talking about?"

He takes a deep breath, his voice heavy with emotion. "I came so close to losing you tonight... I can't even think about it without feeling sick." He pauses, searching for the right words. "And here I am, having not even told you I love you, Dalia. You mean everything to me."

But then his face falls, and he looks away, a shadow of guilt passing over his features. "I failed to protect you tonight," he admits, his voice breaking slightly. He can't even look at me as if he's ashamed of his admission.

Then, slowly, he turns back, his eyes locking with mine, filled with a desperate kind of hope. "Can you forgive me for that? I need a chance to prove to you that I'll move heaven and earth not just to keep you safe, but to make you feel my love for you, every single goddamn day."

His plea hangs in the air, raw and earnest.

Lev's hand gently lands on my belly, his touch careful, full of intent. "And the baby," he whispers, sincerity lacing every word, "I'll do anything for him or her. Just give me that chance."

As his vow sinks in, warmth floods through me, mingling with an ache that's part relief, part love. Tears well up because, let's face it, how could I not melt right now? His promise to protect our future nudges my heart into overdrive.

"I love you like crazy, Lev."

Just then, the sound of cars rolling up breaks our little bubble. I glance over Lev's shoulder to see Elena, Yuri, and the whole gang stepping out.

They catch us right as Lev and I are in the middle of a kiss that feels like it could stop time—a kiss full of all the love and madness of our life together.

As we finally break apart, I can't help but smirk slightly at our audience.

"Perfect timing, folks."

My tone is light, but my heart is full knowing we're surrounded by family who've got our backs, no matter what.

CHAPTER 35

DALIA

Subject: Checking In
Dal,
Hope this email finds you well. Just wanted to see how you're doing. Let me know when you have time.

D*ad*
We're gliding through the skies on a private plane headed for LA, and here I am, laptop open, staring at an email that's enough to give me whiplash.

Known for being more of a man of action than words, Dad's emails usually are as brief as they come.

"It's just a check-in, asking how I am," I explain to Lev, who's lounging next to me. "Simple and to the point," I continue, "but coming from him, it's practically a novel."

Lev cracks a smile at that, his gaze thoughtful as he watches me absentmindedly toggle the cursor. "It's a good thing, though, right? Your dad is reaching out. It's a step in the right direction."

I nod, chewing on my lip as I consider the weight of that simple message. It's not every day you get a semi-warm and fuzzy from the man whose picture is practically under the definition of stoic in the dictionary. "Yeah, it's something. Definitely something good."

Deciding that the perfect response needs more brainpower than I could muster at thirty thousand feet, I snap the laptop shut. "I'll give it some more thought and craft the perfect reply later."

"Forget about that for a minute. We've got a whole weekend in LA ahead of us—think fun, sun, and all the killer food we can eat. No worries allowed."

I flash him a grin, the stress dissolving under the warmth of his smile and thoughts of spending a weekend in LA. "You know what? That sounds like exactly what I need." As I place my hand lightly on my belly, a secretive smile tugs at my lips—there's a little something up my sleeve for him this weekend.

Lev leans close, dropping his voice to a mock conspiratorial whisper. "And I've got something cooked up on our way to the hotel."

"Oh, do tell. What kind of mischief are you plotting?"

He chuckles, shaking his head. "Nice try. But if I tell you, it wouldn't be a surprise, would it?"

I let out a playful sigh, rolling my eyes at his antics. "Keep your secrets, then," I retort, settling back into the plush seat as the plane begins its descent, the LA skyline sprawling out below us like a vast playground.

The moment we land in LA, the thrill of the weekend hits full throttle. Lev has a sleek, red convertible sports car waiting for us. The sun's shining brightly as we zip into the city with the top down, the wind tangling my hair—it's a total movie star moment—minus the paparazzi.

As we cruise, Lev shoots me a mischievous look. "Ready for your surprise?"

"What is it?"

He takes a deep breath, the playful smirk never leaving his face. "So, Maura might've mentioned something about your ex, Chad, and his connections to her family. Turns out Chad's in LA. Want to go see him?"

"I'd love to," I reply, the idea too delicious to pass up.

We head to West Hollywood, pulling up to a fancy real estate company that screams Chad's kind of place. Lev parks the car and hops out like he's James Bond on a mission. He strides around to open my door, offering his hand with a flourish.

As he leads me inside, my mind races with the possibilities. Seeing Chad again under these wildly different circumstances is going to be good.

"Lead the way, darling," I say, squeezing Lev's hand, ready for whatever drama awaits us inside.

Lev swings the door open, and we step into the office. There's Chad, embodying the classic d-bag aura, lounging back with his feet propped up on the desk, chattering away into a headset. The moment he catches sight of us, the color practically vanishes from his face—a picture-perfect moment I wish I'd caught on camera.

Lev calls out in a booming voice for the rest of the staff to take a break. And just like that, they scatter, leaving us with Chad, who sits up straighter, confusion and fear mingling in his eyes as he rips off his headset.

"Are you here to hurt me?" Chad's gaze flicks between Lev and me, sizing up the situation.

Lev crosses his arms, a smirk playing at the corner of his mouth. "That's entirely up to Dalia here."

I can't help the wicked grin that spreads across my face as I step forward, soaking in the sudden shift of power. Chad, who once thought he could toss me aside like yesterday's news, now looks about as stable as a house of cards in a windstorm.

"Well, Chad," I start, "we just thought we'd drop by. You know, catch up, see how you're doing." I pause, letting the suspense hang in the air. "And maybe settle a few old scores."

Lev casually pulls up a chair on the opposite side of Chad's desk, crossing his arms as he settles in comfortably. "Let's get some things straight," he says.

Chad, already looking like a cornered cat, tries to jump in, probably hoping to spin his usual yarn. "Look, I can explain—"

Lev cuts him off with a swift, "Shut the fuck up, Chad," delivered so smoothly it almost sounds polite. Chad snaps his mouth shut, the message received loud and clear.

"Now," Lev continues, "Maura enlightened me about your cozy ties to the Flannigans." He tilts his head, watching Chad squirm under his gaze. "Interesting story there. Seems like you bolted with Dalia's cash because you got cold feet before your fake wedding to a Flannigan."

Chad's eyes flick around, desperately looking for an ally or an out but finding neither. He swallows hard, his Adam's apple bobbing like a buoy at sea.

"Yes, okay, I was scared," Chad admits. "They threatened me, and I thought I was protecting myself."

Lev nods as if he expected as much. "So, you stole from Dalia and ran, thinking you'd save your skin with her cash?" His tone is incredulous but calm, as if he's merely confirming the details of a story he's already pieced together.

Chad nods slowly. "Yes, that's what happened." His voice is barely above a whisper.

Lev turns to me with a smirk that's all too familiar. "There you go," he says. "The cards are all on the table. I've dealt more harshly with rats for much less than this."

Chad's already pale face goes ghostly, looking like he might keel over any second.

Lev continues, his gaze flicking to me, "But it's Dalia's call. So, what do you want to do?"

I flash a grin, the gears turning wickedly in my mind. "Well, I'm really not in a murdering mood today. I think I want him alive and suffering. And I want his suffering to be of the financial variety—hit him where it truly hurts."

Lev chuckles, nodding in approval. "Good call. So, Chad, here's the deal," he leans forward, locking eyes with Chad, who seems to shrink under his stare. "You're going to pay back every last cent you stole from Dalia. And let's tack on some steep, steep interest while we're at it. You pay up, and you get to keep your life and all your limbs. How's that sound?"

Chad, his voice quivering, nearly stumbles over his words, "Please, please, I'll do anything, just... just don't kill me."

I cross my arms, my smile unwavering. "Start writing those checks, Chad. Consider it your penance for messing with the wrong woman."

Lev gives me a satisfied grin, looking like he's wrapping up a routine business meeting instead of extorting an ex. "I think we have an understanding," he says.

He fixes Chad with a look that could freeze lava. "I'm planning an expansion in LA, which means I have eyes and ears in town. My people will swing by every two weeks for your contributions. I'd strongly recommend not being late."

Chad's nodding so fast that I'm worried he might sprain a neck muscle. "I won't."

With that sorted, Lev stands, and we head for the door. Stepping out into the sunshine, he throws a playful glance my way. "Apologies for not bringing a gun this time."

I chuckle, shaking my head as we slide into our car. "This time, your words packed all the bang we needed."

As we pull away, the LA skyline rolling past, I poke at the last bit of intrigue he dropped. "So, an expansion to LA?" I ask, eyebrow cocked.

He flashes me that secretive grin of his and stays mum. Trust Lev to keep things spicy, always holding one last ace up his sleeve.

His gaze drifts, lost in thought as he navigates through traffic. I watch him for a moment, curious about the sudden shift in his mood. "What's up?" I prod.

He flicks a glance my way, something intent sparking in those dark eyes. "I want to marry you," he blurts out, straightforward as ever.

A smile spreads across my face, warmed by the thought but amused by the timing. "I'd love that, especially considering how our last wedding was interrupted before we could be declared husband and wife."

He shakes his head, his expression serious. "No, you don't understand. I want to marry you *now*."

"Now?" My eyebrows shoot up in surprise. This man really doesn't do things halfway.

"Now. Not here in LA, though."

"Then where?"

"Where else? Vegas, baby."

I can't help but grin, caught up in the wild, impulsive plan.

"Let's do it."

Without another word, Lev swings the car onto the freeway, the lights of LA fading behind us as we speed toward Vegas, ready to gamble on a lifetime together in true high-roller style.

CHAPTER 36

DALIA

We burst into our Vegas penthouse suite, and it's every bit the over-the-top, swanky pad you'd expect at the top of the Bellagio.

The view is a glittering panorama of lights and energy, perfectly reflecting the electric excitement zipping through me.

Decked out in the snazzy clothes we snagged last minute, we just had the most fabulously cliché wedding, complete with an Elvis impersonator who had more dazzle to him than the Strip.

Lev scoops me up with a grin that could outshine the neon on Fremont Street, carrying me across the threshold of our suite. His kiss is wild and passionate, with a promise of forever stamped in every touch. He sets me down by the plush king-sized bed, his eyes never leaving mine.

"You look incredible," he whispers. "I can't wait to see you holding our child."

I'm practically a puddle by his feet at those sweet nothings, my heart swelling in my chest. The glimmer of the city below pales in comparison to the love lighting up his eyes. This night, this man, and this wildly impulsive wedding—it's all more perfect than I could have ever imagined.

Lev's grin turns wicked as he pulls me close, his fingers tracing the edge of my dress like he's unwrapping the best damn present he's ever seen.

"You know, I've been waiting all night to get you out of this."

He doesn't waste any time. One tug and the zipper slides down, the fabric whispering to the floor, leaving me in nothing but the lacy panties I'd bought just for tonight. His eyes roam over me, hungry, taking in every curve like he's committing it to memory.

"Damn."

I swear, just the heat in his gaze makes my knees weak.

"I love you," he says, and it's more than just sweet words, it's a promise, a declaration that hits me right in the core. My breath catches, and before I can respond, his lips are on mine. All I can do is kiss him back with everything I've got.

It's slow and deliberate, the kind of kiss that makes you forget where you are, who you are, until nothing else exists but the way his mouth moves, the way his tongue teases, tasting, exploring. One hand slides down my back, the other slipping under the waistband of my panties, fingers skimming over bare skin until they find that sweet spot.

I gasp into his mouth, my hips arching toward his hand, but Lev's got all the time in the world. He's rubbing slow circles, teasing me, building the heat until I'm squirming, desperate for more. My panties are soaked, the fabric rubbing against me with every move, amplifying the ache between my legs.

His lips leave mine, trailing down my neck, over my collarbone, each kiss sending a shiver down my spine. And then he's kneeling, hooking his fingers into the sides of my panties and tugging them down, tossing them onto the pile of discarded clothes on the floor.

"Beautiful," he murmurs, looking up at me with that same hunger in his eyes. "You're so damn beautiful."

And then his mouth is on me again, kissing, licking, making my breath hitch and my heart race. His fingers join in, sliding inside me in time with the flicks of his tongue on my clit.

I'm losing it, the pleasure coiling tight inside me, every nerve on fire, every inch of me focused on what he's doing. My hands are in his hair, pulling him closer, needing more, more, until I'm teetering on the edge, barely able to hold on.

"Come for me," he whispers against me, his voice thick and rough, and that's all it takes.

I fall apart, the orgasm crashing over me like a wave. Lev holds me through it, his touch never faltering, drawing out every last bit of pleasure until I'm trembling in his arms.

When it's over, he pulls me close, his forehead resting against mine, and for a moment, we just breathe together, the air thick with the scent of sex and sweat and something sweet.

Still trembling, I look up at Lev with a wicked grin. That orgasm rocked me, but I'm not done—not by a long shot. I pull him into a kiss, tasting the remnants of my own pleasure on his lips.

I need more of him, all of him.

My fingers make quick work of his buttons, practically ripping his shirt off, and then my hands drop to his belt, unbuckling it with a flick of my wrist.

He's watching me, a smirk tugging at the corners of his mouth, but that smirk falters when I push his pants and boxers down in one smooth motion. His cock springs free, thick and hard, and all I can think about is how badly I want to taste it.

I wrap my fingers around him, stroking slowly, enjoying the way his breath catches, the way his eyes darken with lust.

"You like that, baby?" I purr, my voice dripping with lust and need. But I don't wait for an answer. I'm on my knees in a heartbeat, my tongue flicking over the tip, tasting the salt of his pre-cum. He groans, deep and guttural, and it's music to my ears.

I take him deeper, hollowing my cheeks, sliding my lips down his length until he hits the back of my throat. He's hot and heavy in my mouth, the taste of him making me moan around his cock. I bob my head, my hand stroking what I can't take, my tongue swirling around the sensitive head every time I pull back.

The noises he's making—those low, desperate groans—are spurring me on, making me want to push him closer to the edge.

His hips start to move, thrusting gently into my mouth, and I let him, taking everything he gives.

280 | K.C. CROWNE

"Fuck, you're so good," he groans, his hand tangling in my hair, guiding me, but he's losing control, and I love every second of it. I can feel him tensing, his cock pulsing in my mouth, and I know he's close.

Just when I think he's going to lose it and spill it down my throat, he pulls me off, lifting me up like I weigh nothing, and lays me back on the bed.

"Not yet," he growls, his voice rough with need.

He starts to crawl up my body, but with a sly grin, I suddenly shift, shoving him onto his back instead.

"Oh no, you don't," I tease, straddling him, feeling his cock hot and hard against my thigh.

I don't waste time, I'm too damn ready. I slide down onto his cock, and it's like being split in two in the most perfect way possible. He fills me up, stretching me, and I moan as I take him all the way in.

"Fuck, you feel so good," I whisper, starting to move, rocking my hips, grinding against him.

His hands are on my waist, guiding me, but I'm in control, and it feels incredible. I ride him, the friction sending sparks of pleasure through my whole body, and all I can think about is how deep he is, how perfect this feels.

"God, you're so tight," he growls, his voice strained, and I can tell he's close, but so am I.

I pick up the pace, riding him harder, faster, chasing that high, wanting to feel him come inside me. The dirty talk flows between us, nothing held back, just raw need and love, pushing us both closer and closer to the edge. As I ride him, the pleasure builds until I can't hold back anymore. I throw my head back, my nails digging into his chest, and let go, the orgasm crashing over me in waves that leave me gasping for air. I can feel him twitching inside me, so close to the edge himself, but before he can reach that peak, he flips me over with a quick, determined move.

I wrap my legs around his waist as he slides back inside me, slow and deliberate. His eyes lock onto mine, and suddenly, it's like the whole world fades away. There's nothing but the feel of him, the way his body moves with mine, the way he fills me up so completely.

He's gentle, his thrusts deep and steady, but there's an edge to it, a restrained intensity that makes my breath hitch.

"You're so gorgeous," he whispers, his voice thick with emotion, each word punctuated by a kiss—on my lips, my neck, my collarbone. "I love you so damn much."

And it's those words, that raw honesty in his voice, that makes this different, makes it more than just sex. This is love, pure and simple, and I can feel it in every touch, every thrust. He's worshiping me, treating me like I'm the most precious thing in the world, and it's driving me wild.

His pace quickens and I can feel the tension coiling inside me again, but it's different this time. It's deeper, more profound, like he's reaching right into my soul. I can tell he's holding back, trying to draw this out, trying to make it last, but I don't want him to.

"Don't hold back," I murmur against his ear, my voice a breathless plea. He groans in response, his control slipping as he starts to move faster and harder. It's still tender, still filled with that overwhelming love, but there's an urgency now, a desperate need that mirrors my own.

He's hitting all the right spots, pushing me higher and higher until I'm right on the edge again. "Lev, I'm going to —" The words are cut off by a gasp as the pleasure overtakes me, another orgasm ripping through me, more intense than the last.

My whole body tenses, my nails raking down his back as I hold on for dear life, lost in the sensation of him inside me.

He's right there with me, his breath coming in ragged gasps, his thrusts erratic as he chases his own release.

"Fuck, baby, I'm coming," he groans, his hips slamming against mine as he comes with me, filling me up, his body shaking with the force of it, my pussy milking him for every drop.

It's unlike anything I've ever felt before, this connection, this overwhelming mix of pleasure and love. We're completely in sync, both of us trembling, holding each other tight as we ride out the waves together.

When it's over, he collapses beside me, pulling me into his arms. We're both spent, breathless, but there's a deep satisfaction settling in my chest, a sense of completeness I didn't know I could feel. This man, this moment, it's everything I never knew I needed.

We're lying together, tangled in the sheets, his hand gently moving over my body, tracing lazy circles on my skin. There's a softness to his touch like he's savoring every inch of me, and it makes my heart swell even more. He leans forward, pressing a tender kiss to my belly, right on the little bump that's growing bigger every day.

"Lev," I murmur, brushing his hair back from his forehead, "I've got another surprise for you."

He looks up at me, curious, his eyes warm and filled with love. "What is it?"

I take his hand, guiding it to rest on my belly. "Can you tell what's inside?"

"Our child, of course."

I shake my head, a smile tugging at my lips. "Our *children*, Lev. We're having twins."

For a second, he just stares at me, the words sinking in. Then, his face lights up with pure, unfiltered joy.

"Twins?" he repeats, almost in disbelief. I smile in response, my eyes filling with joyful tears, and his laughter fills the room, bubbling over with excitement.

He pulls me into a kiss, deep and sweet, both of us smiling too much to keep it serious for long.

"I love you," he whispers against my lips, and I whisper it right back, "I love you, too."

EPILOGUE I

LEV

Six Months later...

W e're cruising back from the hospital, the car seats in the back cradling our new treasures—Emma and Laurel.

Fraternal twins, each with her own unique patchwork of features, both equally mesmerizing. I'm behind the wheel, but my focus keeps slipping from the road to the rearview mirror, where I can just catch glimpses of their peaceful, sleeping faces.

Dalia's hand is warm in mine.

She chuckles and nudges me gently. "Lev, eyes on the road, please. They'll still be the most beautiful girls in the world when we get home. But we still have to *get* them home."

"I can't help it," I admit with a laugh, my heart so full it feels like it could burst. "They're just impossible not to look at." And it's the truth; they've already got me completely wrapped around their little fingers.

She agrees with a soft smile as she turns around to look at them.

As we pull up to our new place—a sprawling mansion in Lake Forest—the scene out front is a lively one. A mess of cars lines the driveway, signaling the eager family waiting inside.

I park the car, excitement building. "Ready to introduce them to the clan?"

"Absolutely."

Dalia and I carefully scoop up our sleeping beauties from the backseat. Each of us cradling a twin, we head to the front door where our entire family has gathered, buzzing with anticipation. The moment the door swings open, I'm greeted with eager faces about to erupt into cheers.

Quickly, I press a finger to my lips, and the room instantly quiets down, all eyes now gently admiring Emma and Laurel. Everyone takes their turn marveling at the twins, their coos soft and their touches lighter than air, careful not to wake them.

After a few moments, I lean in and whisper to the group, "We're going to take the girls up to get some rest." The group responds with silent nods and thumbs-up.

Dalia and I make our way to the nursery, a room we've decked out with all the cozy trimmings fit for our girls. We lay each twin down in her own crib, their peaceful faces the picture of serenity.

I flick on the baby monitors, making sure we don't miss a peep.

"They're home," Dalia breathes out, her voice filled with emotion.

Pulling her close, I plant a soft kiss on her lips. "We're all home now."

After planting gentle kisses on the twins' chubby cheeks, Dalia and I head back downstairs, where the house is buzzing with our closest and dearest. Elena, Yuri, and a fully recovered Vanya are chatting by the kitchen island. Luk and Maura are there, too, with little Michael and Sasha bouncing around them. Even Alexei is here, blending into the family scene like he's always been a part of it.

I flip on some music and the drinks start flowing, the atmosphere light and filled with laughter. It feels good to have everyone together, celebrating not just the arrival of Emma and Laurel but the unity of our family.

Gifts wrapped in soft pastels and ribbons are piled up on the side table—tiny outfits, cuddly toys, and all the newborn essentials a parent could wish for. Every so often, I pull out my phone to check the baby monitor app. I'm on high alert, ready to dash upstairs at the slightest whimper. But each time I look, there they are on the screen, sound asleep in their cribs, not a care in the world.

The amount of love in the room is overwhelming, everyone sharing stories and catching up, the joy of the occasion bringing us all closer. Despite the constant pull to check on the girls, I let myself relax, assured by their peaceful slumber, and focus on enjoying the night with our family. This, right here, is what it's all about.

The party shifts out to the pool, with the BBQ sizzling and drinks in everyone's hands.

Vanya, cracking a grin, nudges me. "Hey Lev, look at you, man—classic suburban dad now, huh?"

I laugh, looking around at our assembled family and friends enjoying the serene backyard. "I guess you could say I'm getting the hang of this lifestyle. It's not too bad, you know?"

As we hover around the grill, talk inevitably turns to business.

"So, what's the latest with Vladimir's crew?" Luk asks, flipping a burger with practiced ease.

I take a sip of my beer. "It's all wrapped up. We've disbanded his operation. Those loyal to him had two choices: leave Chicago or join us. Most of them made the wise choice."

Alexei, who's been quietly listening, joins in. "Speaking of joining, my operations are officially merging with the Ivanovs. It's about making us all stronger, more unified."

The news brings nods of approval from around the grill. Yuri raises his beer. "To the Ivanovs. Stronger and more unstoppable than ever."

I clink my beer against his. "Unstoppable indeed. With all of us together, there's nothing we can't handle."

The future, for once, is looking as bright and promising as the afternoon sun glinting off the pool's tranquil waters.

As we're lounging by the pool, Dalia's phone pings with a notification. My immediate reaction is to check if it's something about the twins.

"That the baby monitor app?" I ask.

Dalia gives me a playful look. "It's just Claude," she says, glancing at her phone. "He emailed to say he sold another one of my jewelry pieces. He's got the cash ready whenever we want to pick it up."

"Good to hear he's keeping his word," I reply. I'm satisfied to know that Claude's staying on the straight and narrow under our arrangement.

Elena, who's been listening in while sipping her drink, joins the conversation. "Dal, you should really think about getting back into making jewelry. Claude's going to run out of your stock soon enough."

Maura, half-watching Michael and Sasha play near the edge of the pool, speaks up. "Yeah, your pieces are flying off the shelves. It'd be great to see what you come up with next."

Dalia nods. "You're right. I think it's about time I got back to the studio. Maybe kick off a new collection."

I lean back, taking in the relaxed atmosphere, the sounds of family and friends enjoying the evening's barbecue filling the air. Turning to Dalia, I smile and squeeze her hand gently.

"You know, there's no rush for you to decide what you want to do next," I say. "And you're definitely not obliged to come back as my PA. Then again, I'd be crazy to think you'd stay inside all day."

She laughs, that familiar sparkle in her eye. "You know me too well," she says. "But I might as well enjoy the maternity leave while I can."

We sit there, comfortable and content, watching everyone enjoy the food, the drinks, and each other's company. It's moments like these that remind me of what's truly important.

Suddenly, both our phones chime. It's the baby monitor app, letting us know that Emma and Laurel are awake. We look at each other, the parental instinct kicking in immediately.

"Guess it's time to see what our little angels need," I say as I stand up, ready to head inside. "Let's go, Mom."

Dalia nods, her face lighting up at the mention of our daughters. "Let's do it, Dad."

Together, we head back into the house, love all around us.

EPILOGUE II

DALIA

Two years later...

S itting in my office at Ivanov Holdings, I'm caught up in a FaceTime call with Emma and Laurel, who are now two years old and ridiculously adorable.

Emma, with her dark curly hair bouncing as she giggles, is the spitting image of me. Laurel, on the other hand, has Lev's sharp, gray eyes and his strong-willed personality. Their toddler babble fills the room, and it's honestly the best part of my day.

"All right, my loves, Mama will see you tonight," I tell them, blowing kisses to the screen, which they try to catch with their little hands—a game that never gets old. Marissa, our nanny who's been with us since the girls were six months old, signs off and tells me not to rush home. She knows I have dinner plans with Lev.

Ending the call, I can't help but feel a rush of warmth for my little family. I gather my things, already looking forward to the evening.

I stride into Lev's office, but the room is empty, his desk untouched since this morning. A little pang of disappointment hits me—where could he be?

Just then, Vanya passes by the doorway. I wave him over, my brow furrowing with concern. "Hey, Vanya, have you seen Lev today?"

Vanya pauses, his expression thoughtful as he pulls out his phone. "Actually, no," he says, scrolling through his messages. "And now that you mention it, he specifically requested not to be disturbed all day. Said he had some important business to take care of."

A knot forms in my stomach. In our world, important business can mean anything, and it's not always good. As the wife of a Bratva kingpin, I've learned to brace myself for all possibilities. Worry is a constant companion I wish I could shake off.

Vanya, noticing my sudden quiet, switches topics. "Oh, and Dalia, don't forget the meeting next week about the office building purchase in LA."

I snap back to the present, nodding. "Thanks, Vanya. I'm all over it," I assure him, though my mind is still partly on Lev.

Leaving Lev's office, a touch more worried than when I entered, I decide to head out. There's nothing more I can do here, and sitting around waiting isn't my style. Whatever Lev's tangled up in, I have to trust he'll handle it like he always does.

Just as I'm about to call Lev, my phone buzzes with a text from him. It's just an address, stark and mysterious. I text back immediately, my fingers flying over the screen.

You're being awfully cryptic, I type, a smirk playing on my lips.

His reply comes quickly.

The best surprises are just that way.

All right, Mr. Mysterious, I'll be there soon, I shoot back, excitement bubbling inside me. Tossing my phone into my purse, I can't help but shake my head, amused. Lev never fails to keep things interesting.

I stride out to the parking lot, slide into my Lexus SUV, and fire up the engine. As it hums to life, I check my phone once more. There's an email from my parents. It's short, like always, my dad commenting, *The twins are very cute.*

I smile, heartened by these small yet significant overtures. Things with my parents are thawing slowly—baby steps, but steps, nonetheless. I'm hopeful that it won't be too long before they're ready to visit in person.

With a deep breath, I pull out of the parking lot, the evening ahead promising yet another unexpected twist in the ongoing adventure that is life with Lev. Whatever he's got planned at that mystery address, I'm ready for it.

I pull up to the location, finding myself in front of a quaint, albeit slightly rundown, brick warehouse in Wicker Park. It's got charm; I'll give it that, even if it does look like it could use a little love.

Noticing Lev's Porsche parked out front adds a flutter of anticipation in my chest. I grab my purse, step out of my SUV, and head toward the tall, steel doors of the warehouse. Pushing them open, I step inside and am greeted by a surprisingly tidy interior, with rows of sturdy shelves that look new.

Curiosity piqued, I make my way into the main area. The moment I step through the threshold, I stop dead in my tracks, my mouth dropping open in shock at the sight before me.

As I step further into the main room, what hits me isn't just any surprise—it's a jeweler's dream. A fully decked-out jewelry workshop sprawls before me, its shelves and tables gleaming with newness. My purse nearly slips from my shoulder as I stare wide-eyed.

Lev stands amidst the shimmering equipment, a wry smile playing on his lips. "Surprise," he says, his arms opening slightly as if to embrace my shock.

I rush closer, my heels clicking eagerly on the concrete floor. "Is that a dual-sided polishing wheel?" I gasp, darting from one piece of equipment to the next. "And—oh wow, you've got a laser engraver here too!"

My fingers trace the edge of a high-end metal press, and I turn to him, excitement bubbling over. "And this—this is a micro welder! Lev, this is professional-grade stuff. How did you—?"

Lev's smile widens. "I thought it was time for you to have a space of your own, to create whatever you want, without any limits."

294 | K.C. CROWNE

I circle a beautifully crafted workbench, its surface pristine and waiting for creativity. "This is incredible. You've thought of everything, even the ultrasonic cleaner!" I shake my head in disbelief, already imagining the pieces I could create here.

Lev steps closer, his presence grounding amid the whirl of possibilities surrounding us. "Only the best for my brilliant wife."

Lev watches me zip around the workshop, a gleam of pride in his eyes. "You know, you've been all hands on deck— balancing work, our girls, life. I don't want your own dreams to get lost in the shuffle."

I stop in front of him, looking around at all the shiny new tools, feeling a sudden surge of emotions. "Lev, this is incredible," I admit, feeling tears prick at the edges of my eyes, "but honestly, it just makes me want to cry."

He furrows his brow, stepping closer. "Why?"

"Well, look at my life!" I gesture helplessly. "With the kids and the job, my plate's already overflowing. Where would I fit this in?"

He grins as if he's anticipated this very meltdown. "I figured you might say that," he says, a hint of mischief in his gaze. "That's why I came prepared with a backup surprise."

I raise an eyebrow; curiosity piqued despite the chaos of my emotions. "And what would that be?"

"You're fired."

I blink, thrown for a loop. "Fired?"

"Yep, fired," he confirms. "From Ivanov Holdings. It's high time you ran your own show, don't you think?" His smile widens. "Consider this workshop your new office."

He gestures around the room, his eyes shining with excitement. "Now you can set your own hours, be your own boss. Take a day off to hang with the kids whenever you want. Hell, keep up those weekly lunches with Elena and Maura without worrying about a meeting or deadline."

The reality of what he's done hits me hard, and tears well up, my voice caught in my throat. He's not just given me a workshop; he's handed me freedom and my dream on a silver platter.

He continues, a proud glint in his eyes, "Think of me as your patron of sorts." He chuckles, squeezing my hands gently. "After the way your pieces sold out at Claude's, it's clear people can't get enough of your work. I'm just here to support you in feeding that demand."

I'm overwhelmed, every emotion tumbling over the next. "This is... I don't even know what to say."

"Just say you'll make some stunning jewelry, and maybe let me take you out to show it off now and then," he replies with a wink, drawing a laugh through my tears.

His confidence in me, his support, it's more than I could have ever asked for.

"Baby, this is unreal; thank you so much!" I manage to say between the sniffles.

"Anything to make you happy, my love."

Then, with that devilish smile that always spells trouble—and fun—he looks down at me. "Now, how about we christen your new empire here? What do you say?"

I can't help but grin back, caught up in his playful vibe. "You mean to start the machinery or make a baby?"

He chuckles and dips his head to whisper against my lips, "Why not both? Let's aim for a little gem. Maybe call her Ruby?"

I burst out laughing, loving the ridiculousness of it. "That's going to be one expensive jewel, Mr. Ivanov."

"To make you happy, my love, I'd pay any price."

He seals our deal with a kiss that's deep and promising, the kind that makes me forget about the world outside.

As we part, breathless and more in love than ever, I think to myself, 'Yeah, this is definitely how you start a happily ever after."

The End

Printed in Great Britain
by Amazon

50877995R00167